The Butterfly Moments

S. Renée Bess

Regal Crest

Port Arthur, Texas

ISBN 978-1-935053-37-8

First Printing 2010

9 8 7 6 5 4 3 2 1

Cover design by Donna Pawlowski

Published by:

Regal Crest Enterprises, LLC
4700 Highway 365, Suite A, PMB 210
Port Arthur, Texas 77642

Find us on the World Wide Web at
http://www.regalcrest.biz

Printed in the United States of America

Acknowledgments

Thank you, Andria Shelton, for uttering a form of this book's title during a telephone conversation.

Much appreciation to my former neighbor, Mary Beth Tammany, who painted a verbal portrait of a typical day in the life of a Probation Officer. Thanks for lending me your vocabulary.

A sincere thank you to Lori Johnson for her careful reading and constructive comments.

Thanks to my Facebook friend, Maria T. Watson, for her willingness to answer my questions about police officers.

A big collective hug to all the women who organize and attend the Golden Crown Literary Society's annual conference. Learning has never been so much fun.

Much gratitude to my publisher, Cathy LeNoir, whose loyalty, patience, and persistence in the face of ever-present odds inspire me to continue writing.

A "forever thank you" to Toni Morrison for giving birth to "Sula" and opening a whole new world to me. You showed me language is as important as plot and character.

A ton of appreciation to Lee Lynch, Jewelle Gomez, Cheryl Clark, Becky Birtha, and Ann Allen Shockley, whose work continues to fire my writing engine, especially in the wee hours when memories, fear, and doubts attempt to hijack my efforts.

Dedication

To anyone who has ever searched her/his heart and found forgiveness dwelling there, ready to be offered. You are truly a blessing to your friends and loved ones.

Prologue

Trust and I don't always share the same page; maybe because I've dealt with criminal minds for so many years. I trust direct deposit only when my paycheck is posted on my bank statement. I trust there are stars in the sky only when I see them. I trust tulip bulbs are still planted under my kitchen window when the swollen buds burst into bloom. And I trust the elegance of butterfly wings when I see them flutter gracefully, if only for the briefest moment.

Chapter One

THE MINUTE I heard they'd found the missing girl's body doubled over in an old debris covered plastic bin, I figured she'd been violated. I didn't need the reporter on the all-news radio station to fill in the details. He proceeded to do just that, though. His emotion-deprived voice described exactly where the girl's corpse was found: in the back yard of one of those handsome stone one-story houses just a mile from here. Then, the newsreader segued to a rapid-fire series of questions and answers between reporters and a female police detective.

"What was the cause of death?" an unidentified journalist asked.

"She appears to have been strangled," the cop said.

"Could you tell if she'd been raped, Detective Jones?" a second reporter asked.

"I can't discuss that." The policewoman's voice grew distant toward the end of her terse response.

I pictured the cop turning away from the throng of inquisitors before they could pepper her with additional questions. I imagined also that if the perp had gone to all the trouble of moving the girl's body from the murder scene to a property miles away, arranging the body inside one of those large containers, and covering it with shovelfuls of decayed leaves, he'd been desperate to hide the hellish act he hadn't necessarily planned on committing.

I let the voices on the radio fade as I began clicking through my mental Rolodex of the ex-offenders currently in my caseload. Unfortunately, I was able to name at least half a dozen parolees capable of committing this crime. Any one of them could take advantage of an opportunity to grab a young girl, assault her, and then try to cover it up. Any one of them had the potential to slip back into his drug habit, and fueled by crack cocaine, surprise the freshman college student while she was in the midst of a routine day.

One by one, I proceeded through the list of six ex-offenders whose names I had isolated. I leaned against the frame of the sliding door that separated my kitchen from the redwood deck beyond it. My clients' faces merged with the shadows covering the deck's stained planks. I watched a couple of birds peck at the seed scattered on the wooden platform. The bird food had a habit of falling out of the feeder Catherine, my former partner, had suspended from a branch of the nearby Eastern white pine. I remember arguing with her about how close the feeder was to the deck. I was always the one who had to sweep away the uneaten seeds and shells.

That dispute wasn't about cleaning bird refuse from the deck. Like so many other petty arguments we had, it was a cover for all the hurts and misunderstandings we weren't brave enough to confront. Over time, instead of declaring our troubles, we engaged in silent warfare.

Exactly four months to the day after Catherine filled and hung that birdfeeder, she left our house and our relationship. Numb, I watched her go off in search of a better future while I dug in my heels and prepared to deal with living by myself.

At first, I was convinced I wanted to be loved. I wanted someone, anyone to hold me and swear they'd never felt a heat like the one I inspired. But that longing dissipated like raindrops turning to steam the second they spill onto the sun-scorched cement.

I learned to defend myself from my tears by forgetting the comfort of a soft body lying next to mine at night. To keep loneliness from hovering above my head, I threw away the memory of a hand holding mine and arms wrapped around my waist while lips nuzzled my throat. I no longer needed those tender gestures to keep me company and affirm my existence.

Now, I keep moving, betting that a body in motion doesn't have time to dwell on problems. If I move constantly, my conflicts won't catch up with me. I can continue concealing my feelings and denying my needs. I can bury them deep down in the folds of my day-to-day duties.

I maintain my one-sided conversations with my daughter and my friends because that's comfortable for me. For the time being, it's best if I ask all the questions and supply none of the answers. I smile, even when I'm not remotely amused, and feign interest in mundane events that momentarily distract me from my boredom.

I feel secure at work as long as I'm jogging on the job treadmill. From one day to the next, I never know where my assignments will take me, and I really don't care. It doesn't matter to me if I spend a few hours in the office and the rest of the day in court, in the streets, or at my clients' various job locations. Non-routine days are routine for me, and I'm fine with that.

What I don't enjoy is the prospect of working at my job for the unforeseen future. The work of a probation officer comes with obsolescence factors and my parts are beginning to wear out. Lately I've been thinking less about keeping up with my wily clients and more about being able to afford health insurance, growing my Roth

IRA, and maintaining the major systems of my house versus selling it and buying a condo unit.

My best friend, Katey, swears I was born old, especially when she's trying to convince me to do something I should have done years ago, like snorkeling or skiing for the first time. Katey reminds me my real conflict is looking younger than my age, but acting older than I am. She assures me appearing younger is not the hardship. It's acting so deadly serious 24/7 that's problematic. Katey vows I'll have treads in my forehead as deep as a fault line if I don't learn to loosen up and smile more often.

Being serious is the real me. I've always looked life straight in the eye, examined it for any nasty surprises lurking in the wings, and then gotten a jump-start on being prepared for them. I'm sure it was the combination of my sober attitude and common sense that prevented me from keeping the motorcycle I won two years ago in the Office of Probation and Parole's annual fund-raising drawing. And I'm certain it was my feet-on-the-ground disposition that kept me from going parasailing with Katey and Jean last July.

Me, Alana Blue, up in the air over the Delaware Bay? I think not.

Now that my daughter, Nikki, is grown, I'm responsible only for myself. But that doesn't justify my taking foolish chances gliding in the air above a huge body of water. Not that Nikki would care. My daughter is busy working on her second marriage and still blaming me and my "lifestyle" for the failure of her first one. I surely hope she and her present husband, Owen, make a go of it, maybe even have a couple of children.

If they fail, it'll probably be due to Nikki's self-centeredness combined with Owen's latent anger. Nikki's strong suit has always been anything related to herself, and although I've never witnessed my son-in-law being less than a perfect gentleman, there have been times when I could almost feel his temper brushing against my skin. Nikki thrives on the perfect decorum Owen exudes, but I don't trust what lies beneath his perfect order. I'd rather see him wrinkled once in a while than flawlessly laundered and ironed all the time.

Katey just shakes her head when I give voice to my worries. Then she encourages me to think happy thoughts about the day Nikki and Owen bring a child into the world. Part of me would like to have grandchildren, the part that would read stories to the kids, tuck them under the bed covers, and then retreat to my own house. In my heart of hearts, I don't feel like I'm grandparent material. I'm not ready to be called Gramma, Grammy, Granny, or anything resembling those terms. Let them call me Alana and be done with it.

I'm a planner, however, and I realize another generation is inevitable. Katey knows I think about this issue a lot...

"Get the red coupe, Alana, not that dull gray one." Katey said the day I went to pick out a new car.

"I need the four-door model, Katey, for the grandchildren in my future."

"Dammit, Alana. Nikki just got married and you know she's not planning to get pregnant right away. By the time she has children, you'll be ready for your next car. You can buy a jive-old sedan then, Grandma."

I shivered when she called me the grandparent name. For the hundredth time, I caressed the glossy new-car booklet, running my fingers over all the little color sample squares.

"I like this one." I touched one square in particular. "Charcoal gray is so understated and classy."

"Yeah, but red says you're bold."

Katey snatched the booklet from my hand. She poked her nail into a second color swatch.

"You're willing to be noticed. And you're looking around for a strong beautiful woman to sit right there next to you."

All I could do at that point was glare at her.

"Yeah, right. Grandma's gonna buy a red car and then get a hot chick to ride around in it with her. "

Truthfully, I wasn't thinking about any woman, be she strong and beautiful or weak and homely. That was the furthest thing from my mind. Attracting someone new to occupy the passenger seat of a fiery red coupe was so not me. In fact, it wasn't even a consideration.

THE VOICE ON the radio faded in and out, a symptom of double-A batteries eroding to single-A's, I suppose. I left my perch overlooking the deck and walked to the refrigerator. I reached up and turned the radio off. I still had a couple of hours of comp time left, and I didn't need to leave for work yet.

Hunger pangs reminded me I'd had no more than my customary bowl of cereal and skim milk two hours ago. I was okay with feeling a little bit hungry, though. In fact, not giving in to my rumbling stomach made me feel nobler than I would have if I'd succumbed and eaten a snack. If I could ignore all the temptations in the pantry, I would reinforce my will to live without feeding all my wants. If I absolutely had to have something, I'd grab one of those dry brown crackers with zero trans fats and only a smattering of calories.

I looked up at the apple-shaped clock hanging on the wall

above the cabinets. By now the rush hour was over, and I knew I could drive into the city at a relaxed speed instead of at the Indy 500 pace the other drivers would demand. After all, I had no compelling need to hurry to the job I did so well, but was so tired of doing.

I'm more than a decade shy of the median retirement age, but a few years beyond performing my job with the kind of ardor my clients deserve. I'm burned out, jaded. My ex-offenders' tragic stories are all blending together in the Mixmaster of my brain. Their tales have hammered my once smooth edges into jagged angles.

I realize I've stopped listening to my clients with the kind of sympathetic understanding I'd always managed to muster in the past. My empathy has gone AWOL, and hearing all their hard luck stories no longer touches a soft place. Quite the opposite, their sad episodes leave me skeptical.

As cold as it sounds, sometimes I want to interrupt an offender just as he's reciting, "See, what happened was..."

The frayed threads of my unraveling patience tempt me to bark, "Look, select story A, B, or C, whichever bullshit fable fits."

And just as I've begun praying for the city to offer us an incentive to leave the job, I've been given one more responsibility, supervising other probation officers. The department's satellite offices send us employees who've screwed up one way or another. They're transferred to our office where they get a second chance to do their job the right way. These second-chance Charlies used to receive their walking papers as retribution for the unethical and sometimes illegal tricks they'd pulled. Not now, though. The central office is so short on staff at a time when so many offenders are being released from incarceration, it's a wonder we don't have hardened criminals working side by side with us sharing our cubicles, instead of sitting in front of us, awaiting our guidance and directions.

Currently, I'm working my full caseload of 125 offenders along with being saddled with my third "probation-officer-on-probation," or "POOP" for short. I guess it's not helpful to refer to these folks with that acronym, but no one in the office speaks in complete titles.

My newest "probie" is Rafaela C. Ortiz. She's efficient. She knows her job and she's good at developing contacts in the community, a skill you need in order to make employment and housing connections for your clients. But there's an invisible current running just beneath her surface. I can't quite put my finger on the problem, but it does get my attention. Maybe what I sense between us is a power struggle. I can't blame her for feeling uncomfortable reporting to me, because we're really equals, or we were equals before she had her difficulties in the West Philly office.

Frankly, I don't care how she's earned herself a "POOP" spot. As long as she pulls her weight with her caseload, I don't give a fig whom she dated nor whom she's dating now. If she were to ask me, I'd suggest she stay out of her co-workers' beds. But Rafaela doesn't strike me as the type to ask for advice, and I'm more than comfortable not dispensing it.

She's almost my age. She's got a ton of job experience, and she's more than competent. But she needs to tone down her defensiveness. I don't lord my position over any of my probies, and I've tried to ease the tension between us by being as pleasant and non-threatening as possible. So far though, she just looks at me like I'm the last person in the world she would trust.

I did glimpse Rafaela's smile one day when my colleague, Nannette Warfield, told a joke. I was startled when I saw the dimple pierce her left cheek. Rafaela may have been startled also, because that coy indentation vanished the second after it appeared. I stood there, watching it fade away and feeling disappointment glide into the spot where my amazement had been a moment earlier.

Chapter Two

DESPITE THE WARMTH of the breeze blowing across the campus, Owen P. Reid felt it calm the sharp sting radiating from the abrasions on his face. As he approached Hamilton Hall, he forgot the irritating sensation on his left cheek and paused long enough to smack his pipe against the wooden bench standing yards away from his destination. Owen was unhappy about the campus-wide ban on smoking, and he expressed his displeasure by putting the pipe in his jacket pocket, frowning and then shaking his head. This was the second week of the university's summer session, a period when a few of the regulations should be relaxed, he figured. But none of the rules had changed

Owen strode toward the entrance of the brick and stone building. He had two appointments scheduled during his office hours today. After that, he would be free to meet a colleague for their weekly racquetball match. The first appointment was with a disgruntled student whom Owen expected would debate him about a grade. Owen called meetings like this one "splinters." They were as irritating as tiny shards of wood lodged under a fingernail. The sooner he removed today's particular splinter, the better.

Owen's second appointment was with a doctoral candidate he'd begun mentoring. He looked forward to seeing and talking with Bettina. Having read the last four dissertation chapters she sent him, he was intrigued by both the topic she had chosen and by her writing skills. Owen was so impressed by Bettina's writing, he found himself pondering a scholarly collaboration with her. The only decision he hadn't made was the topic of the article she would co-author for one of the more prestigious academic journals. Surely Bettina was ambitious enough to want her name linked with his below the title of an intellectual essay.

Owen walked along the inadequately lit hallway, oblivious to the usual assortment of announcements and notices haphazardly tacked to the chipped corkboard lining the wall on one side of the passageway. He passed several people, each one too absorbed in thought to really take notice of him. Just short of his destination, he heard his name unfurling in the soprano voice of the woman standing behind him.

"Dr. Reid. Hello. How are you today?"

"Just fine, dear. And you?" Owen smiled briefly. He turned the abraded side of his face away from the teaching assistant.

"I'm great. Always on the go," She said, barely looking at him.

"Aren't we all at this time of year?" Owen's response was clipped.

"Ah, right. Enjoy your day."

Owen didn't wait for the woman's last syllable. He continued his trek. When he arrived at the end of the hall, he turned right and entered a small room filled with faculty mailboxes. Robotically, he took five steps and stopped directly in front of the box assigned to him since his first day as a university staff member. As he opened the narrow metal door, a yellow Post-it note fluttered to the floor.

"What's this?" Owen said as he bent down to retrieve the missive. He read it quickly. "Good. Maybe he's rethought the B I gave him. He was damn lucky to get that."

Pleased that his one o'clock appointment was canceled, Owen grinned. The gift of found time meant he could finish his notes for next week's lectures. And he'd have the moments he needed to once again run through Bettina's dissertation chapters. He was more than eager to do a good job helping her, and he wanted to be sure he hadn't missed anything vital.

Owen shuffled his pieces of mail like they were playing cards and gave each one a cursory look. An errant credit card offer, the minutes from the last faculty meeting, a new English literature periodical solicitation. There was nothing requiring his immediate attention. He headed toward the stairs and energetically climbed the flights to the third floor where his office was located. He could easily have taken the elevator, but he preferred the exercise the climb provided.

Once inside his office, he hung his jacket on the coat tree next to the door and put his briefcase on the narrow console table there. Early afternoon sunbeams streamed through the slatted blinds covering the sole window in the room. Owen deposited his mail on top of his desk and then made his way to the window. He used his thumb and forefinger to separate two of the slats, as he peered at the scene below.

Strips of pavement lay like ribbons dividing the university's grassy spaces into irregular geometric parcels. This area was the very center of the campus from which the cement grids led to all the different buildings that comprised the university.

Owen liked this old structure that housed the English Department's offices. He was especially fond of his office window's vantage point because he believed he could see the school's entire universe, or at least much of its population. He looked down at the book-toting creatures pushing their way forward into the summer sun, and he imagined he knew, simply by virtue of their individual gaits, which students were headed to the Business School, which ones were traveling toward the Science Center or the School of Education, and which few were destined to sit in an English literature class, perhaps one of his.

Owen planted himself at his desk. He pulled some items from his briefcase and arranged them in a neat pile. As he opened the manila cover protecting his doctoral mentee's work, two photos propped near the far edge of the desk caught his eye.

He was most proud of the large portrait taken during last winter's celebration of the university's centennial. There he was, standing between the school's current president and the president-emeritus. The three men, each one cloaked in an academic gown, beamed for the camera. Owen's smile was the widest.

The smaller photograph, snapped a year ago during a faculty picnic, was of Owen, his wife Nikki, and Dr. Caryn Mobley, his department chair. Less formal than the first picture, it froze a moment of unguarded candor and caught both Owen and his department chair focused on Nikki. Owen was staring at her quizzically, as if he were puzzled by his wife. Dr. Mobley gazed at Nikki analytically, as if she were about to give voice to some provocative thought.

Sometimes Owen felt uncomfortable when he glanced at this photo. He thought he spied a proprietary gaze in Dr. Mobley's eyes, and he wondered if indeed she had uttered something to Nikki the second the camera's shutter clicked, something that only she and Nikki knew. He couldn't imagine what they had said to each other, having met for the first time that day, and he found the possibility of his exclusion from their tête-à-tête disquieting.

Shortly after Owen framed the picture and placed it atop his desk, his discomfort got the best of him and he began a new habit of examining his and Nikki's monthly telephone bill. If his wife and Caryn Mobley were exchanging phone calls or text messages, he wanted to know about it. After a couple of months, he felt relieved when he saw they didn't have an ongoing communication with each other. He was perplexed nevertheless by a list of data charges linked to an unknown phone number. He decided to keep his curiosity undercover along with his own personal phone bill which he arranged to have delivered monthly to his university mailbox.

Owen continued staring at the second photograph. He took a long look at his department chair's image. While he respected her knowledge of literature and her sage leadership of the department's staff, he didn't like her. He suspected she didn't like him either.

After working together for the past two years, Owen gave in and accepted his colleagues' gossip as truth. He believed his supervisor was a lesbian. That fact in itself had no bearing on his feelings toward her. She was free to love whomever she wished. Moreover, Owen was quite proud of his liberal attitudes when it came to issues of sexuality. Most black men he knew expressed an aversion to anything even remotely associated with homosexuality. Owen felt a certain amount of superiority about his stance being different.

Besides, his mother-in-law was a lesbian, and that was just fine with him. She seemed to genuinely like all people, male and female alike.

Owen had a different impression of Caryn Mobley. She seemed to dislike him simply because he was a man who was used to receiving attention from most of the women he met, especially the female students who clung to his every word. And he never discouraged them. Wasn't their fawning flattery and flirtatious behavior a part of the politics of academia?

Owen rearranged the photos, nudging the one taken at the picnic to the background and coaxing the larger one forward. Satisfied with the revised arrangement, he settled himself in his chair and began paying homage to Bettina's work. He read a few pages before he picked up a finely sharpened pencil and placed brackets around certain sentences and paragraphs. After reviewing two chapters, Owen stood and walked to the window. Again, he looked at the vista beneath him.

Some of those students down there will be in one of my classes. After their freshman year, that is. I don't enjoy first-year classes. The students aren't old enough to appreciate the beauty of English literature. And they're certainly not mature enough to value my talent as a teacher.

The young professor remained standing in front of the window for a moment longer before he moved back to his desk. He leaned on the back of his chair and let the smaller of the two photos claim his attention once again. His eyes rested on his wife's image. He'd made a good choice in marrying Nikki. She was articulate, attractive in a pampered sort of way, and she played the role of professor's wife with aplomb. She did tend to be emotionally over-involved with her mother's personal life, and she didn't always seem interested in his work, but that was all right with him. He never had any difficulty finding other people who liked to listen to him talk about his area of expertise.

Another moment passed before Owen sat down and resumed his reading chores. He lost himself in Bettina's prose. It was obvious, even in this first draft, that she had mastered the academic patois he found so familiar and comfortable. Needing to busy his hands, he used one to smooth the page before him while he supported the side of his face with the other.

He grimaced the second his hand touched his face.

Remembering the pain, Owen let his fingertips travel the length of the two welts on his cheek. He started to push the manuscript aside to go to the restroom to splash water on his face, but he was too engrossed in his reading to do that.

Owen gazed at his briefcase on the table near the office door, his concentration now broken. More than an hour earlier, he had stuffed his T-shirt into that bag. The gray shirt he planned to wear for his racquetball match was no longer laundry fresh nor neatly folded because he had used it to dab the traces of blood from the scratches on his cheek. He would put the shirt in the washing machine the moment he got home this afternoon.

The briefcase blurred as Owen focused only on his thoughts. Certainly he hadn't foreseen the confrontation he'd experienced this morning. He hadn't predicted the furious physical reaction that occurred less than half a mile from where he now sat. He vowed to plan his actions more carefully from now on, and to pay rapt attention to a woman's maturity or lack thereof before cultivating her friendship. Having made those decisions, Owen summoned a mental picture of the grad student who was due in his office shortly and then returned to reviewing her work.

Chapter Three

JOHNETTA JONES FELT like she'd been asleep only ten minutes instead of four hours when her telephone's jarring ring ended her rest at 3:30 a.m. On the edge of a dream, she opened her eyes, focused on the soft green glow surrounding her alarm clock, and then picked up the phone.

"Detective Jones." She said automatically.

"Johnnie? It's Harold. The captain told me to call you." Detective Harold Smythe's dry-as-toast voice put the finishing touch on Johnetta's wake-up process.

"What's up?" Johnetta swung her legs over the side of the bed. She knew Harold wasn't phoning her with good news.

"We got a murder to look at. Happened sometime early yesterday, but the body's just been discovered. The captain wants you to go to the scene. Seven fifty-four Summit Farm Drive." Harold paused. "Got that?"

"Yeah. Got it." Johnetta chanted the address to herself as she squeezed the switch on the night table lamp. Grasping a pen resting next to an empty glass, she wrote the information in the margin of the previous day's newspaper's horoscope.

"I'm on my way."

She hung up the phone, slid her feet into her worn bedroom slippers, and headed toward the bathroom.

Once there, she loaded her toothbrush with a stripe of minty blue gel and spoke to the disheveled image looking back at her from the mirror.

"Shit. Why'd I think I'd get to sleep all night once I was working out here in the 'burbs? Brighton Township is starting to imitate Philadelphia."

Even as she mumbled those words, Johnetta knew she was exaggerating. Surprise wake-up calls had dragged her out of bed only twice since she'd moved out of the city and begun working for the suburban township's police force. If she suffered from broken sleep, it was because she had to get adjusted to the quiet in her new environment, not because she was habitually awakened by middle-of-the-night emergencies.

Months ago, Johnetta glided effortlessly into retirement from Philadelphia's huge police force. No longer required to live in the city, she bought a small single-level house in a northwestern suburb. She was determined to enjoy her new life, so she took her time painting some of the rooms of her house, hanging art and photos on the walls, and removing the weeds that seemed to grow along the patio's perimeter quicker than she could pluck them. She gave in to a long-held desire and installed three tomato plants and one cucumber seedling in the tiny groomed area next to her garage.

Johnetta was thankful the exterior of her house was practically maintenance free. Aside from removing the handmade wooden shutters a previous owner had installed, she hadn't tackled any other projects. Now Johnetta chided herself every time she entered her driveway and caught a glimpse of the two dark rectangles the missing shutters imposed on the rose-colored brick. She knew she needed to replace them with factory-made models, but the deed remained undone. A benign habit of procrastination, formerly unknown to Johnetta, lived with her now like an unexpected squatter. She dragged her feet when it came to replacing drafty windows and tearing out the old carpet in order to reveal the hardwood floors the real estate agent had promised in his sales pitch. She told herself she had plenty of time to do these projects. Now, a few months later, it seemed as if she had too much time but too little ambition to accomplish these few house tasks.

Johnetta filled some days exploring her new territory. On other days, she drove back to Philadelphia to meet friends for lunch. She spent most of her evenings alone. That's when she noticed how loud the quiet was. She was accustomed to living by herself and had done so since her son went away to college. She was used to the absence of her own voice. Recently the silence had grown more pronounced. Johnetta mulled over the situation. She figured the reason her solitude echoed throughout her home each night was because she no longer heard the tapes of the day's rigorous work playing in her mind. Snatches of conversations, jokes, angry confrontations, and tear-stained confessions...all those things were missing.

Her home's thunderous quiet convinced Johnetta she was not cut out for retirement, at least not yet. When she learned Brighton Township's recent population boom made it necessary to hire more municipal employees, including additional police officers, she cut a deal with the township's directors. She signed a three-year contract on the condition they would hire her at her previous rank, sergeant-detective. Both parties had the option to either re-up or call it quits at the end of the three-year term.

Johnetta guessed this gig would be similar to Andy of Mayberry's, life in the slow lane compared to the mayhem in Philly. At worst, she figured she'd have to investigate traffic scofflaws, a few shoplifters at the nearby mall, and an occasional drug bust at the local high school. Two months into the new job showed her she had underestimated the amount of police action the small borough saw.

Although her murder investigation skills took a holiday, Johnetta quickly developed new professional muscles to help her attend to a rash of house break-ins, more than a few cases of identity theft, an online child pornography ring, and a sophisticated plot to commit mass bedlam in two of the community's middle schools. Life in Brighton Township lacked the lightening quick pace of the city, but it was far from dull. Johnetta pounced on each new situation in her own calm, organized way. She replaced her impromptu lunches with friends in the city with time spent learning the routine of a suburban cop. Her evenings became filled with familiar ruminations as she traded the lonely solitude for mental reruns of her days on her new job.

Johnetta was wide awake by the time she stepped into the shower. She barely let the water acquaint itself with her body before she flung back the vinyl curtain and blotted away some of the moisture with her bath towel. She strode back to her bedroom, groped inside a dresser drawer, and extracted underwear. Rooting around in a different compartment, she felt for a pair of socks. In her haste, she was tempted to scoop up yesterday's slacks draped across the back of a chair next to the dresser. She looked at them and then frowned disapprovingly. She took three long strides to the closet and removed the first pair of pants she touched.

Johnetta stepped into freshly laundered jeans, and then pulled on one of her navy-blue T-shirts emblazoned with the police department's logo. She grabbed the lanyard attached to her badge and slung it around her neck. Seconds before turning off the lamp, Johnetta slid her feet into shoes, pocketed her wallet along with her good luck charm, and picked up her holstered service revolver. By the time she reached the kitchen, she'd managed to strap the holster in place under her arm. She lifted her jacket off its hook near the back door, and slung it over her shoulder. After setting the house's alarm system, Johnetta eased her key out of the ancient lock she kept intending to replace.

That lock is just like me, she mused. *Tarnished, but still working fine.*

Johnetta steered her vehicle in the direction of Summit Farm Drive, a world away from the streets she used to traverse in the moments following murders in her city precinct. The sparse post-midnight traffic made the ride a short one. She imagined murder investigations were rare in Brighton Township, and she wondered if the police force was prepared for this one. She was confident she was. She would ease into the routine. She knew what to do, what questions to ask, and what evidence to look for once she arrived at the address Detective Smythe had dictated.

She would perform with the same skills and concentration she had used so many times during her first police career. She would feel needed and necessary as she looked for evidence and talked with the victim's family members. She would reactivate her style of saying very little while hearing and observing so much.

Having discarded the solitude that encased the early days of her retirement, Johnetta was in her element once more. She felt relief knowing her passion for police work would help her bury the dull pain caused by the absence of any romantic passion in her life. This second chapter of her career would shield her from the moments when she yearned to have a connection with someone. It would be the answer to her unspoken rescue call, her sanctuary from the deep loneliness that accompanied her move from the city.

Chapter Four

"YOU'RE NOT GONNA turn that in today, are you Rafe?"

Sam Arnold shot a look at his co-worker as he pushed his hands against his desk and propelled his chair away from it a good foot or so. He rested his arms across his well-fed belly and grimaced.

"If you start doin' everything early, you're gonna make the rest of us look bad."

Rafaela Ortiz used her knee to nudge the chair under her desk seconds before she scooped up the folder containing her monthly reports. She tucked it under her right arm and then plunged that hand into her pants pocket.

"You don't need my help to look bad. You're doing a good job of that all by yourself."

Rafaela stood facing Sam. She shook her head, making no effort to conceal the disdain she felt for her colleague's work ethic.

"Come on, Rafe. Stop with this ambition crap of yours. We all get paid the same."

Sam's smile was somewhere on the continuum between a leer and a shit-eating grin.

"You're right, Sam. But the difference is I'm getting paid to work, and you're drawing a salary to pretend you're working." Rafaela winked and nodded simultaneously as she opened the office door.

The uneven cooling power of the building's aged air conditioner sent cold air rushing through the hallway. As the frigid currents wrapped around Rafaela's shoulders, she shifted the olive green folder from one arm to the other and tugged her rolled-up sleeves until they reached her wrists. Only a moment ago, the shirt felt confining as scant ripples of cool air struggled to push their way out of the office cubicles' window mounted A/C unit.

Rafaela ignored the shiver now threatening to overtake her while she walked past the elevator and headed to the stairwell. Traveling down from the sixth to the second floor would chase the chill from her limbs. She stiff-armed the heavy, metal door standing between the stairwell and the corridor and then walked to the office where she had to deposit her paperwork.

If I'm lucky, she won't be here. I'll just drop this on her desk and be done with it for another month.

Rafaela imagined the relief of walking into an empty office and not having to feel subservient in any way. She stood near the entrance of her supervising P.O.'s work space and flicked away the errant lock of hair that frequently took up residence over her left eye. She tapped the metal door frame.

"Hi, Rafaela, come on in."

Shit. Now I have to make chitchat, Rafaela thought.

Without looking directly at her supervisor, Rafaela knew the woman was smiling warmly. It seemed to her that this tall, bronze-hued lead probation officer was always smiling.

"Good afternoon. I wanted to turn in these reports along with my tracking forms."

Rafaela kept her face devoid of emotion and her voice expressionless. She hadn't yet figured out her supervisor's motives. Each time they talked, the attractive P.O seemed friendly. But Rafaela remained guarded.

According to the terms of Rafaela's disciplinary transfer, Alana Blue would be her supervisor for the next twelve months. There was nothing either one of them could do to change that fact.

"Great. These forms aren't due until day after tomorrow."

Alana reached over her desk and accepted the papers from Rafaela.

"I love it when P.O.'s are on top of their work. Thank you."

"You're welcome." Rafaela nodded curtly, and then added, "Maybe you could put a note in my file saying how prompt I am with my reports. I need all the props I can get."

"Sure. And I'm certain you'll get a promotion and a reduced caseload as your reward," Alana said.

Rafaela watched Alana blink and then look directly at her. She noticed Alana gazing at her right temple, where half a dozen locks of mixed dark and gray hair trailed down the side of her face and then swept back. She saw Alana's stare follow the braids. Rafaela was willing to bet Alana wanted to see where the trail ended, that her hands would want to trade places with the wooden clip holding her braids in place near the nape of her neck.

"So, how are things going for you here?" Alana tilted her head as she looked up at Rafaela.

"All right. This is the same job it was in the West Philly office."

"Yes, I guess you're right." Alana paused. "I'm curious, Rafaela, do you speak Spanish?"

"Some. Not as much as I used to when my dad was alive."

"Was your father Latino?"

"Yes." Somewhat tentatively, Rafaela added, "He was Cuban."

"You said he's no longer alive," Alana said gently. "Did he die recently?"

"No. He died years ago."

"I'm sorry."

"Thanks. He left me with some great memories."

"It's good to have those, isn't it? Were you born in the States, or in Cuba?"

"I was born right here in Philly. My mom's African-American." Rafaela winked confidently at her supervisor. "So that makes me black, just like you."

Alana smiled. "Your name is Latina, so I was wondering..."

"The only thing Latina about me is the jar of *sofrito* I keep in my refrigerator. It reminds me of my grandmom and my dad."

"They say odors and flavors are powerful souvenirs of the past," Alana said.

Rafaela concentrated on Alana's burgundy red lipstick. She decided the color was a fine introduction to what was probably a pair of very soft lips.

"Why did you ask if I speak Spanish?"

"Because not many of our P.O.'s are bilingual, and I thought maybe you wouldn't mind being assigned some Spanish-speaking clients."

"That's fine with me. Like I said, I don't speak it much anymore. But I meet all challenges head-on." Rafaela shifted her weight from one foot to the other. "Is there anything else?"

"Uh, not really."

"Okay. See you later, then." Rafaela turned to leave.

"Actually, there is one more thing." Alana said.

Rafaela reversed her course and faced Alana.

"Yeah?"

"Do you have any questions about any of our procedures? There may be one or two things we do here that you didn't do in the West Philly office. Are you handling everything okay?"

Rafaela stood tall, her legs slightly parted. She folded her arms across her chest.

"I'm handling the job just fine. But I do have a problem. I'm supposed to have only one supervisor, but it feels like everybody and their mother is constantly looking over my shoulder." Rafaela glared at Alana. "And something else that's bugging me is my caseload. I've been doing this job for twenty plus years, and I've always had male and female clients. Since I've been here, all the cases you've assigned me are male offenders. You've sent male P.O.'s with me whenever I've done home visits, and my three office mates are men? Is this all coincidental, Ms. Blue?"

"I'm aware of the situation, Rafaela." Alana said calmly.

Rafaela reloaded. "Do you think this makes me feel like I'm trusted?" She didn't give Alana time to answer. "Hell no. I don't feel like anyone here trusts me."

"Maybe you're not up to speed with the way clients are assigned in this office," Alana said in even measured tones. "My boss, Conrad Jackson, makes all those decisions. I don't have anything to do with your caseload other than to offer you help and resources."

Rafaela glared straight ahead. By the time she refocused on Alana, she was calm and more composed.

"No one explained that policy to me. You did ask how I was handling things, right?"

"Yes I did, and you certainly answered me." Alana paused. "Is there any other problem we need to discuss? I'm wearing my bulletproof vest."

A flicker of humorless penitence flashed from Rafaela's eyes.

"Not at the moment."

"Well, thanks again for turning in your reports early."

"Don't mention it."

Rafaela did an about-face and walked out of the office before Alana could wish her a good day.

Chapter Five

"YOU DON'T HAVE to keep working with the probies, Alana. You could decline that assignment. Jean told me how that works."

Katey was deep into one of her frequent telephone heart-to-hearts with me.

Holding the instrument close to my ear, I gathered an armful of laundry from the top of the dryer and walked slowly into my bedroom where I dropped the still-warm clothes onto the bed.

"Yes, you're right. I could turn down those assignments. And in retaliation, my boss will add twenty more offenders to my caseload. Ask Jean how that works."

I knew Katey had my best interests at heart when making these suggestions, but sometimes her brainstorms weren't practical.

"You're going to burn yourself out, Alana."

That's how these conversations went. In her zeal to help me, Katey would give birth to an idea she thought was valuable, and she'd punctuate it by adding how much Jean supported the notion. I'd counter her proposal with logic grounded in my on-the-job experience. Then Katey would become exasperated and change the subject completely.

"Why is Rafaela such a difficult assignment for you?"

I could see Katey was in the mood to interrogate me, and she hadn't reached her frustration point.

"It's her attitude."

"Is she one of those young know-it-all types?"

"She's not what I would call young."

Rafaela Ortiz was exactly five years my junior, but I didn't think I needed to share that statistic, not even with my best friend. Nor was I willing to tell Katey why Rafaela required a supervisor. That information was confidential, and even though I was burned out, I still cared about being professional.

"Well, why does she bug you?"

Katey seemed more curious than usual. I wondered if Jean knew the scuttlebutt about Rafaela and if she'd shared it with Katey. After all, Jean stayed in touch with folks in our office. It was possible she was privy to more information about Rafaela than I knew.

"I've asked myself that very question, Katey, because it takes a lot to ruffle my feathers."

I picked up a bath towel and folded it in thirds.

"Rafaela is going along with the program, but she's barely tolerating being supervised."

"I thought you liked rebels. I've heard you say they make the best parole officers." Katey said.

I smiled into the phone, appreciating the way Katey always listened to me.

"I do, usually. But not when they're being rebellious with me. The job is hard enough. I don't need roadblocks from within the ranks. I'm not the enemy and I don't make demands."

I visualized Rafaela glaring at me with that customary insolent expression on her face while I sputtered my way through some inner-office directive.

"Is that all that's bugging you about her?" Katey asked.

"No, that's not all. She's got this defiant way of tilting her head and then gazing right through me, especially when I try to give her a heads-up about something."

"Wow, Alana. Sounds like you've already analyzed her behaviors."

"I haven't analyzed her at all."

Indignant, I freed a freshly washed sock from a bra hook and reunited it with its mate.

"I said analyzed her *behaviors,* not her." Katey's voice shifted to sarcastic mode and she added, "Am I getting too close for comfort, dear?"

"Not in the least, madame."

I hoped I'd done a good job pretending to be nonchalant. I'd spent more time than I should have mulling over the reasons Rafaela got to me the way she did. I'm one of those honest, look-you-dead-in-the-eyes women. Every time Rafaela Ortiz stared at me with that semi-arrogant attitude of hers, I had to look away from her. That's not like me at all.

"You can believe I'm not staying awake at night thinking about Rafaela."

Even as I made that declaration, I knew damn well my nightly review of my work day included freeze-frames of Rafaela staring at me. Searching for any memory of Rafaela's sending me the slimmest sliver of a smile had become a nightly ritual.

"Good. You don't need her interfering with your rest."

"You're right."

I was eager to change the subject.

"My boss showed me a memo about the state's early-leave legislation. The ink the governor used to sign it isn't dry yet, but I've already brought in empty boxes to pack my things." I balanced a squat tower of towels and washcloths over one arm and escorted them to their shelf in the linen closet.

"Oh, Alana, that's wonderful. I remember the day Jean finally made up her mind to file her retirement papers. What a relief." Katey laughed. "Living with her became bearable again."

"Yeah. It's tough trying to make such a huge decision." I shook my head thinking about my current situation. "Some days I want to walk out of that office and never come back. Then, other days it's not so bad."

"Would it be easier if you had a smaller caseload? What if you could get rid of the Rafe Ortiz assignment?"

"You call her Rafe?" I was startled by the familiarity embedded in Katey's shortening of Rafaela's name.

"Jean calls her that. They know each other pretty well from having worked together years ago." Katey said. "You know Rafe is gay, right?"

"Yes. But as far as I'm concerned, she's simply another P.O. whose paperwork I'm accountable for," I said, almost too quickly to be believed.

I recognized Rafaela was family before we sealed our introductions with a hand shake. I didn't need the rumors preceding her sudden arrival to confirm the obvious. As her supervisor, all I cared about was her job performance. I wasn't interested in her personal data. It was no more than gossip by the watercooler discussed for half a minute and then forgotten, swept up with the scraps of paper littering the brittle, cracked tile floor.

Whenever my imagination threatened to turn toward Rafaela, I convinced myself the only thing the buzz about her proclivities did was remind me of my fatigue. I was tired of all of it, the hearsay, the minor scandals, the work following me home, the numerous failures threatening to overwhelm me and make me feel most of my caseload was teetering between stints in prison instead of recovering from the time they'd served.

I wanted out from the army of social service workers trapped on a mountainside of bureaucratic forms burying our clients' humanity. So the moment the city put an early exit-with-benefits package on the table, I pulled up a chair and sat down to the meal. I was more than eager to move on to a different job in a place where I could really help folks.

During the past twenty years I've seen enough examples of brotherly hatred and sisterly violence to last me several lifetimes. Some of that brutality has come perilously close to me, warning me of uglier events just waiting in the wings. Maybe that's why the murder of the high school honor student, practically in my own back yard, saddened more than shocked me. There seemed to be no respite from the psychotic anger rubbing out young lives before they had a chance to reach adulthood.

I've shadowed and counseled more con artists, get-over experts, and just plain crazy-ass fools than I can remember. Every sign I've seen or heard recently, including the phone message from a police detective who wants information about one of my offenders, is pointing to the exit. It's time for me to say adiós to all the bullshit, all the malcontents, and all the lives so wrapped in the tentacles of poverty they can hardly breathe. I need to see what lives on the other side of my office door.

"So have you filled out your papers?"

Katey's voice jolted me back to the here and now.

"Yeah. They're completed and sitting upstairs on my desk."

"Well, you have to mail them, you know."

"I know that, Ms. Bossy."

I laughed and hoped my amusement concealed my annoyance with myself. I hadn't been ready to admit to having one foot outside my office door, perhaps because I didn't yet have a new place to put my feet once I'd left the Office of Probation and Parole.

"I'm taking the packet to the post office tomorrow morning. Tomorrow is soon enough, right?"

"Oh sure it is." Katey paused. "I know you don't like your business on everyone's lips, but I can tell Jean, can't I?"

"Of course you can. I wouldn't want you to keep anything from her. Besides, you two need plenty of time to decide on an appropriate retirement gift for me."

My friend's laughter trickled through the phone.

"Don't worry. I already know the perfect present for you."

"Really? Already?"

"Yup. And don't ask because I'm not telling."

"That's a deal. Besides, you know how much I enjoy surprises."

"Do you know what you're going to do after you leave?" Katey asked.

"No, not yet

"Well, I hope you can take some time off before you jump into your next job."

"What makes you think there'll be a next job?"

"Because you're like Jean. You need to keep accomplishing something."

I nodded, my ear fused to the telephone.

"You may have something there." I said.

"How long did it take Jean to find her niche?"

"About two days." Katey giggled. "Not really. It just seemed like we went to Rehoboth Beach for a week, and then right away Jean started her consulting job."

"I might want a longer break than that." While I spoke the

truth, I was mindful of a lesbian-run social service agency that always welcomed volunteers. If I could do without being on anyone's payroll, I could always work for that outfit.

"Hey, does Nikki know about your plans?"

"No. I haven't talked with her in a while."

"Are things strained with her again?"

"When are they not strained?"

"Hmm. Sorry I asked." Katey sighed. "I don't know why she refuses to accept you for who you are. Honestly, she's a throwback to another era. People in her generation are usually more liberal than she is."

"I must have kept her home from school the day the liberal lesson was taught, because she missed it completely

"Well, for your sake, I hope she grows up soon. She's missing out on good times with a great mother."

"Thanks, Katey. It's kind of you to say that."

"Maybe she'll come to your celebration dinner." Katey paused. "You'll have one of those, you know."

"I know, especially if I'm not the only one leaving the job

"Are you planning to leave in August or in the fall?"

"I haven't decided, but I'm inclined to choose a date in early autumn, before the next court decision about the overcrowded jails."

"That's a smart move."

"No one ever accused me of being stupid. Stubborn? Yes. Dumb? No."

"You are a stubborn one. Maybe that's why you don't get along with Rafe Ortiz." Katey said.

"Excuse me? Did I say we don't get along with each other?" I pretended to clear my throat.

"Not exactly. I retract that."

"Retraction accepted, girl. So, are we going to see each other one of these days?"

"You can count on it. How about meeting for dinner one night next week?" Katey said.

"Just name the day, time, and place."

"Okay. Let me check my calendar and get back to you tomorrow."

"That sounds good. Talk to you then."

I hung up the phone, but continued thinking about Katey. We're only two years apart, and we share a lot of things in common. Because Katey and I come from opposite ends of the rainbow, our biggest difference lies in how we confront everyday issues.

I'm black and Katey's white. Our racial identities impact the way we look at the world. God knows the ethnic difference affects the way the world looks at us.

Katey goes through life thinking nothing is impossible. She can plant her feet and move them just about anywhere she chooses, anywhere except those places where her footsteps might get in the way of white men. I've explained to her how I have to look in all directions simultaneously before I even think about moving one of my feet. And even then, I must move with caution.

Despite our close ties, I don't expect Katey to understand me completely. The subtleties of race are frequently beyond the reach of someone not born black. I give Katey credit for wanting and trying to understand, though. She has a wonderful incentive, her partner Jean.

I've never been in an interracial romantic relationship, but I imagine it comes with its share of challenges. Once in a while Katey talks to me about the speed bumps they encounter. Jean keeps these situations to herself. She's quiet about her life with Katey, and I honor her desire for privacy.

I met Jean shortly after I arrived at the Center City Office of Probation and Parole Services. A couple of years my senior, she was a top-notch P. O., admired by her peers and her clients. She was also the first African-American lesbian mother I was aware of, other than myself. Jean's son Mark and my daughter Nikki took each other to their respective senior proms.

Mark was a handsome teenager, as nice and responsible as he was good looking. He would have been the perfect boyfriend for Nikki if he weren't gay. It took Nikki most of her last year in high school plus all four years she was away at college to come to terms with her prom date's sexuality. Once she claimed she'd gotten over it, she was able to appreciate Mark's friendship. She claimed he was the brother I had neglected to supply her.

Nikki wasn't the only one who had a problem with my not producing a second child. Her father, my ex-husband, objected also.

Years earlier, I had done what was expected of me and married Charles Evans without really thinking about it. I'd followed the pre-written script and wedded the first appropriately educated black man with potential who asked me out on more than one date

Charles was intelligent and ambitious. Spawned by a family of laborers, he eschewed working with his hands. He decided early on to become a lawyer. After going on two dates with me, he knew I would be the perfect accessory for his right arm. Through long days and even longer nights, Charles basked in the comfort of looking at my two university degrees hanging on the den wall a good eight inches below his framed credentials. By Charles' estimate, he was a good catch; certainly the best catch I could have hoped to reel in.

I gave birth to Nikki halfway through the second year of our marriage. The day she took her first wobbly steps, Charles told me something was missing from the family portrait, a son. Not completely satisfied with our daughter, Charles wanted to be able to boast to the world about a smaller version of himself. My glee at having finally seen my way clear to returning to work melted.

Despite my half-hearted willingness and Charles' frequent efforts, a second pregnancy didn't happen. After a while, Charles' frustration with "my failure" persuaded him to test the potency of his semen with other women; several other women.

I ignored his recreational activities with the spirit of a tourist in Egypt, cast adrift on a raft in the middle of a river called De-Nial. Nikki sailed along petulantly through her first years of school. And I answered the invitation to seek shelter once again with the Department of Probation and Parole. The job welcomed me with open arms and caseloads brimming with hardened criminals who practiced their trade on my soft mannerisms. While I seemed to be learning-disabled regarding the state of my marriage, I was a quick study on the job. My demeanor toward my offenders toughened quickly, and I brought some of that vinegar home with me each day.

About that time, Charles met a woman who refused to be locked in his box labeled "piece on the side." Their affair began while Nikki was in middle school. When I realized how seriously Charles felt about her, I was more surprised by my reaction to their relationship than by its existence. I was only mildly annoyed by his attachment to her, the same way I would have been momentarily irritated by a mosquito bite.

When I stopped to really think about it, I understood what I felt was relief. I could drop any pretense of remorse I had about not becoming pregnant again. I could begin to see my way out of a marriage to a vain, self-consumed man. I could stop burying the feelings I had those mornings when I awoke on the border of a vaguely pleasant dream of soft arms encircling me. I could give myself to the pleasure I felt watching certain women pass by, and I could feel at home with those good sensations. I could stand in front of my mirror and later in front of a female lover and pronounce the word that identified who I was and whom I truly desired.

I encountered not more than a second's worth of argument when I told Charles I intended to divorce him and retake the name I'd owned since birth. Nikki shed the only tears that fell during our rancorless separation and perfunctory legal proceedings. An angry, hurt, and bitter child, Nikki blamed me for exiling her father from her day-to-day life before she'd had a chance to arrive at her potential. She was sure she could have made him prouder than any younger brother would have. A male child would have grown up to disappoint him. Of this Nikki was certain.

During her early adolescence, she was certain also that my being a lesbian was the reason I never conceived another child. She flirted briefly with organized religion, and that flirtation bolstered her belief. She argued its merits and asked me if I weren't afraid of going to hell. I entertained her debate once, for about five minutes, before I stated how appalling I found her intolerance. I strongly suggested that being stuck in such profound ignorance is a hell right here on earth.

One way or another, Nikki has waged war against my right to express my sexuality since she's been aware of it. She blamed me for the failure of my marriage and the collapse of her first one. I refuse to claim ownership of either happenstance

Chapter Six

NIKKI REID ARRIVED for her Monday afternoon appointment at exactly four o'clock. She pushed open the door and entered the softly lit room. As usual, the space smelled of lemon and orange, the lingering odor of room freshener hurriedly sprayed in the wake of a previous client. Dr. Suzanne Greene was already seated in the overstuffed floral armchair. The therapist waited until Nikki came into full view before she greeted her.

"Hello, Nikki."

"Good afternoon, Dr. Greene."

Nikki approached the old tweed sofa against the wall. The day's dying sunlight shared its weakened beams with the far end of the seat, highlighting its years of use. Nikki sat down and avoided the worn spot where the thin twists of fabric threatened to snag the clasp of her bracelet. She knew every inch of that side of the sofa, and she wouldn't let it trap her jewelry, any more than she'd allow Dr. Greene to lead her into revealing something she wasn't ready to bring to light. Nikki's palms met the sofa's familiar surface, as she made a bargain with her fingers to stay still for once and not betray her restless mood.

Nikki wanted to get right down to business. She was here for one reason only, to continue her conversation with Dr. Greene, the psychotherapist one of her friends had recommended after the practitioner had saved the friend's marriage. Nikki was determined her union with Owen was going to succeed. If it failed, it wouldn't be due to lack of effort on her part.

"How was your week?"

"Fine. Routine." Nikki stared into Dr. Greene's eyes.

Dr. Greene returned Nikki's gaze. "Tell me about that dinner you were planning to have with your mother."

"It didn't happen." Nikki redirected her gaze from Dr. Greene to the bookcase standing against the wall, yards away from the therapist's wide chair.

"How did that come about?"

"I didn't think having dinner with her was necessary." She removed her hand from the sofa's cushion and smoothed back her perfectly coifed hair.

"Had you invited her to a meal?"

"I'd only mentioned it casually. I hadn't set up anything definite."

"How do you feel about changing your mind?"

"I'm fine with it." Nikki's raised eyebrows punctuated her short response. She pursed her lips in anticipation of Dr. Greene's next question.

"Have you talked to her since then?"

"No. I didn't think that was necessary either."

Staring at the bookcase, Nikki zeroed in on two books standing side by side on the middle shelf. She couldn't decipher their titles, but their identical bindings signaled they were twin volumes. After a long moment of silence, Nikki began concentrating on Dr. Greene's hairstyle. *She wouldn't be able to wear those corkscrews and work in corporate America. That's for damn sure,* she thought. *She has to be self-employed. Or maybe she's like my mother, who refuses to straighten her hair. Yes, she's probably just like my mother, one of those natural-headed lesbians.*

"You might want to consider discussing the missed dinner with your mother." Dr. Greene's face held a neutral expression, as if she had no particular ownership of her suggestion.

"As you know, I call her only when I absolutely have to. My free time belongs to my husband and me." Nikki raised her voice a half pitch.

"And how have you and Owen been spending your free time in the last week?"

The abrupt switch from her mother to her husband caused Nikki to flounder for two seconds.

"The usual stuff."

"Talk a little about the usual stuff."

"You know, the routine things most husbands and wives do."

Nikki stared at Dr. Greene. *This is more like it. This is why I'm here, to talk about Owen and me, not about my mother. I'm not spending 125 dollars an hour to talk about my dyke parent.*

"Did you and Owen do anything this week that wasn't routine? Anything special that you particularly enjoyed?"

Nikki stole a glance at Dr. Green's left hand. No bracelet, no rings, no nail polish. Nikki remembered asking the friend who recommended Dr. Greene whether the therapist was married or single. Her friend had no clue. After a couple of therapy sessions, Nikki concluded the absence of a wedding band proved how scrupulously careful Dr. Greene was to guard her privacy. A few visits later, Nikki decided Dr. Greene was unmarried.

"When you talk with Owen about your mother, do you feel he supports you?"

"Of course he does."

Here we go again. Back to my mother. Why does she keep bringing her into this?

Nikki recalled the session when she first disclosed her mother's sexuality. She remembered watching Suzanne Greene blink quickly several times after she uttered the words "My mother is a lesbian." Now, that recollection flitted through Nikki's mind and forced a sly smile across her lips.

"Does Owen listen silently or does he participate in the discussion?"

"He listens mostly. He'd better be on my side."

"How would you describe your side? What does that look like?" Dr. Greene asked.

Nikki turned slightly, attempting to make her back more comfortable against the sofa. "It looks like the right side to be on."

"Does anyone validate your opinion?"

"Does anyone validate my opinion? Let's see." She held up both hands and one by one raised her fingers as she spoke. "The federal government, organized religion, state law, most of my colleagues at school, and every one of my married friends."

"You don't have any friends who would support your mother's being a lesbian?"

"Not a single one." Nikki's lips formed a smug line above her dimpled chin.

"What about those people who say it's okay to be gay or lesbian, that one's sexuality is biologically based?"

"Those people don't have offspring or parents who deceived them for twenty-five years." Nikki spit out her words and dug her finger nails into the armrest.

"You sound angry," Dr. Greene said.

Nikki struggled to contain the sparks blazing on her surface. "Of course I'm angry."

Dr. Greene leaned forward. "Nikki, what's more painful for you, your mother's lesbianism or her keeping that part of her identity from you for many years?"

"I'm pissed about the whole thing. It's bad enough she hid behind a curtain of fake heterosexuality for most of my life, but what's worse is she's a lesbian. She's unnatural and she does unnatural things."

"So, if I'm hearing you correctly, you're angrier about her being gay than you are about her having concealed it from you."

Nikki nodded. "That's right."

Dr. Greene paused, then asked, "Is there anything positive you could say about your mother?"

"Yes. At the moment, she's not shacking up with anyone."

"You're pleased that she lives alone, without a partner?"

Nikki nodded angrily.

"Why is that a good thing?" Dr. Greene's gentle voice

continued questioning Nikki.

"Because if she were living with someone, then everyone would know she's a lesbian," Nikki said calmly.

"Is that important to you? Would you prefer people not know about your mother?"

"Extremely important. It's a small world."

"What would happen if people knew about your mother's sexual identity?"

"Anything could happen. It could affect Owen's career. And what about her grandchildren?"

"I guess you're talking about the future?"

"Yes, I am. What happens when my children have to answer to their friends' taunts about their grandmother? Grandmothers shouldn't be sexual anyway."

"Some people believe we don't cease being sexual until we die."

"Well that makes me feel a hell of a lot better. Thanks," Nikki said.

"Do you want to take some time to talk about why your mother's sexuality disturbs you so much?"

"No. I don't believe in frittering away moments, and talking about that topic would be a serious waste of my time here. Frankly, I'd rather discuss how to be a good wife despite my mother's sexuality. I don't want that to screw up my second marriage." Nikki's voice communicated her determination.

"That's fine. If it's agreeable to you, I'd like to suggest we invite Owen to join us during some of our sessions. It takes two people to avoid screwing up a marriage, you know."

Nikki thought she saw the edges of Dr. Greene's mouth soften. She observed the beginning of what looked like a set of parentheses border her lips. *Good*, she thought. *She does have a sense of humor.*

"Okay. I'll mention it to him. But I warn you, he's not a big talker."

"That's all right. I'm sure we can coax him into saying something." Dr. Greene offered a generous smile. "And when he's not talking, we can check in with him to make sure he's listening well."

Once again, Nikki looked to the space above Dr. Greene's head. *Listening well? That's Owen. I could tell him we're having dinner in a UFO with Martians, and he'd just nod and ask me if I needed help with anything.*

"Our time is about up. Should we plan on the same time next week, or do you want to ask Owen to come also and then get back to me about the day and time?"

"The latter. I'll phone you as soon as I've talked to Owen."

"That's fine, Nikki. I'll wait for your call."

Nikki pushed herself away from the seat. She stood, opened her handbag, and extracted the check she'd already written.

"Thanks, Nikki. Have a good week."

Nikki opened the door and left the office. Smiling as if she'd just told herself a salacious joke, she identified the short bursts of sound she heard in her wake. Although she exited the office too quickly to be able to smell the tangy aroma of the lemon mist air freshener, she knew for sure Dr. Greene had sprayed away the remnants of her therapy session.

Chapter Seven

LORIN WILKES LOOKED at her watch as she entered the austere lobby of the old granite building. She was five minutes late for her appointment and grateful that her friendship with Rafe Ortiz would erase the annoyance any other P.O. would feel about her tardiness. It wasn't her fault the southbound buses chugged sluggishly down Broad Street, determined to ignore any semblance of a schedule. In desperation Lorin had resorted to half-walking and running most of the way to the Office of Probation and Parole.

Lorin stabbed the elevator button and uttered a barely audible curse word. The ancient, square box yawned open and creaked in response to Lorin's impatience. Three flights later the decrepit box stopped abruptly. The door strained its way ajar, and a handsome burnished-brown woman with salt and pepper hair stepped inside.

The woman acknowledged Lorin's presence."Good afternoon."

"Hello." Lorin said, returning the woman's greeting. For a second she thought she saw a flash of familiarity in the woman's easy smile.

"I'm already late, and this old contraption is making me even later," Lorin said.

"You have to treat Molly with kindness. At least she's working today."

As the woman reached past Lorin and tapped on the elevator car's wall, Lorin inhaled deeply. She didn't know the name of the other passenger's fragrance, but she knew immediately she found the vaguely floral odor pleasant.

"You mean this elevator wasn't running yesterday?"

"Nope. She's some-timey. If you'd been here twenty-four hours ago, you would've had to use the stairs," The woman said.

"In that case, I'm grateful she's working today, because I'm headed up to the sixth floor."

"You would have made the climb okay. You look like you're physically fit."

Lorin felt her cheeks grow warm. She tightened her grip around the handle of her briefcase. "I'm just as happy to ride all the way up instead of climb."

A blast of cold air filled the elevator as its old door labored open. Relieved to have arrived at her destination, Lorin took a last look at the box's shabby interior. She stepped into the hall and then turned around quickly.

"Which way to Rafe, uh Rafaela Ortiz's office?"

"It's on the right, the third office past the double doors."

The elevator's scratched door lumbered shut, sealing its remaining passenger and her pleasant fragrance inside.

Lorin headed toward her destination. Startled by the sound of her phone ringing, she pulled it out of her pocket and glanced at its small screen.

"Hi, Kim. This is a surprise," Lorin said.

"And it'll be a quick surprise, too."

The familiar voice made Lorin's pulse accelerate.

"I can't see you this evening. I have to change our plans."

"Why?" As suddenly as Lorin's heartbeat increased, it slowed.

"As it is, I'll be late getting home. Then I have some things to do for work tomorrow."

Lorin sighed. "Okay. I understand. I'm disappointed though."

"I know you are, baby. I'll make it up to you." The voice purred in Lorin's ear.

"Promise?"

"I promise."

"If I had a dollar for every promise you've made and broken, I wouldn't have to work, you know?"

Silence greeted her response.

"Kim? Are you there?" Lorin spoke louder.

"I'm here. I just don't have an answer to that."

You could say you love me. Lorin thought. She knew waiting to hear Kim's declaration of love for her was as fruitless as trying to empty the ocean with a teaspoon.

"Can we see each other before next weekend?" Lorin asked.

"I'm not sure. I'll try."

"All right. Talk to you later, then."

The phone went dead, a lifeless good-for-nothing collection of plastic and circuitry board, valuable to Lorin only when it was alive with Kim's voice. She tucked it back inside her pocket and continued her short walk to Rafe's's office.

"As I live and breathe, it's Lorin Wilkes."

Rafe left her chair and sauntered over to Lorin. The two women hugged.

"So, this is your new headquarters."

Lorin rocked back on her heels and turned 360 degrees.

"Not bad. Smallish, but not bad at all. At least you're closer to my office than you used to be."

"If I'm so close, you'd think you could get here on time, Wilkes." Rafe smiled at her friend.

"It's not like I didn't leave my office on time. The damn buses never run on schedule," Lorin said.

"Schedule? There's a schedule?" Rafe laughed.

"I ended up jogging most of the way. And then I had the misfortune of getting into the oldest elevator I've ever seen." Lorin shook her head. "I'll bet Benjamin Franklin invented that thing the day after he tried to electrocute himself flying his damn kite."

"Nothing would surprise me." Rafe shook her head, and then gestured to her cubicle. "Care to enter my office?"

"Thanks." Lorin walked the few feet separating her from Rafe's desk. She sat down in the chair Rafe pointed to. "A woman I saw in the elevator told me sometimes the thing doesn't even run."

"She was right. It doesn't." Rafe laughed. "Some mornings it starts, but by noon it stops working."

"Has anyone ever gotten stranded on there?"

"Probably." Rafe paused. "Come to think of it, I wonder if the alarm works."

"Hmm. You know, I wouldn't mind getting stranded in that scrap metal trap if I could be marooned with the woman who was on it with me a few minutes ago."

Rafe playfully nudged Lorin's arm.

"And who would that be?"

"I have no idea who she is, but she's certainly attractive."

"Somebody in this office building?"

"Yes, I guess so. She seemed to know all about the habits of your unreliable elevator."

Rafe narrowed her eyes. "What did she look like?"

"About your height, copper colored skin, short curly graying hair, dark eyes, a slow smile, a deep dimple on the right hand side..."

"Not that you noticed any details or anything."

"Hey, I appreciate feminine beauty, that's all."

"And I see you're still trying to talk to the sistahs." Rafe grinned at Lorin.

"When it comes to women, I don't see color. You know that." Lorin returned her friend's smile.

"Right, I do know that about you." Rafe tilted her head back and winked at Lorin. "So what's up with you and your secret lover these days?"

Lorin's smile evaporated.

"We're still seeing each other — when we can. I just wish "when we can" were more often than it is," Lorin said.

It must be tough, not being able to see her when you want to."

"What's tougher is not being sure if she wants to see me as often as I want to see her."

Rafe reached for Lorin and patted her arm.

"You know, I could tell you there are other fish in the sea, but I know damn well when you're in love with someone, you're not interested in going fishing."

Lorin nodded slowly and then let a smile return to her face.

"Except that elevator woman. She really smelled good."

Rafe laughed. "You know what? All of a sudden I don't feel sorry for you."

"Good. I hate being a charity case. Now, can we talk about the business that brought me here?" Lorin straightened her posture.

"Sure."

"Her name is Selena Garrett. Have you met her yet?"

"Only on paper. It's taken forever for me to be assigned any female offenders."

"With all the women coming out of jail recently? How is that possible?" Lorin asked.

"It's a strange coincidence, isn't it? I spoke to my supervisor about that the other day."

"And?"

"I figured some idiot here might think because I got involved with a female co-worker in West Philly, I'll get involved with another one in this office. Or worse than that, I'll hit on a female client."

Lorin shook her head vigorously. "That's ludicrous."

"I know. But that's where my imagination took me."

"What did your supervisor say when you approached her about this?"

"All she did was remove herself from any responsibility for my assignments. Somebody else farther up the chain makes all the decisions about our caseloads."

Lorin sat back in her chair. "Well at least you don't have to battle the person who's directly over you."

"Nope. At least not about this point."

"What's your supervisor's name?" Lorin asked.

"Alana Blue."

"Hmm, sounds like a detective's handle. Is she as cool as her name is?"

"She's professional, I'll give her that. I was angry when I asked her about my assignments, but she didn't flinch. For a second I wondered if she'd heard what I said."

"Does she treat you fairly or is she riding your butt about every little thing?"

"So far she's been fair. Word is she's counting the days 'til her retirement. She'll be outta here in another month."

"Maybe after she leaves they won't reassign you to anyone."

Rafe grimaced."No such luck. I have to report to a supervising P.O. for an entire year."

"That sucks."

"Majorly. But I didn't have a choice."

Rafe twisted her mouth into a sardonic grin. "Wish I'd thought of that before I started dating my married co-worker."

"Yeah, or before your married co-worker's jealous husband found out about you two and decided to stage a very public scene in your office."

"Please don't remind me of all that shit. I was trying to have a good day." Rafaela sighed. "So what's up with this new client of mine, this Selena Garrett?"

"Two words...buckle up."

"Trouble?"

"Potentially."

Lorin unfastened her briefcase and removed a bundle of papers. "The good news is she's intelligent and employable, so you won't have a problem connecting her with a job. In fact, she already has one."

"Why is it I can sense bad news getting ready to jump off the tip of your tongue?" Rafe telegraphed a thin smile.

"Well, the bad news is it might be hard finding her someplace to live. She's got one of those I-dare-you-to-ignore-me personalities, and she lives each day like she's on *The Jerry Springer Show*." Lorin smiled at her own description.

"Just what I need, a problem." Rafe rubbed her forehead. "Is she an instigator?"

"Let's just say she's extremely aggressive and not in a good way."

"Then she won't be out of jail for very long

Rafe's fingers tapped a quick rat-a-tat on the edge of her desk. "I'm scheduled to meet her tomorrow. Guess I should make the anger management sessions mandatory for her."

"She's been there, done that." Lorin skimmed one of her documents. "Yup. It says here she attended each and every session and she exhibited improvement and a desire to be conciliatory."

Rafe tucked her feet under the front of her chair and rocked it an inch or two off the floor. "So what else is going on with Ms. Garrett? Baby daddy issues?"

"I seriously doubt that. She's childless and she's gayer than you are." Lorin watched for Rafe's reaction.

"Oh. An aggressive butch?"

"No, more like an aggressive femme. I'll bet she's broken quite a few butches' hearts without working up a sweat." Lorin pursed her lips.

"Has she tried to work her aggressive feminine wiles on you?"

"I think she's considered it, especially when she saw how

frustrated I was trying to keep a roof over her head. She's run through five different roommates in our two group homes."

"Damn. When I looked at her arrest records, I didn't see any violent crimes, just retail theft and identity fraud. Now you're telling me she's a lesbian nutcase."

"Sorry, my friend. But at least you know what you're dealing with. I've given you fair warning."

"This is true."

"My boss told me there's a good chance we'll drop Ms. Garrett from our client list, especially if she screws up again." Lorin sent Rafe a sympathetic glance."I didn't want to dump her into your lap without your knowing something about her."

"I appreciate that."

"And considering what you're up against here in this office, I wanted you to understand you really have to watch your back with her," Lorin said. "She's going to end someone's career before she's through, and I don't want it to be yours."

Lorin put her papers back into her work bag and stood up. "Guess I'd better hoof it back to my office."

"Let me walk to the elevator with you." Rafe gestured toward the door.

"Thanks. Do you think I should take a chance on riding in that thing a second time?"

"Sure. Maybe you'll be lucky and meet that good-smelling woman again."

As Lorin and Rafe walked slowly toward the elevator, they saw a woman emerge from the stairwell and enter the office near the end of the hallway. Lorin nudged Rafe's elbow.

"That's her. That's the woman who was in the steel deathtrap with me."

"Really?" Rafe feigned surprise.

"Do you know her?"

"Uh-huh. That's Alana Blue, my supervising P.O."

"I don't believe it." Lorin slapped Rafe playfully on the back. "Aren't you the fortunate one?"

Rafe cocked her head to the side and flashed a circle made with her thumb and third finger. "You can put money on it."

"So you think you have this supervision thing sown up?"

"Not by a long shot."

"Then she's straight and married?" Lorin asked.

"No, she's not married." Rafe said."As a matter of fact, she's family."

"Well...?"

"Well nothing. I'm not going there." Rafe tried to sound resolute.

"Because she's a co-worker?"

"Right." Rafe avoided Lorin's stare. "And she's not my type. She's too serious."

"Actually Rafe, I find serious women seriously attractive because everything they do is done with intensity."

"That's fine if you're ready to get married. But I'm not looking for a wife, and I'm seriously intense about that."

"All right, I hear you." Lorin laughed and then pointed to the elevator. "My ride's here. See you soon?"

"You bet."

Lorin hugged Rafe before she stepped gingerly into the ancient elevator.

"If you don't hear from me in the next twenty-four hours, check on this damn rat trap."

Rafe threw her head back and laughed. She waved good-bye and then retraced her steps to her office. When she passed the room Alana had entered, she peered quickly past its open door, hoping to see some trace of her supervisor without being seen herself. Rafe wondered why she'd never noticed Alana Blue's fragrance. She decided to make that discovery the very next time an opportunity presented itself.

Chapter Eight

NIKKI PARKED HER Mini Cooper next to her husband's car in their generously sized garage. Owen had arrived home from work early, and Nikki figured correctly that he'd be in the den, reading a student's research paper or writing his lecture notes. She tiptoed past him and made her way to the kitchen. She was tired, completely spent after a day at school that should have been routine, not carved into slices by one emergency after another. Her head felt as if it were wedged in a vise filled with screaming first-graders on one side and plastered with demanding parents on the other.

At that moment, Nikki's only goals were to reach the bottle of aspirin she kept on the bottom shelf of one of the kitchen cabinets and to avoid any interaction with Owen. Although she was always happy to see him, right now, she wanted simply to swallow a painkiller and then sit in a warm bath, out of talking range. She didn't want to read her mail, respond to any phone messages, nor open her mouth to speak because she knew the mere effort of moving her jaw would cause her more discomfort

Noiselessly, Nikki opened the cabinet door, extracted the plastic bottle bearing the yellow label, and removed two pills. She sidled up to the water dispenser and touched its lever, praying the liquid would fall soundlessly into the mug she tilted beneath the stream. She placed the aspirin tablets on her tongue. As she sipped the water, an errant droplet fell from her bottom lip and silently hit the tiled floor.

Nikki put the cup in the sink and then removed her shoes. She glided out of the kitchen and into the hallway. The den's door stood ajar, letting the smoke from Owen's pipe drift into the hall. An odor akin to cherrywood filled the air. Nikki tried valiantly not to inhale. She hated Owen's smoking habit, and she told him that every time she watched him reach for his pipe. She accused him of using the pipe as one of his academic role-playing props. It was part of his costume, as were the tweed jackets in his closet, and the nattily-trimmed goatee he wore. Seeing Owen with that pipe in his mouth, hand, or pocket forced Nikki to give voice to her annoyance. As was his way, Owen merely looked at her passively whenever she railed against his smoking. Then, he'd turn around and walk away without defending his right to do with his lungs whatever he pleased.

Nikki paused in front of the open door and looked at her husband. All five feet, eight inches of Owen Phillip Reed's wiry frame was stretched out on the leather easy chair. His legs and feet were perched on the ottoman and his right hand supported the bowl of his pipe which jutted from his mouth at an awkward angle.

Nikki didn't doubt her love for Owen, even if he was less a physical presence than her first husband, Harold, had been. It was enough for Nikki that Owen had rescued her from divorcee hell. He had restored her reputation as a "marriageable woman of color." And he'd promised he'd be willing to be a father to the two children Nikki planned to gestate and give birth to.

Nikki figured she could be married to Owen for quite a while. He was a reliable companion, and she could count on the regularity of his routines. Nikki never needed to look at a calendar to see what day it was. She could always calculate the date and the time by checking Owen's schedule. An atomic clock couldn't be as regulated as he was. She often thought the way he clung to his daily schedule could enable a wife to slip away easily from the bonds of marriage to seek excitement with a secret lover.

The university semesters transitioned one after the other with little change. A well-respected expert in English Romantic literature, Owen taught the same courses fall after fall, spring after spring. His willingness to present the same material year after year baffled Nikki. His readiness to ignore African-American writing amazed her. Owen was completely out of touch with an entire world of letters; a world to which he might have related as naturally as his heartbeat had he believed in its academic relevance.

Determined to continue her journey to a warm bathtub, Nikki glanced at the floor-to-ceiling bookcases covering three of the den's walls. She glanced at Owen's desk, a paper-strewn oak island festooned with a stack of ungraded research projects. Remembering her vow of silence in deference to her pounding headache, Nikki backed away from the den before Owen could sense her presence.

At that second, her cell phone rang.

"Shit!"

"Hey. I didn't hear you come in." Owen twisted his upper torso in the chair and looked toward the doorway.

Nikki glared at her phone and then silenced it.

"I just got here." Nikki massaged her forehead. "And I'm going upstairs to soak in the tub and get rid of this horrendous headache."

"Oh. All right."

Owen returned to his reading. Less than a second later, he squinted over the top of his eyeglasses. "Do you want me to make dinner?"

"Whatever. This headache is so bad, I don't really care."

"All right then. I'll see what's in the fridge." He tapped the contents of his pipe into the ashtray nesting on the old wooden table beside his chair. "Nikki?"

"Yes?" Already at the staircase, Nikki dispatched her answer over her shoulder.

"Please remember to turn off your cell phone. You're at home now."

"Right." Nikki mumbled her response.

She was annoyed she'd forgotten to press the phone's power button before entering the house. She bristled whenever Owen reminded her to do this. He was dead set against any electronic intrusion into their lives. Owen had purchased a phone only after his father became gravely ill, and his mother insisted on being able to reach him. He'd bought the phone reluctantly and he routinely neglected to turn it on. It was turned off the day his father died, and to make matters worse, Owen failed to see the pulsing red light on the answering machine in his office at the university. He didn't find out about his father's death until late that afternoon when he arrived home from work. Forced by Owen's distaste for modern communication technology, Nikki had the sad task of telling him his father had passed away and his mother was desperate for his loving support and attention.

Owen responded, "Oh, well. What could I have done five hours ago that I can't do now? Nothing. Absolutely nothing."

Drawn to the clothes drier's low hum, Nikki stopped in front of the louvered doors concealing the second floor laundry alcove. In disbelief she opened the door on the right to verify the sounds she heard. In the relatively brief time they'd been married, Owen had never done the laundry. Never. Nikki checked the dial to see how much longer the drier would be on. Ten more minutes.

She closed the door, muffling the drier's dull noise behind it, and stopped in the bathroom long enough to start filling the tub with warm water. After adjusting the faucet, Nikki spotted the wicker hamper under the window. It looked exactly as it had that morning, almost filled and slightly askew with the sleeve of one of Owen's T-shirts belching over the side.

Nikki strode toward the hamper and flung it open.

What in the world did Owen put in the washing machine if all of these dirty clothes are still here? I knew it was too good to be true, she thought.

Shedding her garments piece by piece, Nikki stuffed as much as she could into the hamper.

Now I have to do this tonight on top of everything else, lesson plans, my journal, erase the messages on my cell —

"Nikki!"

Owen's voice cut through her contemplation.

"Yes, Owen."

"I forgot to mention something important. Your mother called soon after I got in."

"And?"

"And she wanted to say hello. She said you didn't need to return the call unless you wanted to, especially if you had a lot to do tonight."

"Thanks for the message, Owen." Nikki projected her voice toward the hallway, hoping Owen would hear her and not yell his inane mini-lecture about trying to talk to him from another part of the house. Even though he had the habit of using his raised voice to talk to her from some other room or floor, he always ridiculed her when she tried to answer him from a remote location.

"What did you say? I didn't hear you?" Owen shouted.

"I said thanks for the message. What with the laundry and everything else on my agenda, I don't intend to phone my mother this evening."

Silence greeted the last of Nikki's words. Slightly annoyed, she went into the hallway and looked down the stairs.

"Owen?"

"Yes, Nikki." Owen bellowed from the den.

"The dryer's running and the hamper's still full. What in the world did you wash?"

Nikki heard Owen's chair scrape against the floor. A second later she saw his shadow precede him as he approached the staircase. She saw the silver dollar-sized shiny spot on his prematurely balding head before she looked at any other part of him.

"My gym clothes. I played racquetball at the faculty courts after my office hours today."

"Oh." Nikki nodded.

"I got so sweaty; I didn't think you'd appreciate it if I mixed my shorts, socks and shirt with the rest of the laundry."

"You're right." Nikki said. She was pleased Owen was following through with one of her frequent requests. She redirected her stare from her husband's bald spot to his face.

"What are those red streaks all over your left cheek?"

Owen touched his face. "I got in the way of Bill's racquet. It was an intense match. I was really into it, honey."

"Well I'm glad you took care of your sweaty gym gear."

For the briefest of seconds, Nikki looked down on Owen and sent him an angelic smile. He riposted with a gentle glance of his own before he turned around and retreated to his work.

Chapter Nine

DETECTIVE JOHNETTA JONES dug her heels into the brown tweed industrial carpet and pulled her swivel chair closer to the computer's monitor. She typed her password and waited for the short "persons of interest" list to pop onto the screen. Rubbing a sudden chill from her forearms, she peered at the three names printed in bold black letters against the light gray background. She highlighted the first name and then clicked on it.

This character was nearing the end of his parole after doing a stint in Graterford Prison. He'd been convicted of carjacking and robbing the vehicle's occupants at gunpoint. Rape and murder weren't part of his criminal arsenal.

Johnetta continued reading. She ruled out the second possibility. He was in his early seventies, and his most recent physical description suggested his frail arthritis-wracked body would not permit him to force a healthy eighteen-year-old female to submit to rape and strangulation before lifting her corpse, putting it in a car, and later stuffing it into a compost bin.

There was evidence the victim tried to defend herself from her attacker. Johnetta was certain the lab results would show the blood and skin fragments found under the girl's fingernails belonged to the perp, whoever he was.

"Johnnie, I'm goin' out for coffee. Want a cup?" Harold Smythe stood in the doorway, smiling at his co-worker.

"Uh, no thanks, Harold." Johnetta's eyes left the computer screen long enough to answer him. "I'm trying to cut back to two cups a day, so I can fall asleep at a decent hour."

Detective Smythe grinned. "I got that sleep thing all figured out. All I have to do is listen to my wife. She never shuts up. Puts me to sleep better than a pill, and it's cheaper, too." Harold laughed, amused by his own comments.

"I hear you." Johnetta barely smiled. Even though she hadn't been anyone's wife or partner in a long time, she didn't relate to wife-bashing humor. She had never related to it.

"Okay. I'll be back in two shakes

Johnetta watched her partner's dark-blue gingham checked shirt disappear from view. She liked Harold well enough, and she appreciated his welcoming her from day one. Johnetta had been surprised by Harold's lack of resistance to partnering with Brighton Township's first female African-American police detective. She'd been convinced she'd encounter at least a few blatant displays of resentment from the suburban boys in blue, especially when they took note of her rank. So far, she hadn't experienced anything that left the bitter taste of racism in her mouth.

They must be more subtle out here than they are in the city, she had thought more than once. *Surely, they're not more evolved.*

Johnetta shifted her attention back to the computer. She dragged the cursor over the third name on the list.

Reginald Harris, age thirty-six, released and paroled two months ago after serving five years of a ten-year sentence for raping a minor. Harris' address was in West Philadelphia's Mantua area, "the Bottom." According to the information on the screen, so far he'd conformed to the rules governing his parole.

Johnetta read further, searching for the name of his parole officer. She moved the blinking arrow to a drop-down menu, and then clicked on the "print" command. A low humming noise on the other side of the room assured her the printer was doing its job.

She put her hand in her pocket and absentmindedly fingered the good-luck charm ensconced there. The metal lambda keychain—that had long ago belonged to Pat Adamson, Johnnie's partner in the Special Victims Unit—was a source of comfort. Johnetta touched it often, finding both consolation and strength in the contact.

Pat Adamson's murder was the first of two deaths that changed Johnetta irrevocably. It ushered in caution the way no amount of police training or any anecdote told by another seasoned cop could have. It reordered Johnetta's priorities. Clearing the Philly streets of criminals became secondary to staying alive in order to be a mother for her son. The decade it took to find and arrest the person who pumped the bullet through Pat's chest taught Johnetta perseverance and gave her the gift of Zen-like patience.

The other death that transformed her was Khalif Baxter's. One suffocating humid August afternoon, Khalif tried to outrace her, first in a stolen car, then on foot after the car flattened an innocent pedestrian. Johnetta shouted a warning as Khalif turned to face her, his hand wrapped around a shiny black object that looked so much like a gun. In the split second that changed several lives, Johnetta fired her service revolver.

Whenever she remembered that day, she heard the sharp boom of her weapon discharging. Her right hand recalled the gun's recoil. Her ears replayed Khalif's monosyllabic scream as his body crumpled to the ground. She felt the hollow echo of her disembodied voice shouting into her shoulder-mounted two-way radio.

It seemed to take an age for the ambulance and the squad of backup officers to arrive that afternoon. And during those long moments, the blood spurted rhythmically from Khalif's throat. The vital red liquid became a stream punctuated with the shards of glass and cigarette butts already littering the street. Flushed with terror and anger, Khalif's sister, Jaie, indicted, tried, and convicted Johnetta of homicide right there on the spot. Johnetta knew if she'd been a white cop, she would have been the victim of the ugliest side of mob violence. All she ever wanted to do was serve and protect, not murder a young male car thief pointing something at her that appeared to be deadly, but turned out to be a cell phone.

What followed were ten years of survival, a decade of doggedly chasing every shadow linked to Pat's murder, of downing endless glassfuls of scotch as she played tag with her guilt about Khalif Baxter's death. Getting through that period left Johnetta spent. She avoided forming long-term romantic relationships, and instead, embraced ambivalence whenever one appeared on the horizon. Few women provoked her curiosity. No woman claimed her attention for more than a couple of dates. She was content being uncoupled. All she needed was her job, an assortment of friends, and her son.

Johnetta rubbed the fatigue from her eyes. She lowered her head, turning it first to the left and then to the right, stretching the muscles in her neck. Then she arose from her chair and walked to the Formica-topped table where the printer continued spitting out sheets of paper. She examined the pages. Satisfied they contained the information she needed, she picked them up and returned to her desk. Methodically she reviewed each paper's contents, highlighting certain sections. Concentrating, she read one bit of information twice. Then, smiling slightly as she recognized a name, she lifted the telephone from its stand.

"Good morning. This is Detective Johnetta Jones from the Brighton Township Police Department. I need to speak to one of your probation officers — Alana Blue."

Chapter Ten

RAFE ORTIZ WAS restless. While the demands of her job didn't offer her the luxury of spare time, she had just enough moments between her last task and the next one to be reminded of the void in her life. A familiar need shadowed her. Like an unwelcome guest, it pulled up a chair and made itself at home. Rafe knew she wouldn't ignore this persistent need much longer.

She pushed open the door to the office she shared with three other parole officers. She entered the second of four cubicles and glanced down at her calendar. This would be an easy afternoon, she thought. Two clients had appointments, and she had to visit a third at his job. Rafe picked up a cup of lukewarm coffee with one hand and a half-eaten package of peanut butter crackers with the other. Biting one of the crackers, she chastised herself for failing to eat a better meal. *Even a piece of fruit would be better than this shit.*

"Ms. Ortiz?" A thin voice floated Rafe's way.

Pushing the crackers aside, Rafe looked in the direction of the small voice and smiled at her first appointment of the afternoon. After handling a roster filled with male offenders, this woman was only the second female client in her assignment list.

"Hey, Delilah. Come on in. Have a seat."

She pulled the chair from under her desk and sat down as she motioned to Delilah to do the same.

Her head bowed, as if she were trying to shrink her nearly six-foot frame, Delilah Harris walked slowly toward the chair. She kept her hand soldered in place atop a wide greasy splotch spread over her right pant leg. It was bad enough she had to present herself weekly to the always neatly dressed Ms. Ortiz. Today she had to make her appearance wearing an old ill-fitting blouse and badly marred cotton slacks.

Rafe struggled to avoid looking at the finger-length peninsulas of darkened fabric migrating from Delilah's mid-thigh downward toward her knee. She concentrated on her client's face.

"How are things going?"

"Fine." Delilah stared at the frayed label taped to the front of a file cabinet behind her parole officer.

Rafe looked down at the torn cellophane package with the two remaining peanut butter crackers. She picked it up.

"Would you like one?"

Delilah shook her head quickly. She barely looked at Rafe.

"No, no thanks."

"So tell me about your job. How do you like working with the hospital's dietician? Is everything okay?"

"Yes. Everything's goin' good." Delilah nodded vigorously. "Ms. Johnson, my boss, she said to tell you she's behind with her paperwork, but she'll give you a call tomorrow morning."

"Okay. I'll expect to hear from her."

"She said I'm doing my job real good. And they might be able to give me overtime in a couple of weeks, if that's okay

"That's fine." Rafe sought her client's gaze. She wanted to be sure Delilah understood the next thing she was going to say. "We just have to be careful that any additional time you spend at work doesn't interfere with your going to your AA meetings."

"Oh it won't, Ms. Ortiz. I can still make it on time. Or I can go to a later one."

Rafe picked up a manila folder from her desk. She opened it and removed a form, giving it a cursory glance.

"Your latest D&A tests are clean, Delilah." Rafe smiled. "I'm really happy about that."

Delilah looked up, offering Rafe a slow smile. "Thank you, Ms. Ortiz."

"Are you still getting along well with your aunt and your cousins?"

"Oh, yeah. It's kinda crowded in the apartment, but they give me my space. I'm all right."

"Good."

Rafe spread her fingers over the edge of the desk. The notion of paying Delilah a home visit streaked through her mind. Just as quickly, she decided against it.

"Okay. I'll see you here next week at the same time."

"Sure, Ms. Ortiz." Delilah looked at the file cabinet one final time. "And if my schedule gets changed because of the overtime, I'll let you know."

"Sounds like a plan, Delilah."

Rafe stood up and offered Delilah her hand. Delilah rose and stood next to her chair as awkwardly as an hours-old fawn stands next to its mother. She inclined the upper part of her body and timidly accepted Rafe's handshake, returning it with a weak grip of her own.

She barely muttered,"See you next week, Ms. Ortiz."

Rafe nodded and watched the young woman slip her handbag over her shoulder and walk out of the office. She picked up the thin folder containing all she knew about Delilah Harris. After meeting with her a half dozen times, it was easy for Rafe to imagine how Delilah could have been on the stupid end of a drug-dealing enterprise, literally holding a bag of weed while her boyfriend phoned from three blocks away to tell her he'd just sent the next customer to pick up the product. All Delilah had to do was give the drugs to the buyer. She never saw any cash trade hands. What she did see was as much bottom drawer vodka as she could drink.

And when her boyfriend's entrepreneurial spirit led to his expanding his business from peddling small amounts of marijuana to distributing stolen liquor and methamphetamine, Delilah upped her choice of beverage. She transitioned from drinking the clear Russian-influenced alcohol to downing top-shelf champagne, or premium cognac blended with prescription cough syrup. She would have continued her sales assistant career for some time if a particularly scruffy looking customer wearing a wire and concealing a badge had not arrived on her corner one cold January morning. Following his arrival, Delilah Harris had one hard, ugly-ass time substituting water and decaf coffee for Courvoisier and codeine.

Rafe felt a smile pull at her mouth when she took a last look at Delilah's most recent substance report. Clean as a bathtub scrubbed twice with Bon Ami. Delilah was doing just fine. Rafe tucked the file folder under two others and pondered her reactions to Delilah's history. She was well acquainted with the temptations of alcohol and the struggle to stay free from its pain-soothing clutches. Delilah didn't need to tell her how hard it was to turn away from drinking in order to stop the pain from seeping through her pores like sweat on a hot August day.

Rafe thought about her own battle to pull away from the liquor haze filling her head before and during her self-destructive affair with a married co-worker. She wondered if anyone in this Center City office knew about that part of her life. Did anyone know she had struggled to remain sober night after night, drinking nothing more than her memories of an ill-conceived episode that looked a lot like love when it began but ended in bitter disappointment? Did her old boss, Conrad Jackson, have any idea she'd been in as much pain as many of her clients? Did her new supervisor have any clue how hard it was for her to come to work after scarcely sleeping two and three nights in succession? And if she did know that about her, did Alana Blue care?

Rafe had thirty minutes before her next ex-offender was due to arrive. She pushed away from her desk and stretched. Glancing at the cubicles flanking hers, she remembered all three of her colleagues had left word they'd be out in the field today. Usually Rafe welcomed the stillness their absence lent the office. But today the quiet atmosphere bothered her. The lack of chatter made the windowless room feel like it was a cavern closing in on her.

She scooped up her keys from the bottom drawer of the file cabinet, and set out to take a walk through the building. Striding through the hallway, she waved at one or two people and kept going until she reached the east stairwell. She descended two steps at a time, going from the sixth floor down to the fifth. Once there, she went through the double doors etched with the words Probation Services, Philadelphia County Division, Administration

A couple of Rafe's friends, Nannette and Marsha, worked in these offices. They always gave Rafe a heads-up about any procedural changes floating through or clogged in the pipeline. Rafe was always one of the first to know about any new job opportunities or personnel switches.

She peeked in the office where she usually found her two friends. Failing to see either one of them, she waved to a sweatshirt-clad guy talking on the phone, his feet propped up on a table. She continued on and walked the length of the hallway before reversing her route.

Then, she descended the stairs, this time more slowly than she had climbed moments earlier. She paused to gaze out the landing area's window. The bright September sunshine emphasized the coat of dust on the surface of the old marble sill. Rafe controlled her urge to engrave a hieroglyphic on the old stone. Instead, she pictured her ex-lover, Cynthia, and thought about the last time they enjoyed each others' bodies. Rafe spoke softly through the open window.

"If I could do it again, I would. Cynthia was some of the best sex I've ever had. Next time though, I won't get caught by anyone's crazy-ass husband."

Rafe took one last look at the sky and then left her perch by the window. She returned to the second floor landing and elbowed her way through the door.

Nannette Warfield stood on the other side of the door. She pretended to throw a body block Rafe's way. "Hey, girl. Where've you been? I was looking for you."

"Hey, yourself. I was just upstairs in your territory." Rafe grinned broadly. "What's going on?"

"Nothing much. Thought I'd come down here and harass you for a minute." Nannette's smile took up only half her mouth.

Rafe stole a glance at her watch. "A minute's all I've got."

"You've got less than that, girl. A client came sashaying through here, asking where your office was and acting like you'd better be there

"You must be talking about Selena Garrett." Rafe said.

"She's something to get ready for, girl. I remember the first day she showed up for her intake interview. I was praying they wouldn't put her in your caseload. You don't need that crap, Rafe.

Hell, no one needs that. " Nanette narrowed her eyes. "Are your office mates sitting at their desks?"

"Nope. They're all out."

"Then you better keep the door wide open, or meet with Ms. Garrett out in the hallway. I wouldn't trust her as far as I could throw a Hummer." Nannette shook her mop of reddish-blond curls.

"I hear you." Pressed for time, Rafe asked, "Anything going on that I need to know?"

"Not really. I did hear my boss say he'd like to hire two P.O.s to take the place of your supervisor." Nannette peered over the top of her eyeglasses. "She's leaving next month, you know, and he's really gonna miss her."

Rafe returned Nannette's curious stare with a thin smile.

"Well, since she's my supervisor, I don't know if I'm going to miss her or not."

"Hmm." Nannette barely concealed a grin. "Too bad she's leaving before you two really get to know each other."

"Yeah? If you say so." Rafe was in motion. "I have to go. I'm late."

"All right, then." Nannette waved. "Hey, watch out for that sly little minefield waiting for you in your office."

"Will do

As she speed-walked back to her cubicle, Rafe visualized her life at work without Alana Blue. At least she knew what to expect from Alana. The woman never questioned her decisions, nor sent her any vibes indicating she cared a whit why she'd been lifted out of the West Philly office and plunked down in this one. Plus, there was that contagious smile of hers. If she absolutely had to be supervised, Rafe felt lucky to have drawn Alana's number.

Rafe made the last turn in the hallway before arriving at her office door. Before entering, she smiled at the memory of her friend Lorin's elevator encounter with Alana, and she reiterated the pledge she'd made to herself about getting close enough to her to breathe in her fragrance. No sense in getting any closer though, since Alana would be gone in a matter of weeks.

"Hey, Rafaela."

Selena Garrett was already seated next to Rafe's desk, her legs crossed provocatively under a form-fitting skirt. "As you can see, I'm right on time."

"Good afternoon."

Rafe yanked her chair out from her desk, matching her quick action with a facial expression devoid of even the slightest trace of a smile

"As you can see, I'm one minute late. And please call me Ms. Ortiz."

Rafe opened Selena Garrett's folder and took a moment to reacquaint herself with her client's circumstances.

"How did everything go this past week, Selena?"

Selena cleared her throat before answering in a cool manner.

"I can't complain."

"I see you're in your second community-living arrangement." Rafe shot Selena a practiced stare.

"You mean my second group home?" Selena asked.

"Yes. How are you getting along with the other women?"

"Them? They're all right."

Selena uncrossed her legs.

"As long as everybody's cool with me, I'll be cool with them. I don't usually have problems gettin' along with women." Selena dropped her voice half an octave.

"You know what I mean, Rafaela?"

Rafe frowned so intensely new wrinkles rippled across her forehead.

"Oh, my bad. I forgot what you just told me about calling your name. I shoulda said, Ms. Ortiz."

Rafe ignored Selena's attempt at familiarity. She'd dealt with this brash kind of offender before, and she'd been wise enough to let their behaviors pass without responding.

"Your last random drug screening was clean. That's a good sign."

"Thanks, Ms. Ortiz." Selena flashed a smile. "You proud of me?"

"You need to be proud of yourself. It's how you feel that counts."

Rafe leveled her gaze at the younger woman. She knew saying she was proud of her would be a golden invitation for Selena to say something more personal. Rafe had no intention of screwing up this assignment with anything even remotely resembling flirtation.

"How are things going for you in the office supply company? What's a typical day like?"

"Boring." Selena turned her head away and rolled her eyes.

"Describe it for me."

"I clock in. I go to Ms. Myers. She gives me some of the overnight orders. I start filling them. When I've finished, I let delivery know and they come and pick them up."

"Then what? What's the rest of the day like?"

Selena glanced sideways at Rafe.

"Then...I go to lunch and talk mucho bullshit with anybody who's there. After that, I come back to the floor, and Ms. Myers has more orders for me to fill."

"Anything else?"

Rafe paid rapt attention, refusing to be discouraged by Selena's this-shit's-just-too-boring-for-me-to-recount attitude.

"Oh yeah. I clock out." Selena pushed her hips farther back in the chair. "You wanna know about everything I do after work too?"

"No. Not everything." Rafe, unperturbed by Selena's attitude, perused the hand written notation she'd made at the bottom of one of Selena's forms.

"Are you getting much from the group sessions with Dr. Fields?"

Selena leaned forward in her chair. She rested her forearm on Rafe's desk and stared into her eyes.

"I get a lot out of those sessions, Rafe...Ms. Ortiz."

"What, for example

"Well first of all, Dr. Fields lets us talk about anything we want." Selena lowered her voice. "And second, for an older woman, Dr. Fields is fine. I don't know for sure if she's gay, but if she's not out, I'd love to be the one to pull her. Know what I mean?"

Rafe countered Selena's leer with a dispassionate glance.

"I hope you'll continue to respect Dr. Field's skill and her professionalism. She's there to offer therapeutic help to you and the other women." Rafe left a meaningful pause before adding, "Know what I mean?"

Selena straightened her posture

"Sure, Ms. Orteeez."Selena smiled as she stretched out the second syllable of Rafe's surname.

"I think we're finished for today." Rafe closed the manila folder. "Next week I'll visit you at work, so please ask Ms. Myers to have all her forms finished for me by then."

"Okay."

Selena stood. Using both hands to smooth nonexistent wrinkles from her thighs, she turned to Rafe. "You take care, Ms. Ortiz. Or do you have someone who takes care of you?"

"That's something you don't ever need to be concerned about, Selena."

Selena grinned. "Good, 'cause I do have a lot on my mind these days."

"I imagine you do."

"One more thing, Ms. Ortiz."

"Yes?"

"I'm glad I got you as my P.O. instead of Ms. Blue."

Rafe took the bait. "Why is that?"

"'Cause one of my girls on the inside told me she's a real bitch."

Rafe's jaw tensed. Her instinct to defend her supervisor was on automatic pilot.

"You shouldn't believe everything you hear, especially from another offender, Selena."

Selena smirked at Rafe's advice. "I heard about her on the outside, too. From one of my associates. He said she really keeps up with all her clients and you can't do no side-stepping with her."

"Are you sure your friend wasn't talking about me, Selena? Because that description fits me to a T."

Selena laughed. "Thanks for the warning, Ms. Ortiz."

Rafe was aware of Selena's gamesmanship, and knew Selena had been evaluating her every minute of this office visit. She'd done her best to present a tough exterior, because she figured Selena had broken down more than a few women who'd been determined to avoid her before they gave in, weakened by Selena's will to conquer and dominate. Rafe knew she was no more than a weekly distraction in Selena's otherwise dull routine of work, group home, drug tests, and court mandated talk-a-thons with a therapist who might or might not be a lesbian.

Rafe placed two folders back in the file cabinet, and put a third one in her work bag. Then she removed her jacket from the ancient row of hooks next to the office door. She reached into her desk's side drawer for her car keys and prepared to visit one of her clients at his jobsite. She felt grateful to be headed out into the field, because she knew traipsing around the C and R Roofing Company would be less stressful than sitting a foot away from Selena Garrett.

Rafe walked out of the office, feeling lighter and breathing easier than she had for the past half-hour. As she walked toward the parking lot behind her office building, she began her daily ritual of blaming her weakness for women for the affair she'd had with Cynthia Hall. Cynthia, whose seductive behaviors were very similar to Selena Garrett's, was the reason all of Selena's attention-getting tricks were doomed to fail. Rafe had traveled down that destructive road once and she wasn't planning to go there again. So far, avoiding temptation at work had been easy. Until Selena Garrett's bold flirtation, she hadn't run into anyone who had piqued her interest, no one that is, except her supervisor. She'd looked more than once at Alana Blue, but as much as she enjoyed the view, Rafe decided looking was all she would allow either of them to do as long as they both worked for the city's Office of Probation and Parole.

Chapter Eleven

THE SECOND SHE entered the street where she lived, Lorin saw Kim's car parked at an awkward angle. Its rear end blatantly crossed the white line separating her property's two parking spaces from her neighbor's slots.

She must have been in one hell of a rush, Lorin thought. *Trying to beat the clock, as usual.*

Lorin steered her white Toyota SUV into one of the visitors' parking stalls on the other side of the driveway. In one motion she grabbed her backpack and sprang out of her vehicle. The prospect of seeing Kim on the other side of her condo's front door sped Lorin's feet. She slipped her key into the lock.

Kim stood in the middle of the spacious living room, cell phone in hand.

"Hey, baby." Lorin approached Kim and thrust out her arms in anticipation of holding her lover close.

Kim held up her unencumbered hand and pointed to her phone. She placed her forefinger on her lips and whispered, "Shhhhh, I'm talking."

Lorin nodded and backed away obediently. She walked into the kitchen, deposited her backpack on a chair and opened the refrigerator. She stared inside, more interested in listening to Kim's phone conversation than in finding something to drink. After grabbing a bottle of water, Lorin went to the other side of the room and retrieved a glass from the cabinet. As she concentrated more on Kim's voice than on the task at hand, Lorin poured some of the water. Suddenly, she jumped back as she felt a stream of cold liquid bounce off her knee and trickle down her leg.

"Oh, shit." Lorin tore a paper towel from the holder and wiped the water from her leg.

Kim strolled toward Lorin. "What happened?"

"I spilled some water, that's all

"Hey." Kim sidled up to Lorin. "Let me give you a better greeting."

Lorin softened and embraced Kim. "Hello, you. I'm glad you're here."

"Sorry I was on the phone." Kim's voice sounded like spun sugar to Lorin. "But I had to take that call. It was Lawrence."

"I thought so. Otherwise you would've dropped the phone immediately and rushed to kiss me hello."

Lorin tried to hide her wishful thinking under her sarcastic response.

"It was important. He was telling me what time he'd be coming home."

"And what time would that be?" Lorin asked, hoping to hear Lawrence wouldn't be ending his work day until many hours later.

Kim held up her left hand and looked at her watch.

"We have exactly one hour before I have to go."

"Is that all?" Unable to disguise her disappointment, Lorin pouted.

"Look, it's better than nothing. Right?"

"I suppose so."

"Hey." Kim reached for Lorin's hand. She guided her fingers over Lorin's wrist and danced them up the course of her arm, until they arrived at Lorin's shoulder. "You're wasting precious time standing here sulking."

Lorin grasped Kim's fingers and brought them to her lips. She kissed each one tenderly.

"You're right. I don't want to squander another second."

As Lorin turned and began walking toward the back of her townhouse, she tugged Kim's hand gently, yet insistently. Kim followed without uttering a word. Again, she checked her watch.

By the time they reached the bedroom, Lorin had begun to caress Kim mentally. Knowing exactly how her hands would feel as they moved over Kim's body elicited an audible moan from Lorin's throat. Kim heard the sounds of her lover's desire and she responded by undressing. Removing one piece of clothing at a time, she carefully draped each garment over a chair. Lorin watched her. She revered each movement and gesture Kim made.

Naked, except for a pair of earrings, her wristwatch, and two deep dimples at the crest of her round hips, Kim sashayed to the pine armoire on the far side of the room. She looked over her shoulder at Lorin, who continued to watch her. Then she opened one of its doors.

"Let's play with my favorite toy," she said.

A smile spread over Lorin's face.

"Whatever you want, honey."

Chapter Twelve

MOST PEOPLE WHO know me would bet I, Alana Blue, would spend my free time finishing my paperwork and putting everything in order, since I'm so close to saying adiós to my job. Nine times out of ten, they'd be right. For some reason I've been nursing a yen to visit the zoo, so this morning I decided the hill of work piled on my desk at home could wait until evening. I was going out to enjoy this early autumn day.

I took my time wending past the carefully groomed gardens near the zoo's entrance. I meandered through the primate house and taunted my fear of reptiles long enough to half look at the crocodiles and alligators lounging in their swampy display area. After stopping to watch the zebras, hunger propelled me to the zoo's open-air cafeteria. I picked out a tuna wrap and a cup of coffee and sat down at a vacant picnic table, near a young woman with a little boy who could barely sit still.

"If you eat half of this hot dog, I'll let you have the candy cigarettes."

The mother used her most convincing let's-make-a-deal voice to coax the child into eating his lunch. She glared at her little boy's legs as they swung frantically back and forth, threatening to lift him into flight any second.

"I don't want a hot dog," the child said.

"Then you can't have any candy."

The woman punctuated her statement by poking the nosepiece of her sunglasses and pushing them snugly against her face. The boy stared at his mother as he stood up. Wearing a grimace of determination on his otherwise cherubic face, he figured out how to extricate himself from the one-piece table and bench. Triumphant, he climbed free and strutted around the table.

"I wanna see the hippos," he said.

"We'll go there after you've eaten more of your lunch."

She spoke, but didn't look at the child. The glimmering diamond on her finger commanded her attention. The stone shimmered in the noon sunshine.

"No. I'm not hungry."

The boy picked up his pace and walked to the end of the raised deck where he challenged gravity by rocking back and forth on his toes.

"Michael, if you don't come back here this instant, we're going home."

Stomping his feet, the somber-eyed preschooler returned to his mother's perch on the picnic bench.

"Do you want to eat your lunch, or do you want to leave and go home?" The mother revealed her trump card.

"I wanna go home. I don't like the zoo."

Bingo. I shot a look at the young diamond-sporting woman in the sunglasses and smiled at her. We both knew the contest was over and the child had won.

I'm sure I made my share of mistakes when Nikki was young, but I bet I never bargained with her. I didn't believe in the bartering brand of parenting, unless I considered the unspoken contract between us. I'm referring to the agreement whose terms were about Nikki's living comfortably under my roof as long as she followed my rules, did well in school, and was always respectful. I don't remember exactly how I communicated these expectations, but I must have enforced them successfully, because Nikki remained in my house until her first wedding. She's been independent since then and I've been joyfully grateful.

I eavesdropped again and heard the woman tell her child to pick up his juice cup and napkin. A second later, when I noticed her doing the clean-up chores, I kept my smile to myself.

I leaned back, surprised I felt so relaxed. I could practically hear the clock ticking away the hours in the countdown to my last day at the office. I'd almost finished clearing my files, discarding what no one would need, and putting semi-active paperwork into the boxes I'd brought from home. I wasn't a collector, so there weren't many things I intended to pack and keep, just some photographs, a few books, a pair of old shoes I used when it rained unexpectedly, a jacket, and gifts some of my clients had given me over the years.

I reached for the Styrofoam cup, and took a sip of coffee. Two months earlier, the summer heat would have persuaded me to buy iced tea instead of a hot drink. But coffee was the right beverage for me this afternoon. And taking the time to sit here and drink it slowly was a step in the right direction for someone who's habitually in a rush to do everything.

"Are you enjoying the weekend, Ms. Blue?"

I looked upward, searching for the owner of the quasi-familiar voice. If I'd been at work, I would have recognized it immediately. But here, outdoors and completely disassociated from the office, I wasn't sure who had spoken to me until I could see all of her.

"Rafaela. Hi

"Hey." Rafaela grinned down at me.

"I didn't expect to see you here." I didn't expect to see anyone I knew here.

"I could say the same thing to you"

Rafaela continued sharing her rakish smile with me. She lifted a cardboard tray full of food chest high.

"I'm hungry."

"I can tell." I laughed as I perused the cheeseburger, onion rings, fries, and lemonade that threatened to overshoot the tray's boundaries.

Rafaela moved closer to the table."Mind if I join you?"

"No, not at all. There's plenty of room."

"So what are you saying? I have so much food I need a lot of space?" Rafaela pretended to be indignant as she placed her tray opposite my empty cup.

"You do have a tad more than a Happy Meal," I teased.

"Hey, I'm a growing girl."

Rafaela stood in front of me, her hands on her hips, emoting more than her usual defiance.

I couldn't avoid noticing how the sleeves of her polo shirt emphasized her well-defined upper arms.

"Well, it doesn't look like you're outgrowing anything."

I hoped my comment wasn't overly familiar. I was usually more subtle when I took in a woman's appearance.

Rafaela didn't respond, at least not verbally. It may have been my imagination, but I thought I saw her steer her gaze on a round trip, beginning with my mouth and traveling down to my throat, my breasts, and back up again to my smile.

"Did you say you come here often?" she asked.

"Hardly ever. Today's visit is strictly spur of the moment, like yours."

"Do you do a lot of things spur of the moment?"

Rafaela tore the corner off a mustard packet and squeezed out a ribbon of the yellow condiment.

"Not really. I'm a planner." I watched Rafaela remove each item from her tray and then push the cardboard tray to the side.

"You can't plan everything in life." She picked up the cheeseburger and took a hearty bite.

"You're right. But I don't like to deal with the unexpected."

I spoke plainly. I had never learned how to hide some of my truths from people, no matter who they were. As I answered Rafaela, I realized that aside from our conversation about her caseload's male-to-female client ratio, this was the longest exchange we'd had.

Rafaela pushed the box of fries in my direction.

"Help yourself."

"No thanks. I'm trying to keep my waistline measurement at a reasonable number."

"They say a waist is a terrible thing to mind." Rafaela grinned. "And from what I can see, you don't appear to be outgrowing anything either."

Rafaela's candid appraisal surprised me. The scintilla of discomfort riding on that surprise wedged its way under my composure.

"Do you know how quickly you can gain weight when you're my age?"

I wanted to rebalance us. After all, I was Rafaela's supervisor, and she was my polite but subtly defiant probie.

"Alana...I can call you by your first name, right? We're not at the office."

Rafaela's serious tone was at odds with the pose she struck, burger in one hand and an onion ring jutting from the thumb and forefinger of her other hand.

Momentarily flustered by her request, I stammered my response. "Of course you can. Of course. And for the record, I don't have a problem with your using my first name when we're in the office."

"Good." Rafaela slipped the strip of fried onion into her mouth, wiping away its slick residue with a napkin. "First of all, Alana, I'll bet we're practically the same age. Second, it's obvious you care about staying in shape. And third, one french-fried potato now and then is not going to ruin your body."

Despite my knowing Rafaela's age was close to mine, I felt like I was years older; maybe because I had a grown daughter, or different responsibilities at work. Maybe because I knew instinctively I'd looked at life more seriously than she had.

Rafaela selected a potato sliver from its box and quickly popped it into her mouth, savoring its flavor. "Oh man, this is delicious."

Infected by her over-acted joy, I gave in.

"All right, I've changed my mind. I'd like to have one of those onion rings."

"Be my guest." She nudged the container closer to my side of the table, but she continued holding on to it. "On one condition. You have to agree to stop calling me Rafaela."

I reached over her hand and stole a ring from the box.

"Do you prefer 'Rafe'?" I asked, my tongue acquainting itself with both the shortened version of her name and the crunchy sweet vegetable I'd lusted after from the first minute they'd arrived at the table.

"Yeah, I do prefer that."

"We have a friend in common, and I've heard her refer to you as 'Rafe.' "

"Who's that?"

"Jean Thompson. Her partner, Katey, is a close friend of mine. She told me you and Jean used to work together."

I watched Rafaela relax and savor another bite of her burger. She chewed slowly while she looked at me.

"Yeah, we did ... back in the day." Rafaela leaned back. "If you're tight with Jean and Katey, does that mean the two of us share something else in common?"

"It's quite possible we do, Rafe." I smiled slightly.

"Then I'm glad I ran into you."

Unable to think of a clever response, I looked down at my empty coffee cup. I'd lost my equilibrium and along with it, my self-assurance. I was used to holding my own in all sorts of conversations. Something different had found its way into this encounter.

"So, you've finally been assigned a couple of female clients, huh?"

"Yeah. Did you have anything to do with that

"Sort of."

I'd had everything to do with it. I'd shamed my boss Conrad, into changing his less-than-official male-clients-only-for-Rafaela-Ortiz policy.

"Thanks. And thanks also for putting Selena Garrett in my caseload." Rafe's voice took on a sarcastic tone.

"She's a doozy, isn't she?"

I recalled glaring at Conrad when he dropped a copy of Selena's file on my desk and directed me to forward it to Rafaela.

"Apparently, she's a legend. A social worker friend of mine has been struggling to keep Ms. Garrett in one of her agency's group homes."

I recalled perusing Selena Garrett's file. "With the Baker organization?"

"Yup."

"Is she still living there, or did they drop her?"

"She's hanging on by a press-on nail. One more dispute with a roomie, and she's out on the street," Rafe said.

"I don't remember all of her details."

"Based upon all I've read, she's been a royal pain since she was born; extremely aggressive, never accepted authority, manipulative as all get out, and determined to do everything her way," Rafe added.

"Looks like you'll have your hands full."

"That's exactly what she'd like." Rafe pulled her lips into a tight line and looked off to the distance. "But I'm not playing that game."

I wondered to which game Rafe was referring, but my sixth sense kept me from asking her to clarify her comment.

"I'm giving Selena enough rope to hang herself. Sooner or later she's going to challenge the wrong person, and it'll all be over," Rafe said.

Every P.O. had to deal with a Selena Garrett type sooner or later. And conventional wisdom dictated a client with Selena's reputation stood on a tightrope, precariously balanced between another prison term or a violent death.

Rafe eyed the remainder of the onion rings scattered on the cardboard plate. "I shouldn't eat all of these. Please help a sistah out here."

I grinned. "Sorry. One's my limit."

"Well that's the last time I ask you for help."

"You know, Rafe, you never ask me for help. Supervising you has been a breeze so far."

"Glad to hear it." The trace of cockiness in her voice softened. "Once I understood who assigned the offenders to the P.O.'s, I realized you weren't the enemy. And, you never make me feel like I'm being supervised, Alana."

"Good. That's been my goal."

"Your goal with me, or with every P.O. you supervise?"

"With everyone." I paused. "In your case, it's clear you know what you're doing."

A smile spread slowly across Rafaela's lips. My eyes followed that smile from one side of her face to the other. I looked at the prominent cheekbones delineating the slight hollows that led down to her mouth. Startled when I realized I was staring at her, I looked away.

"I'm gonna get a refill. Can I get one for you?" Rafe's voice brought me back.

"Thanks. That would be great."

"What are you drinking?"

"Coffee, please. Black."

"Gotcha."

Rafe stood and deftly swung each leg up and over the bench. She reached for my cup, smiling the whole time. I watched her walk toward the bank of beverage dispensers. She seemed to possess both an aggressive masculine energy and a feminine sensibility. For months now, I'd been aware of Rafe's presence in the office, and I'd been puzzled by her attitude toward me. This afternoon, I was intrigued by her company.

"Wanna stroll for a bit and check out the animals?" Rafe said as she handed me my coffee.

"Sure."

We ambled in no particular direction, pausing long enough to avoid colliding with children and stopping whenever we found ourselves in front of an enclosure.

"I never knew foxes were so small." Rafe watched the silky, red-haired creature trot to a shady area and then look around cautiously.

"They're smaller in real life than they are in our imaginations, aren't they? Must be the effect of all those fairy tales we heard when we were kids," I said.

The fox stood completely still, as if on alert. He seemed to be staring at a stony outcropping about twenty yards away. I followed the animal's sightline.

"Look. Behind those rocks over there. Do you see movement?" I grabbed Rafe's arm. "There must be four...no five babies."

Rafe put her hand atop mine, fusing me to her forearm.

"Wow. I've never seen baby foxes before."

I paid more attention to the warm palm resting on mine than I did to the kits.

"They're so cute," I said.

Rafe released her hold and looked at me. "You've got to be somebody's mother, 'cause you're making maternal noises."

"Guilty as charged." My uncovered hand suddenly felt cool. "I have a daughter."

"How old is she?"

"She's twenty-eight."

"That means you're finished with the tuition payments and she's on her own."

"When it comes to Nikki, I'm finished with more than tuition payments."

"That sounds somewhat serious." Rafe stared at me expectantly.

"It's not anything I feel like thinking about seriously right now."

This was neither the time nor the place for me to describe the state of my relationship with my daughter. Besides, I didn't know Rafe that well.

"That's fine with me." Rafe continued looking at the foxes. "So how old do you think these babies are?"

"I don't know. Maybe we can ask someone who works here."

We walked the breadth of the metal fence protecting the foxes and approached a placard tacked on a pole.

"It says the mother gave birth two and a half months ago."

"If these were domestic kittens, you'd be able to separate them from their parent and take them home with you," Rafe said.

"Sounds like you're speaking from experience. Do you have a cat?"

"No way. I'm not a cat person." Rafe kept shaking her head. "I'm too much on the go to have a pet. But if I did, I'd have a dog."

"There's a canine for you, right over there." I pointed to a lone gray wolf lying on a patch of grass inside his enclosure.

Rafe approached the barrier that separated the animal from us. She and the wolf stared at each other.

"He's beautiful," she said. "Look at his thick fur. I wish he'd stand up and walk. Better yet, I wish he'd stalk something. I love seeing them when they're on the prowl."

"He's probably so well fed he doesn't have to be on the prowl. If he was born in captivity, he may not know how to hunt for his food," I said.

"Oh, he remembers. Hunting for food is instinctive." Rafe spoke with authority. She crouched down. "Look at his front paws. They're huge."

I suppressed my urge to quote Goldilocks and comment on the size of the wolf's eyes and teeth. I preferred to observe Rafaela as she watched the gray predator. After a moment she straightened her posture and hooked her thumbs into the diamond-shaped openings in the chain link fence. I scanned the habitat's rocks and trees, searching for a second animal.

"Do you think there's a female in here? His mate?" I asked.

"Not that I can see."

Clearly awed, Rafe added, "He's probably happier being alone...the legendary lone wolf."

I wondered if she were speaking more about her own preferences than the wolf's. Unwilling to entertain my curiosity, I banished her comments from my mind.

Rafe pulled the sides of her jacket closer together across her chest. "It's getting late, and I need to get going."

Disappointed, I managed a tentative smile. "We've almost covered the entire zoo."

"If you say so." Rafe sounded skeptical.

"I've enjoyed spending time with you, Rafe." I meant that.

"Same here. I knew you couldn't be serious 24/7."

I smiled at her backhanded compliment. "I do relax from time to time."

"So, are you ready to say goodbye to the animal kingdom for today, or is there more territory you're going to explore?"

"In fact, there is one more stop I have to make." I pointed at the last building between us and the path leading to the zoo's parking area. "I can't leave without going into the butterfly house."

"The butterfly house?"

"Yes, butterflies," I said emphatically. "They have some very exotic ones with brilliant patterns on their wings."

"I guess I never thought of butterflies as zoo animals. People actually capture them?"

"It does seem a little strange. But then, the whole concept of putting animals in enclosures for most of their lives so people can walk by and look at them is a little cruel, don't you think?"

"I guess so." Rafe pursed her lips. "But I wouldn't lose sleep over it."

I wondered what would rob Rafe of sleep. Did her affair with her co-worker in the West Philly office cause her insomnia?

"I'll see you at the office on Monday." I extended my hand.

Rafe took it in hers and held it.

"I imagine you will, Alana. Enjoy the rest of your weekend."

We parted. I walked toward the butterfly house and paused when I reached the entrance. Before I opened the door, I turned around to look for Rafe, but she'd already disappeared. Eager to get lost in the beauty of iridescent wings, I entered the building. I moved a few feet through the darkened interior until I reached the first display case.

Blinking rapidly as flashes of blues, greens, blacks, and oranges darted in front of my eyes, I thought how quickly the years pass and how close I was to my last day on the job. In less than a month, I wouldn't be responsible for checking Rafe's work and wondering how she was handling her caseload of ex-offenders. The possibility of running into her at the office in the midst of any given day would no longer exist, and I wouldn't need to speculate about the reasons for her attitude. I knew better than to attach any importance to how I felt when her hand pressed down on mine. The wiser course for me to follow was to remember the words Rafe had uttered about the wolf preferring to be alone.

Chapter Thirteen

"BE CAREFUL WHERE you step." I waved my hand toward the boxes flanking both sides of the doorway to my office.

"It looks like you're packing to leave, Ms. Blue."

The strikingly handsome woman stepped carefully around the stacks of cardboard containers.

"You figured that out, huh?" I didn't have to read the name printed on the badge she held up, because I remembered her well. "I guess that's why you're a detective."

"Right. That's why my suburban police department pays me the big bucks." Detective Johnetta Jones' wide smile belied the sarcasm of her answer.

"Please excuse the mess in here. I'm retiring two weeks from tomorrow and I'm trying to clear out a lot of these files."

"Congratulations." Johnetta's face brightened. She gave the room's disorder a cursory glance. "It's amazing how many things you accumulate during a career, isn't it? Have you been in this office for a long time?"

"Yes, I've been here for a number of years."

She didn't seem to recall having met me more than a year earlier right here in this very room. I remember I answered each of her questions and launched a few of my own. I also remember I stared at her almost to the point of rudeness. I pretty much noticed everything; from the sparse jewelry she wore to how well her slacks and shirt conformed to her body. Her frameless glasses seemed to disappear into her high cheekbones. Her expressive eyes narrowed each time I responded to one of her questions. I remember speculating she probably did that in an effort to search for any subtext I might have woven through the threads of my answers.

She smiled at me only twice that day, and when she did, I decided the sharply defined contours of her lips were more at ease without a smile on them than with one. Although the controlled tones of her voice challenged me to contradict her assertions about one of my clients, I mounted a debate anyway. We went back and forth several times during the interview. Detective Jones seemed certain my client was guilty, and I stuck to my guns about his post-prison reformation. Despite our contentious moments, when the interview ended I was left wondering how this woman spent her off-duty hours.

"You might have forgotten, Detective, but you interviewed me here once last year."

"Yes, eighteen months ago. The Judson case."

"If I remember correctly, you linked my client to a pattern of M.O.'s in three separate rape cases."

"That's correct, Ms. Blue. You've got a good memory."

"That's because he was one of only a few ex-offenders who've been able to fool me. I never would have suspected Malik Judson of serial rapes. He was a model ex-con." I still felt the need to explain why I had defended Malik in the face of all the evidence Detective Jones supplied.

"But it turned out he was the perp. I recall you felt angry with yourself for trying to convince me he wasn't." The lines etched around Detective Jones' mouth softened.

"Now you're the one with the excellent memory, Detective. That's why your police force pays you a high salary."

"Actually, I was still on the city's payroll when I worked that case. I retired shortly afterward."

"And now you're back on the job, after your retirement?" There was no use in guessing what this woman did during her off-duty hours. She didn't have any free time.

"I stayed retired for a minute. Then I discovered I'm a happier person when I'm working, and policing is what I know best."

I pointed to the boxes scattered around the room.

"Well, I can't say I envision myself coming back to this office in a month or two. When I walk away, I'm out of here."

Detective Jones allowed herself the vaguest suggestion of a smile. "Most people are able to leave their jobs and stay away. I couldn't." Her resolute manner put a period on the topic and signaled she was ready to move on.

"I can see you're very busy, Ms. Blue, so let me explain why I'm here this morning."

I'd been curious about this interview ever since she set up the appointment. I'd played her phone message twice, because hearing the name of her jurisdiction threw me for a second. I had a vested interest in whatever concerned Brighton Township and I had an uneasy feeling Detective Jones' visit was related to the unsolved rape and murder that still occupied my local newspaper's headlines.

"I'm investigating the murder of a young woman whose body was found in Brighton Township. I need some information about one of your offenders, Reginald Harris."

Damn it! I knew she was talking about the college student who was discovered so close to my home. Of all the possible suspects in the five-county area, what were the chances she was investigating a criminal in my caseload?

"Have a seat, Detective, if you can find a chair." I smiled weakly and made my way to the file cabinet. I opened the second of four "Active" drawers and withdrew a thick folder.

"I've probably read a lot of the info you have in his file already, Ms. Blue." Detective Jones leveled her gaze at me. "What I need to find out today is more subjective stuff, like your take on Harris' personality and his temperament."

"You're interested in my opinion even though I argued with you about Malik Judson?"

"I'd never hold that against you." She seemed as sincere as I was eager to have her risk trusting my judgment about an offender. "That guy was a sociopath. He could've fooled God."

If I were listening for affirmation, I heard it in her words.

"I know Reginald Harris has been rule compliant. Can you recall anything he's objected to?"

Detective Jones opened a leather-bound notebook and thumbed past several pages.

"He complained once about the frequency of his drug and alcohol tests," I said.

"What did he say? Did he use any threatening body language?" Her eyes shifted from the page in her notebook to my face.

"He raised his voice. Not enough to intimidate me though." I visualized my client's mini-outburst. He'd sounded frustrated and claimed he was being singled out and given too many unannounced D&A tests.

"Was he persistent?" Detective Jones homed in on me.

"He mentioned it a second time, but by then he seemed resigned to the reality of being a parolee."

I pictured Harris sitting across from me, his voice little more than a whine the second time he mentioned "too much damn peeing in a cup."

Detective Jones lowered her gaze and wrote quickly in her notebook before she focused on me again.

"Has he ever said anything angry about any of his female relatives?"

"Not that I can recall."

"About any of his girlfriends or female acquaintances?"

I looked down at the floor, trying to remember if I'd ever heard Reginald Harris blurt out any irate comments about women.

"No. We usually discuss his job and his living conditions. When I ask him questions, he gives me short answers. I'm sure he never wants to prolong his appointments with me any more than necessary."

Detective Jones put Reginald Harris' folder on my desk. She

sighed and then raked her fingers through the neat waves of her closely trimmed salt-and-pepper hair. After a second or two, she fixed her eyes on mine with an unnerving intensity.

"Has Mr. Harris ever threatened you? Has he ever said or done anything in this office that made you believe he was contemplating harming you or hurting anyone else?"

Up to now, her calm voice had been just this side of smoothly seductive. These questions however, shot out like exploding firecrackers.

"No. I never got that vibe from him."

"Are you certain?"

"Absolutely." I'd know for sure if Reginald Harris had ever made me feel unsafe. He hadn't.

Detective Jones kept staring at me. "Have you ever gotten that threatening vibe from any of your clients?"

"A few times." I paused and wondered why she had asked me this question. "It comes with the territory, and it's never affected the way I handle my job."

I noticed an expression of mild surprise cross her face. Perhaps she was like other people who, from time to time, mistook my quiet demeanor and graciousness for timidity.

I switched gears and became the questioner. "Do you have children, Detective Jones?"

"I have a grown son. Why?"

"Sometimes our children train us how to face threatening behaviors. They play the intimidation game with us so often, when someone else tries it, we recognize it for what it is and we can more than hold our own."

I thought about Nikki's earliest attempts to manipulate and skirmish with me.

"Well, for as long as my son has been on this earth, he's known better than to try anything with me." Detective Jones' eyes lost their kind expression. Already erect, she sat straighter in her chair.

"I believe you, Detective, even though I don't really know you."

"Trust me. It's true," she said.

I did trust her iron tone.

"I've always heard the relationship between sons and mothers is quite different from the rocky road mothers and daughters travel."

"Yeah, I've heard that also." Her strict façade relaxed a bit. "All that aside, my son Thomas is a real good guy. He would have gotten along with any parent."

"It's nice to hear that. It's got to be tough rearing a boy in this city."

"I won't lie to you. We had our tense moments." She paused for a second. Then she gazed at me, almost shyly. "Did you and your husband go through rough patches with your daughter?"

"No, we didn't. I went through all the rough patches with her by myself. Her dad dropped out of the picture early on." It had been such a long time since anyone referred to my husband, that for a moment, I wondered if Detective Jones were still talking to me.

"How about you? Did your husband help rear your son, or were you a single parent also?" My curiosity didn't surprise me, but the flash of anxiety I felt as I awaited her response amazed me.

"I was single for most of Tommy's childhood." Detective Jones' lips parted, as she teetered on the edge of saying more. Instead of continuing, she kept her next thoughts to herself.

"He must have been proud of his mom's being a detective," I said.

I own up to being mildly intrigued by most female police officers, and Detective Jones was no exception. That she'd been tough enough to survive a career in the Philly Police Department, and then resilient enough to seek a spot on a suburban force piqued my interest.

"I'd like to think he admired me." She looked away for a second before continuing. "I'm being modest. I know he admired me, or at least he did until he reached his late teen years."

I watched her eyes blink quickly. She looked down at her hands.

"What happened then? The usual teenage-era monster?" I tried to brighten what suddenly appeared to be a stormy topic.

"Yeah, adolescence took its toll. And smack dab in the middle of it, I told him I was a lesbian." She looked directly into my eyes.

I hoped she saw a look of subdued elation, not censure. I'd assumed she was gay when she interviewed me last year. Or maybe I'd hoped she was. My only surprise was how openly she declared it.

"It's hard for some kids to adjust to their parent's sexuality, especially if it's an alternative lifestyle." I realized my response sounded more clinical than I'd intended.

"It's not a lifestyle, Ms. Blue. It's my life," Detective Jones fairly snapped at me.

Slightly wounded by her defensiveness, I leaned forward in my chair and spoke gently.

"Please call me Alana. Could I call you Johnetta?"

"Yes." Curiosity streaked through Johnetta's eyes.

"I understand what you're saying, and I appreciate your trusting me enough to say it," I continued. "I'm a lesbian, also."

"You are?" Johnetta's seriousness vanished as she extended

her hand to me.

"Yes, I am."

We locked hands conspiratorially. Her grip was firm, but the palm of her hand was surprisingly soft.

"In that case, don't call me Johnetta, call me Johnnie." She beamed. "It's a damn small world, Alana."

"Indeed it is." I grinned at her. After a few seconds, I asked, "How's your son treating you these days? Has he recovered from your disclosure?"

"Completely. He's as good a man as he was a child." Johnnie couldn't contain her grin.

"Does he live in the area?"

"No. He had a job transfer about a year ago and he got married the year before that. He's happy, and most importantly, he's at peace with everything that concerns me." Johnnie's face took on a beatific glow. "Does your daughter know all about you?"

"She does." I suppressed a sigh "And she's less than pleased. I don't know how it happened, but my daughter turned out to be ultra-conservative. She's the most homophobic person I know."

Johnnie shook her head. "That's too bad."

"It is what it is, and there's nothing I can do about it. Does your son get along with your partner?"

"He liked both of my exes, although neither one was a live-in."

"Was that because of his earlier attitude about you?"

"Not really. It was more about my not feeling totally committed to either woman."

"I see." I wondered if Johnnie had been more dedicated to her career and her son than she'd been to her former partners.

"How about you? Are you with a partner?" Johnnie stared at me, her eyebrows raised.

"Not currently."

"Because of your daughter?"

"No. She's not a factor at all." Despite my willingness to question Johnnie, I didn't feel a pressing need to share anything further about my love life. Although my last relationship ended without much drama, I was ambivalent about entering another one.

Johnnie glanced at her wristwatch. "Oh, man. It's later than I thought." She stood up and once again offered me her hand. "Thanks for meeting with me and answering my questions, Alana. All of them."

I stood also.

"No problem. Uh…could I ask you two more questions?"

"Certainly."

"Number one, the case you're working on…is it the college student's murder? And second, how closely are you looking at

Reginald Harris?"

"Yes, it's that case and Harris looks good for it. My partner and I are getting close to arresting him and requesting a court order to haul his ass from Philly out to our jurisdiction. All we need is a positive DNA sample."

I shifted my weight from one foot to the other. "I live near the property where the girl's body was discovered."

Johnnie beamed. "That means we're neighbors, Alana. I live in Brighton, too."

"You're kidding. These coincidences are too much."

"They're pretty unbelievable."

"You know what? We should get together sometime. Maybe meet for coffee," I said.

"I'd like that, Alana. And since you're going to be happily unemployed soon..." Her voice went up at the end of her unfinished sentence.

"Yeah, I'll be out of here. But you've been rehired. I might have much more free time than you have."

Johnnie pulled a business card from her wallet.

"Well, I don't work 24/7, you know." She wrote on the back of the card. "That's my cell number. Give me a call sometime, neighbor."

"I'll do just that," I said. "And do me a favor. Find someone else to arrest for that murder, someone who's not in my caseload."

Johnnie grinned at me.

"Look at it this way, Alana. If you have to testify about his parole record, you won't have to travel into the city. You'll report to a courtroom in Montgomery County, close to home."

"Thanks a lot," I said sarcastically.

"Don't mention it. See you in the neighborhood."

I thought about the possibility of spotting Johnetta at the local supermarket or gas station and realized I wouldn't be sorry to run into her, not sorry at all. As I watched her leave my office, I recognized a subtle feeling I had relinquished some time ago. I couldn't tell if the recognition brought relief or fear.

Chapter Fourteen

LORIN WILKES STRETCHED every fiber of her five-foot, seven-inch frame before sitting down awkwardly on the flat rocks that divided one side of Cape Henlopen State Park's beach from the other. Even though she wore sunglasses, she held her right hand above her eyebrows and gazed across the expanse of sand. Several female couples, some with preschool-aged children orbiting them, were constructing temporary shelters against the cool September wind.

Lorin dug her heels into the sand and contemplated putting some sunburn lotion on her legs. She started to reach into her backpack, then decided not to search for the tube of lotion. *I'm not going to be here that long, so why bother?*

The autumn sun, a faint shadow of its summertime self, shared the day with the cool breeze kissing the sea's surface. Lorin squinted as she watched a person walking toward her. At first, the figure was a hazy silhouette, genderless, without color, almost floating above the strip of sand that welcomed the waves' final ripple. Then, as the person came into soft focus, Lorin could see that indeed, the phantom was female. She was wearing a visor, and although the glare prevented Lorin from deciphering the cap's logo, she knew it was the kind of head covering Kim always wore to the beach or to the golf course. The woman moved the same way Kim did, assertively.

Lorin leaned forward, ready to stand and leave the rocky outcropping at a second's notice. A fine mist covered her sunglasses and made it difficult for her to see the approaching woman's face. Lorin figured in another moment her moisture compromised vision wouldn't matter. She'd be able to see Kim clearly, call out her name, and half-trot to greet her. In this lesbian-friendly part of Rehoboth Beach, she'd actually be able to hug her lover in broad daylight and then find a spot where they could sit and talk for a couple of hours. Afterward, they'd retreat to the women-owned bed and breakfast where Lorin had already checked in and left her overnight bag. If Kim weren't too tired after her work day and her drive from Philadelphia, they'd ease one hunger by making love and then assuage another by going out for dinner.

Lorin braced herself with her hands and pushed against the sides of her jagged seat. She arose quickly, her smile spreading, her tongue tasting the air's salty residue on her lips. How would Kim's mouth feel and taste when she kissed her?

The beach walker was closer now, her tanned skin glowing. Lorin watched the woman slow her pace, cast her eyes downward at the sand, and search for some unknown treasure washed ashore with the tide. It was clear to Lorin the woman was looking for some object, not for a person. It was equally clear the woman wasn't Kim.

Lorin's disappointment tore through her. Unwilling to return to her perch atop the ashen-gray rocks, she bent down to pick up her backpack. Dejected, she flung the bag over her shoulder and walked reluctantly to the water's edge. Children's voices wove in and out of the thundering waves that broke just yards away from Lorin.

"Mommy! Mommy! Whales!"

Lorin stared at the ocean. A short distance away she could see three dolphins, their blue-black bodies slick with the sea and their movements perfectly choreographed. She glanced at the children, who by now were jumping up and down frantically and screaming for their two mothers' attention.

Lorin liked kids, but she was grateful she didn't have any. And she was even more grateful for Kim's childlessness. It was bad enough Kim was married. If she were to become a mother, Lorin feared they would see each other less frequently than they did now.

Lorin followed the dolphins' progress, becoming so lost in their rhythmic dives in and out of the ocean that she almost missed hearing her cell phone ring. She ripped open the side compartment of her backpack and yanked out the phone. The letters of her lover's name spread across the display. Lorin knew this couldn't be good news because Kim was supposed to be beside her on this beach right now.

"Kim? Where are you, honey?" Lorin struggled to absent fear from her voice.

"I'm at home. I just got in from work."

Lorin tensed. "Is anything wrong? I expected to see you here a while ago."

"I know. I'm sorry." Long seconds of silence stretched Lorin's patience. "It looks like I'm not going to be able to make it."

"Why?"

"Lawrence called. He claimed he saw how nice the weather forecast was, and he wondered if I could cancel my getaway with the girls and instead, go to Cape May with him."

Lorin felt her throat tighten and go dry. "But what about us?"

"Please understand. I'll try to make it up to you, I promise."

"I've already checked in at the B&B. What am I supposed to do?" Lorin's stomach took a rollercoaster ride.

"Don't worry. I'll pay for my half."

"I don't care about that, Kim. I care about not seeing you. This isn't fair."

"Did someone tell you dating a married woman would be fair?"

Instead of hearing contrition in Kim's voice, Lorin heard a challenge. "No. No one said anything to me about fairness."

Kim sighed into the telephone. "Look, I don't like this any more than you do. But what can I do? Lawrence would be suspicious if I turned him down to spend a weekend with my girlfriends. And then, he might start asking questions I can't answer."

"I'm trying to deal with this, Kim. But it's hard." Lorin stared out at the gray sea.

"I know it is. When we first started seeing each other, I told you it wasn't going to be easy. Remember?"

"Yeah, I remember." Pivoting her ankle back and forth, Lorin's toes etched a squiggly design in the sand.

"Look, I'll call you later on. Maybe we can see each other sometime next week."

"Kim?" Lorin stilled her foot.

"What?

"Never mind. We'll talk later."

"Okay. Bye."

Lorin slipped her phone back into her backpack. She bent down, picked up a piece of shell, and hurled it over the water. Oblivious to other beach strollers, she muttered,"Shit! Another one of Kim's half-ass promises down the drain."

She took a last look at the female duo sitting on the sand, surrounded by their laughing kids.

"Doesn't look like that's going to be Kim and me anytime soon."

With her shoulders hunched, she trudged past sparse beach grass. Finally, she reached the sand-covered walkway leading to the parking lot. Questions, like hungry seagulls, swirled above her head. The only decision she had the will to make was whether she wanted to spend the night at the B&B or drive back to the city right now.

Chapter Fifteen

"WELCOME, OWEN. I'M glad you decided to come here today." Dr. Greene parceled out a quick smile before turning her attention to Nikki.

"How are you, Nikki?"

"I'm okay." Nikki looked at Owen and pointed to the sofa.

"Nikki, how did you feel about asking Owen to be here today?"

"It was easy," Nikki said confidently. "Owen and I are both invested in our marriage. We'll do what we need to do to make it succeed."

"Do you agree with that, Owen?"

"Yes, I agree. I don't mind being here at all," Owen said quickly.

"Good." Dr. Greene let a few seconds of silence pass. "What was this past week like for you?"

"The regular. Routine," Nikki said.

Dr. Greene turned to Owen. "Was it routine for you as well?"

Owen nodded quickly. "Yes. Yes, it was."

"Since this is the first time you're meeting with me, Owen, could you describe your weekly routine? I'd like a sense of what that word means to you." Dr. Greene sat in her easy chair facing them. Her hands, palms open and turned upward, rested in her lap.

"Oh, sure." Owen cleared his throat. "I'm teaching two courses this semester, so that's four classes a week."

"He always teaches two courses, two sections of each, Monday through Thursday, with office hours on Wednesday and Friday," Nikki added.

Owen nodded his approval of Nikki's explanation.

"Do you enjoy your work, Owen?" Dr. Greene asked.

"Yes, immensely." Owen fixed his eyes on the therapist.

"What makes it enjoyable for you?"

"His young female students," Nikki blurted out.

Owen turned his head toward Nikki. He frowned at her, cleared his throat, and then resumed answering the question.

"Uh, I enjoy all of my students, Dr. Greene. All of them. I like helping them discover English literature doesn't have to be dull and boring."

"It sounds like you value what you teach, and you value your students."

"Yes, I do." Owen's expression brightened.

"Tell me, what kinds of activities do you enjoy when you're not teaching?"

Owen looked up at the ceiling. "Uh...racquetball, reading, research."

"The three R's," Nikki said.

"I play racquetball every chance I get. There's a faculty league at school, and some of us have been playing for years now. Other than that—"

"Owen leads a scholarly life." Nikki reached out and patted her husband's knee. "And he's always writing. It's still publish or perish in the university world."

Owen stilled Nikki's hand.

"Nikki, a moment ago you said Owen derives enjoyment from his young female students. Do you want to talk more about that?" Dr. Greene gazed directly at Nikki.

Nikki stole a glance at Owen. "I don't know. I guess I shouldn't have made that comment."

"Just a quick detour here." Dr. Greene held up her right hand. "This is a "should-free" zone. We don't make any judgments about what you should or shouldn't say. Okay?"

Owen smiled."That sounds good to me."

"I forgot about that. And I forgot to mention it to Owen." Nikki looked contrite.

"You forgot to tell me something? That's a rare occurrence." Owen's retort dripped with sarcasm. He looked directly at Dr. Greene and explained, "Nikki covers all the bases. She never forgets to mention anything to me."

Dr. Greene gazed at Owen and Nikki.

"Nikki, you've told me why you wanted to include Owen in our work here. Have you shared your reasons with him?"

"Yes. He knows how uptight I get dealing with my job and all the things I have to keep up with at home, and he's been very patient with me, especially when I've been stressed out." Nikki removed her hand from Owen's leg. She looked down at her lap, and lowered her voice along with her gaze. "I'm afraid one of these days his patience will wear thin. In fact, I think he's running out of patience already."

"Why do you think that?" Dr. Greene asked.

"Every time I want us to discuss an issue, I'm the only one doing the talking. Owen clams up. I don't know what thoughts are going through his head."

Owen nudged his right shirtsleeve up and away from his wrist and glanced down furtively at his watch. Then he rolled the fingers of his left hand into a fist and moved it from left to right between his thigh and the arm of the sofa.

"Is Nikki's perception accurate, Owen? Do you think your patience with her is wearing thin?"

"No. Not at all. We have talks whenever the need arises."

Nikki stared at Dr. Greene and shook her head. She turned slightly toward her husband. "You get totally quiet, Owen. You know you do."

Owen's lips formed a thin line. His chest expanded and contracted with deep breaths.

"It's just that I do a lot of talking at school. I lecture, you know?" He paused. "When I come home, I like to relax. Home is my place of solitude."

Owen began moving his fist from side to side more quickly. "Not much TV, a little music from time to time, no long-drawn-out telephone conversations, and absolutely none of that singing, ringing cell phone nonsense while I'm at home. I need quiet in order to read and write. I need to be able to concentrate on my work."

Owen's last words shot out of his throat with the speed of an archer's arrow. His voice became a piercing, high-pitched staccato. "I'm sorry. I didn't mean to have an outburst."

An astonished Nikki stared at him.

"You don't need to apologize for anything, Owen," Dr. Greene said softly. "This is a safe space for the two of you to be able to talk as well as listen to each other."

Owen nodded once, curtly. "Thanks."

"Nikki, is your stress the most immediate issue you want to discuss with Owen?" Dr. Greene asked.

Nikki nodded vigorously. "That and the constant tension I feel whenever Owen mentions my mother."

"I like my mother-in-law. I respect her."

"That's because she's not your mother. Your mother is a respectable woman." Nikki tilted her head to one side as she spat her response at Owen.

"So is yours, Nikki." Owen said. "Everyone who knows her respects her."

"You don't know what everyone says about her behind our backs." Nikki's voice grew louder.

"Maybe I don't. But neither do you. Look, we can't control what other people think and say," Owen said.

"I know we can't control them, but I can be hurt and embarrassed by what they think and say. All of that hurt and embarrassment stresses me out, Owen. And when I'm on stress overdrive, I can't be the kind of wife you deserve."

"What do you mean by the phrase, 'the kind of wife you

deserve'?" Dr. Greene asked.

Nikki looked plaintively at Owen. "You know what I mean, don't you?"

Owen didn't answer.

Nikki scowled angrily at Dr. Greene. "When I'm constantly stressed out by one thing or another, I don't want to have sex. How the hell am I going to get pregnant if we don't have sex?"

"An immaculate conception would be my guess," Owen said. "Then you can be anointed into the sainthood and purity of character you believe your mother gave up the day she came out of the closet."

"Damn you, Owen," Nikki spewed her venomous anger. "You respect my lesbian mother, but you don't respect me, your straight wife!"

"Let's slow things down and get some clarity here, all right?" Dr. Greene said. "Owen, it sounds to me like you may not share Nikki's feelings of anger and embarrassment about her mother."

"Bingo. You're right."

"Can you feel empathy for Nikki? Can you try to imagine how she feels about her parent?"

"He doesn't have to imagine my feelings," Nikki said before Owen could utter a word. "I communicate how I feel just fine."

Owen lowered his voice and unclenched his fist.

"Nikki is always harping about what our friends probably think of her mother's sexuality, and how their opinions make her feel."

"And you still don't get it, do you?" Nikki glared at Owen. "No matter how many times I try to explain how ashamed I feel, you don't understand. But what really hurts is your lack of support."

"Why should I support you? Your attitude is provincial and homophobic." Owen crossed his arms in front of his chest and turned to look directly at Nikki. "We're not talking about a stranger here, or a celebrity. We're talking about your mother. As far as I can tell, she did a great job raising and providing for you. What difference does it make who she chooses to love?"

"It makes a hell of a difference to me, Owen." Nikki gritted her teeth.

"What if your mother was heterosexual and you were a lesbian? Would you want her to reject you the way you reject her? Huh?"

Nikki jumped up from the sofa. Towering over Owen, she screamed at him, "What the hell kind of question is that?"

Owen looked up at Nikki and spoke to her in a calm voice. "I'm asking you a hypothetical question, that's all. I wish you'd stop and consider how your mother probably feels every time you shut her down."

"When do I shut her down?"

"Any time she's tried to talk to you about her break-up with Catherine, or about civil rights for gays and lesbians," Owen said.

"That's not true." Nikki sank back into the sofa.

"Isn't it? You accuse me of not talking to you when you want to discuss an issue. Well, Nikki, you're the role model for shutting down. The only opinion you want to hear from me is condemnation of your mother and of all gay people. And that's just not going to happen."

Owen patted his jacket pocket, in search of something.

Nikki sneered and thought, *He doesn't have his pipe. He won't be able to continue talking without holding his goddamn pacifier.*

Newly composed, she spoke. "Look, Owen, all I'm asking is do you want your children to have a lesbian for a grandmother?"

"I want my kids to have a loving grandmother. I don't care if she's straight or gay. I'm sick and tired of your using your mother's sexuality as a wall between us."

Nikki said nothing

"Nikki, how do you feel about what Owen just said?" Dr. Greene asked.

"It's a pile of bullshit."

"Oh, that figures." Owen shook his head in disgust. "Whenever I speak my mind, you label it bullshit."

Owen and Nikki stared in silence at Dr. Greene. They'd dug an emotional trench and jumped into it, feet first.

"It's important for us to agree on a couple of things before we end our session today." Dr. Greene directed their attention away from each other and back to her.

"First, it sounds to me like you're struggling with the ability to communicate effectively. Second, you each have needs that aren't being met."

Owen nodded. Nikki remained motionless.

Dr. Greene reached for her appointment book. "Shall we set up an appointment for next week at the same time?"

"All right." Nikki broke her silence.

Owen reached for the phantom pipe once again. "I'm not sure. I'll have to check my datebook."

"That's fair, Owen. Will you phone me to either confirm or reschedule?"

"Sure."

"In the meantime, I have a homework assignment for both of you. I'd like you to list all the needs or desires you have that aren't being met right now within your relationship. Then, I'd like you to review your list and highlight the two most important needs."

"Only two?" Nikki asked.

"For now, only two." Dr. Greene smiled and stood up. "I'll see you next week."

"Thank you, Dr. Greene." Owen removed a check from his wallet and handed it to her.

Nikki walked briskly to the door. She looked back to make sure Owen was following close behind. The couple made their way to their parked cars.

"Are you coming straight home?" Nikki fingered her key fob.

"No. I have some material to duplicate for tomorrow's classes."

You're going back to the university?"

"Yes, I am. Everything I need is in my trunk." Owen gestured to the rear of his Volkswagen. "I won't be long. I'm going to the Quick Print."

"All right. See you later."

Nikki slid into the driver's seat and started her car. As it idled, she watched Owen open the trunk of his car and push aside a dark green sheet of plastic covering a stack of papers.

Probably some precious lecture notes, Nikki thought smugly. She shifted her car from neutral to drive and accelerated past Owen who stood near his car door, waving impotently at her.

Chapter Sixteen

ONCE I'D MADE the decision to leave, I never looked back, not even this early October night when I walked into the banquet room where most city departments held their celebrations. I was so resolute; I assumed the silvered veins in the ancient mirrors lining the room's walls reinforced my decision to retire.

A silent army of burgundy damask-covered tables filled the banquet space. Here and there, a deeply etched crease announced the length of time a particular tablecloth had been in storage, awaiting its call to duty. The unmistakable odor of industrial-strength starch competed with the smells of food, perfume, and aftershave filling the room.

A platform stood at one end of the area. It held a podium along with a table festooned with the same kind of burgundy cloth that covered the imperfections on all the smaller tables. A routine assortment of pink, red, and white carnations filled crystal vases on each table.

Carnations are safe, I thought. *They're sweet, undramatic, unassuming.*

"Alana, there you are!" My boss navigated his way toward me, steaming ahead of his wife, who followed in his wake. He brushed aside my outstretched hand and pulled me into a bear hug.

"Hey, Conrad." Eager to avoid his strong-arm tactic, I stepped back a pace or two.

Conrad inspected me. "You look wonderful, doll."

"You clean up pretty nicely yourself." A quick perusal of his navy blue suit, pale pink shirt, and expensive tie confirmed his reputation as a clotheshorse. Some of my colleagues and I were convinced Conrad worked for two reasons only: to pay his health insurance premiums and to keep his closet filled with designer outfits.

Conrad looked to his side. "You remember my wife, Celia, don't you?"

"Sure I do." I reached for Mrs. Conrad's hand. "It's nice to see you again."

"Same here, Alana. And congratulations to you." Celia gave me half a pump before her hand slid from my grasp.

I had met Mrs. Conrad at a holiday party shortly after she and Conrad married. She seemed shy then, standing next to his garrulous persona while balancing a cocktail in one hand and a small plate of hors d'oeuvres in another. I had trouble reconciling the fact that this same, almost mousy woman was the principal of one of the city's largest and most difficult to manage high schools. Try as I might, I couldn't picture Celia being in charge of a box of Kleenex, much less a huge public school. Imagining she could direct three thousand students in addition to the staff strained my belief system.

"How about a drink, Alana? A scotch?" Conrad was off to the bar before I could answer.

"Thanks." I muttered to his back. Celia eked out a thin smile.

"So, how does it feel to be leaving your job?" Celia pasted a pleasant expression on her face.

"It feels good." I wouldn't let her attempt at a genuine smile prevent me from favoring her with mine. "How is your work going? Are you off to a good semester?"

I saw the muscles in Celia's throat tighten.

"Oh, you know how it is. Never easy. Always challenging."

"That's what my daughter tells me." I rushed to agree with her, hoping that would help her feel more at ease. I sympathized with anyone who had to attend a retirement party to honor people they didn't really know.

Celia perked up."Is your daughter in the system?"

"Yes. She teaches at Pemberton Middle School." I nodded. "She seems to like it, although from time to time she does mention the problems she encounters."

"Oh, I'm sure she does." Celia lowered her voice and used her hand to cup one side of her mouth. "It's been a couple of months since it happened, but we're still dealing with the fallout from our latest murder."

"Excuse me?"

"Shantay Taylor, the girl whose body was found in a compost bin somewhere out in the suburbs? She graduated from my school last year. A lot of her friends are a year or two younger than she was, so they're still with us. It's a terrible thing." Celia exhaled audibly.

"I'm familiar with that case." Familiar was an understatement. I couldn't escape its tentacles. Johnetta Jones phoned me just yesterday to ask if my client, Reginald Harris, had shown up for his last appointment. I assured her he had, and he hadn't acted any differently from any other time he'd been in my office. Johnetta listened quietly and then reminded me of our promise to meet for coffee sometime soon.

"They haven't arrested anyone yet." Celia leaned closer to me. "And you know, although it looks like the murder happened out in Brighton Township, Conrad is all paranoid about the perpetrator belonging to one of his parole officer's caseloads."

"We've all thought about that possibility, Celia." I knew Conrad wasn't suffering from paranoia. No doubt the Brighton Police Department had gotten his okay to interview me before they sent Detective Jones to my office.

"Well, one more reason you must be happy to be leaving. The world's going crazy." Celia turned up her volume and punctuated her conclusion about universal insanity with a quick shake of her fashionably long reddish-brown tresses. She swiveled her head from left to right with such intensity, I wondered if she were truly in control of it or in the early stages of a tremor associated illness. I wondered also if Conrad had gone all the way to a Scottish distillery to get my drink.

On a roll, Celia continued. "Shantay lived with her aunt in the city."

"I didn't know that." If I'd read that fact in the newspaper, I hadn't retained it. Johnetta hadn't mentioned it either. Or, maybe she had, and I'd been too preoccupied, staring at the determination I saw on her face and wondering if she'd ever shot anyone with her service revolver.

"The television reporters made it sound like she lived with her mother, but she didn't. The court took her away from her mother because she's a drug addict."

"The mother or Shantay?" Despite being distracted by all the activity in the banquet room, I was trying to listen carefully to Celia.

"The mother," Celia said. "Shantay was so nice, one of the few really serious students we had in our school. She had a future in front of her. She could write rings around her classmates, probably around some of her teachers, too."

I flashed back to the photo of Shantay Taylor I'd seen on TV shortly after the murder occurred. It was one of those cap-and-gown head shots that incline you to believe in the young person's promise. The girl's bright eyes held an expression of hopefulness. Her easy smile showed a complete absence of guile and conveyed a youthful innocence. Buried under all the chores I needed to accomplish before leaving my job, I hadn't thought about her picture for the last few weeks. I had thought about the crime though. It loitered at the edge of my mind every time I passed the house where her body was found. I'd become especially vigilant during my weekly meetings with Reginald Harris, and wondered if he had any idea the cops in Brighton Township were examining him under a microscope. And of course, if it weren't for Shantay Taylor's murder, I wouldn't be looking for Detective Johnnie Jones as I tooled around the streets and businesses in my neighborhood.

Once again I focused on Celia. "It's so sad someone ended her life. I'm sorry you and your students have had to go through this emotional trauma."

"Oh, honey. My students have gone through so much by the time they reach high school. This is simply one more tragic chapter." Celia reached out and touched the back of my hand. She began shaking her head again. "Such a waste. That young woman wrote some wonderful poetry. She could have become a writer or a journalist."

"Here you are, Alana." Conrad's booming voice ripped the pall off Celia's somber conversation. He arrived with a glass in each hand. One he surrendered to me and the other he held to his mouth, swallowing at least half of the liquid.

"I didn't think you'd want a second drink, Celia."

"No, you're right, dear." Her smallness replied.

"Thanks, boss." I tipped my glass in his direction before turning my head slightly to more easily peruse the room. Surely by now, other folks I knew had arrived.

"If you'll excuse me, I see some friends over there." I stretched the truth as I gestured toward a group of total strangers who were congregated around one of the other retirees.

"Oh sure, Alana. Enjoy. This is your night." Conrad squeezed my arm before I could slide away from his range. Gritting my teeth, I quickly reviewed all I remembered about the state's sexual harassment regulations. Did my official retirement date correspond with his sudden touchy-feely behaviors? The very thought of a public apology from Conrad followed with a check representing several years' worth of salary garnishments coaxed the biggest smile to my face. By the time I approached the small knot of people I'd never seen before, they were all smiling back at me.

Although I wasn't the only employee being recognized tonight, I was the only person taking advantage of the city's expedient buyout offer. The other three P.O.'s seated at the head table were retiring with more years of service than I had accumulated. In my mind, they were more entitled to this party than I was.

After taking a few sips of my drink, making small talk with some of my co-workers became easier. I didn't know about the others, but I'd begun to feel a sense of lightness as the weight of my job drifted from my shoulders. All of the crappy days were floating away, carried off the same way our used plates of fish, chicken, or vegetarian eggplant casserole were at the end of the meal.

A few days from now I wouldn't have to worry about job and housing placements, random drug tests ensnaring the more addictive personalities, and all the temptations waiting out there in the streets to trap the ex-offenders in my caseload. I could say goodbye to the endless paperwork, the reports no one really read before filing, and the ridiculous "P.O. on probation" policy that kept me busy with a succession of employees needing my signature on their forms. I would see no more resentful glares from employees who had messed up one way or another. There would be no more subtle pushbacks from Rafe Ortiz.

Too bad I never had a chance to win her confidence. Maybe I should have let her know how much I trusted her to do her job correctly; how I gave her free rein and signed off all of her work without checking it; how I never second-guessed her decisions.

I walked the plank and argued with Conrad about Rafe's lack of female clients. At the time, I didn't figure he'd swing to the other side of the pendulum and assign that slick career criminal, Selena Garrett, to her caseload. If Conrad were out to trap Rafe instead of capitalizing on how valuable she was to our department, he was wasting his time. I was sure Rafe had learned her lesson, albeit the hard way.

Her infractions weren't any more serious than those of others I'd heard about. What made Rafe's misadventure so memorable was how public it was paired with her yeah-I-did-it-so-what attitude. She accepted her penalty without moaning and groaning, but she's made it clear she feels defensive with her co-workers and excluded from our office's inside track. Maybe that feeling of exclusion outweighs her professionalism and explains why I haven't seen her here tonight.

We reached the part of the evening I'd been dreading, the unscripted remarks and anecdotes some people found entertaining, but I thought were embarrassing. Conrad stood at the podium, introducing co-workers who took turns pelting the three retirees and me with memories of our crazy times on the job. They spun their own versions of the days when our absurd circumstances forced logic to take a vacation. Laughing about those times was easy for us now, but when that crap was happening, it was far from amusing.

My career-long demeanor, the only one I'd known to present to my work world, kept most of my colleagues off balance when it came to teasing me publicly. They seemed uncertain about breaching the border separating a scathing memory from a humorous one. Consequently, their comments were gently droll, not bitingly critical. That was fine with me. I wanted the people in the Office of Probation and Parole to remember me as efficient but kind, knowledgeable and gently humane, always humane. So what if I was no nonsense 24/7? I'd earned everyone's respect, hadn't I? Everyone's that is, except my daughter's and perhaps Rafe Ortiz's.

The speeches ended, and one by one we received our plaques.

For the umpteenth time, I scanned the room in search of Nikki and Owen. I didn't expect to see them, but I perused the crowd just the same. Halfway through my exploration, a familiar figure darted in front of me.

"You know what I'm going to miss the most about you, Alana?" Sally Lindstrom, the lead administrative assistant in the office, didn't wait for my answer. "Your smile. Seeing your beautiful happy smile first thing every morning."

"Really?" I wasn't aware I smiled every morning. Some days when I arrived at work, I'd barely felt conscious, especially if my arrival followed a late night of reading or a dinner date with someone pleasant but not at all exciting. My morning smile must have been a reflex, timed to appear automatically the moment I opened the office door.

"You always brightened the whole place," Sally said.

"I'm glad I could do that for you."

"Uh, huh. You kept smiling even after they loaded you down with those extra assignments. And no matter what news I had for you, sad or happy, you always thanked me," Sally paused before adding, "like you meant it."

"Well I did mean it, Sally." I winked at her. "You were the messenger. No need to shoot you just because you brought bad tidings."

"That's what I'm talking about. I wish everyone had your attitude, Alana." A cloud of sadness passed over Sally's eyes.

"You've got some good people working there with you. The job is tough and sometimes overwhelming. From time to time some of us forget who the real enemy is."

"Isn't that the truth?" Sally turned and peered over her shoulder. "Now where the Sam Hill did Tom go?"

A moment earlier I'd noticed Sally's husband withdraw from the banquet room and walk toward the door. "I saw him head out of here. He's probably looking for you."

"Well, I'd better get going. Can I give you a big hug, Alana?"

I nodded. "You'd better."

As I embraced Sally, I noted how fragile her thin upper body felt. Taking care not to hug her too fiercely, I gazed over her slight shoulder, and caught a glimpse of a woman braced against the room's far wall.

"Come see us sometime, Alana. Don't forget about your friends in the trenches."

"I won't forget about you, Sally." I inclined my head just a little bit. Then I peered at the spot across the room where I'd seen the female figure a second ago. The only person I spotted now was a waiter stacking plates and silverware onto a huge tray. The woman was gone as quickly as she'd appeared. I wondered if I'd really seen her or only imagined it.

Shaking the mirage from my mind, I sought out Katey and Jean.

"Hey, it feels good saying adiós to all these people, doesn't it?" Jean grinned and touched my arm.

"Mostly," I said. "It feels a little bittersweet, too."

"I know what you're saying." Jean added. "You've worked so long and hard with these folks, it feels like you're leaving part of your family. But trust me, you'll get over it quickly."

"Now you can do whatever you want, Alana. You can get up late, go to bed when you please, read all those books you've been stockpiling..."

My mind wandered over Katey's ideas, and I thought about Johnetta Jones. Would I feel the need to get another job, as she had?

Katey spoke to me, but the glazed look in her eyes suggested she was pondering her own future. Jean must have translated Katey's words exactly as I had.

"Baby, you know you can stop working anytime you want."

"According to my financial planner, I can't join your little club for another three years, and even then I have to be thrifty for as long as I'm retired." Katey spoke authoritatively.

"So what's it like lounging in bed all day while the little woman here gets up and goes out to work?" I teased. I knew darn well Jean never lingered in bed. Her ambition drove her to a new career, teaching a course in the criminal justice program at the local community college.

"Oh, I don't let that happen." Katey shot a grin at Jean before shifting her attention to me. "Jean jumps right up in the morning and gets the coffee going."

I winked at them. "Sounds like a system."

Jean grinned. "It works for us."

"Thanks for inviting us to the celebration, Alana." Katey leaned closer to me. "This has been real nice."

"Your being here made me happy."

"I'm sorry Nikki and Owen missed hearing what your colleagues said about you. Nikki would have been proud."

"Well, that's up for debate. I can't remember the last time Nikki felt proud of me."

"Put all of that in your rear view mirror, Alana. If Nikki wants to act like a brat, let her," Jean said.

"That's easy for you to say, Jean. She's not your daughter," Katey said.

"And we know she's not at all comfortable being my offspring, so let's drop the subject." Although I was smiling, I couldn't banish the little worry lines from my forehead.

"Good idea." Jean smiled at me and reached for Katey's arm. "Let's not spoil the evening. This has been such a great send-off for you, Alana."

Katey and Jean took turns hugging me before they drifted toward the door. I saw them pause and speak to others whom, no doubt, wanted to catch up with Jean's latest news. I delayed my getaway long enough to speak once again to Conrad and Celia, as well as to a few other co-workers I knew I would miss. I thought I had uttered my last "see you later" when I felt a hand come from behind and rest itself on my right shoulder.

"I hope you weren't about to leave without saying goodbye to me."

I turned around slowly, happy I recognized the speaker's voice. I hadn't simply imagined seeing her fine-featured olive brown face as I hugged Sally Lindstrom. She hadn't been a hallucination framed by a somber-hued wall. Rafe had been here, staring right through me the same way she had every time we'd found ourselves in the same space at work, the same way she had looked at me when we walked side by side at the zoo that Saturday afternoon not long ago.

Chapter Seventeen

TIRED AS SHE was, Rafaela knew she had little choice about where to spend the evening. Going to the Office of Probation and Parole's retirement dinner was the politically expedient thing to do, considering her status as a recently arrived P.O. whose supervisor was retiring.

Maybe Alana Blue will show up with a girlfriend, she thought. *And I might as well earn some points with that asshole, Conrad. He's the one who's going to harness me with another supervisor.*

After visiting her last client of the day, Rafe dragged herself home, showered, and put on the charcoal gray pantsuit she saved for occasions when she wanted to leave an impression.

Rafe smiled as she smoothed the vaguest hint of a wrinkle, by flat-handing the fabric draped over her slender thigh. She recalled the first time she'd worn the suit. Her running buddy gave her the once-over and proclaimed that a suit as sharp as that one deserved to be worn by a woman named "Rafe," not Rafaela." Rafaela" was a name belonging to someone utterly feminine. It was the name her Cuban-born father sang out any time he'd called for her. In contrast, the monosyllabic, urban-tinged "Rafe" was a name that stood up and strutted. She owned it proudly, and thought its very sound represented the flip side of her Cuban heritage; the side imbued upon her by her African-American mother.

"Rafe" was how she carried herself. She entered spaces quietly but in control. She never sought attention. Attention seemed to find her. The second Rafe appeared, her aura charged the environment with an energy that drew people close.

Rafe intentionally arrived late. Even so, she killed time sitting in the dimly lit bar adjacent to the banquet room. She ordered two drinks, a chocolate martini and a club soda. She stared at the former before offering it to a woman seated nearby. When the woman smiled her thank-you, momentarily Rafe considered skipping the retirement fete completely and spending her well-dressed good-looking self on this stranger. Reconsidering, Rafe looked at her watch, left some money on the polished marble counter, and stood up.

The image staring back at her from the smoky mirror behind the bar pleased Rafe. She didn't particularly mind the strands of gray intertwined with her dark brown hair. In fact, she thought the mixture suggested a certain amount of gravitas mature women found attractive. She was proud of the way the suit jacket emphasized her broad shoulders and minimized her breasts. She stared at her likeness a second longer, and found it hard to believe this was Friday night and she had an obligation to spend the evening with some of the deadbeats she'd just seen at the office a couple of hours ago.

Rafe walked toward the entrance of the banquet room and read the message on the easel standing near the door. She paused for a split second and questioned her resolve to go any further.

Almost imperceptibly, she shook her head. She gripped the door's handle and entered the large space. The bar's subdued lighting instantly morphed into the brightness of the neighboring room's celebration. Rafe was aware of the bar's hushed voices and bland nameless background music spontaneously changing to raucous laughter and a static-filled public address system. On sensory overdrive, she moved toward the comfort of a dark wall where she could get the lay of the land while standing in the shadow of a nearby column.

She perused the room, searching for familiar faces, and wincing every time feedback from the microphone screeched everyone into silence. She heard Conrad Jackson gruffly ask for silence. She watched him hold a plaque in his fleshy hand and summarily read the generic congratulatory words inscribed on it. It took Rafe only a second to zero in on her supervisor. Alana Blue stood proudly behind her chair at the table of honor, her mocha skin's warm glow enhanced by the soft peach of her jacket.

Rafe remained immobile. She ignored the applause filling the room and the people rising to their feet in appreciation of the honorees. With laser-like accuracy, she fixed her gaze on Alana, watching as she exchanged handshakes with various people. Rafe remembered experiencing the warmth of Alana's hand the first time they were introduced to each other. Their palm-to-palm contact was brief and pleasant. She recalled resting her hand on Alana's arm the day they met at the zoo. That experience also, had been quick and enjoyable.

A waiter dropped a knife nearby. As it crashed to the floor, its clanging ripped Rafe's concentration away from Alana and took her to the place she usually visited when vulnerability threatened to swallow her.

Alana is not all that special looking. And she's too serious. The last thing I'd ever do is get involved with a serious woman. Life is too short for that.

She watched Alana step down from the dais and hug the high-strung secretary who was always flitting around the office. Quickly, Rafe left her shelter against the wall and slipped through the open doorway, leaving the celebration behind.

Returning to the safety of the mahogany bar, Rafe caught the server's attention and just as quickly, waved him away. She didn't need alcohol to help her get through the evening. She needed to return to the retirement dinner. Attending the function was part of the penance she had to perform to atone for her lack of good judgment and self-control. And although she was more than curious about Alana Blue, the opportunity to see her away from the confines of the office wasn't enough to make the evening palatable.

Rafe shook off her lingering temptation to down a quick drink and returned to the banquet room. As soon as she reentered the celebration, she saw Alana standing not more than a foot away.

Rafe reached out and touched her shoulder. Taking advantage of the second of hesitation she spied in Alana's eyes, Rafe smiled and took control.

"I hope you weren't about to leave without saying good-bye to me."

Rafe extended her hand.

"Yes, I was about to leave." Alana briefly grasped Rafe's hand." Did you just arrive?"

"I've been here for a while," Rafe said.

"You're keeping a low profile tonight. That's not the Rafe Ortiz I was beginning to know." Alana's smile was tentative.

"Maybe that's the new me." Rafe cocked her head to one side.

"Right." Alana's eyes challenged Rafe, her mouth turned up.

"Okay, so there's not a new me," Rafe said. She gestured to the room. "This event belongs to you and the other three lucky ducks getting out of Dodge City."

Surveying the dwindling crowd, Rafe changed course. "Is your family here?"

"No, they're not."

"Your close friends?"

"A few."

"Well, that's good." Rafe took a deep breath. "You've had a great career and your friends and family should celebrate with you."

"I agree." Alana paused before adding, "I didn't expect my daughter and son-in-law to be here, so I'm not disappointed they aren't."

"I remember that afternoon at the zoo when you said you didn't get along with your daughter. We should talk about that when we go out for dinner."

"What?" Alana seemed surprised.

"I'd like to take you out to dinner, Alana. To celebrate your leaving the department and the end of our working together."

Alana let half a laugh escape her lips. "The end of our working together?"

"Yes." Rafe leaned forward and lowered her voice. "I had to wait until now to ask you out. I don't date co-workers any more, remember?"

"Oh, I recall that very clearly."

Turning toward the exit, Rafe continued."Could I buy you a drink? The bar's only a few paces away."

"No thanks. I don't think that's a good idea."

"What about dinner some time?"

"That might not be a good idea either."

"Why?" Rafe asked, puzzled.

Before Alana could answer, she heard someone call her name.

"Well, Alana, we haven't been able to get out of here yet." Katey returned to Alana's side.

"So I see." Alana smiled gratefully at Katey and then gestured to Rafe. "You know Rafaela Ortiz, don't you?"

"Hell yes." Jean's contralto boomed, drowning out Katey's answer. She clutched Rafe's hand and squeezed it. "Where have you been, woman?"

"Here and there." Rafe shot Jean a sly smile.

"Mostly there, by the looks of it. 'Cause we sure haven't seen too much of you here recently."

"That's because I'm trying to be a good girl and stay out of trouble."

"That's always a wise path to follow," Jean said. She turned to Alana. "This poor misguided soul used to work with me years ago in the Germantown office."

Alana smiled benignly.

Jean placed her hand at the small of Katey's back and turned to Rafe.

"You remember my telling you about Katey, don't you?"

"Sure. It's nice to finally meet you."

Katey grabbed the hand Rafe offered. She pumped it and then stared at her. A second before her examination became awkward, Katey gestured to Alana.

"How about our friend, huh? Do you believe she's leaving the rank and file?"

Rafe grinned. "I'm happy for her. She deserves our good wishes."

"Oh, it's a good move for her all right," Katey said. "I'm not so sure about all her clients, though."

Alana smiled. "They'll survive without me."

"Yeah, they might, but what about your co-workers?"Katey turned to her new acquaintance.

"Right, Rafe?"

"They'll be okay without me, too," Alana said before Rafe could respond.

"Not this one." Rafe hooked her thumb at herself. "I depend upon her guidance and advice."

"Rafaela Ortiz, how many times did you come to me with questions or problems that needed to be resolved?"

"Well, truth be told..."

Alana laughed. "Not even once."

"It's true. But I always knew you'd support me." Rafe looked quite satisfied with her comeback.

"Nice recovery, Rafe," Jean said dryly.

"You know your job inside and out. The supervision thing was just a formality," Alana said, offering Rafe an indulgent smile.

"This sounds like a double testimonial," Katey teased.

As the other three women laughed nervously, Jean kept her gaze fixed on Rafe.

"Well anyway, I'm going to miss you." Rafe offered her hand to Alana.

"I'll miss you also, Rafaela."

Alana's response was tinged with surprise, as if the notion of missing Rafe had occurred to her only a second ago.

"Ready to go, Katey?" Jean motioned to the door.

"Sure." Katey looked at Alana. "I made this offer earlier, but this time it looks like we're all ready to leave. Want to walk to the parking lot together?"

"Good idea." Alana turned to Rafe. "Good luck to you, Rafaela."

"Same to you. And thanks." Rafe stared at Alana. "I have a feeling we'll see each other again soon."

Alana didn't respond.

"Give me a call sometime, Rafe," Jean said. "And remember to leave trouble wherever you find it." Jean shot Rafe a humorless look before she followed Katey and Alana.

"Tell trouble to leave me alone," Rafe said.

She watched the trio walk toward the exit. Raising her hand to wave, Rafe calculated how many days she'd let pass before phoning Alana. A week at the most, she figured. Maybe Alana wouldn't resist the need to call her first.

Chapter Eighteen

CURIOSITY COMPELLED JOHNETTA to leave home for work fifteen minutes early. She used the extra time to satisfy her curiosity by taking a different route to police headquarters. Driving slowly, Johnetta aimed her car toward one of the township's main roads. It wouldn't be congested this early in the day. As she cruised by a small commercial area, she peered into each of the strip's store windows. She'd memorized how much light usually illuminated the optician's business, the butcher shop, and the tanning and nail salon during their pre-opening hours. Nothing was amiss this morning.

The faint aroma of freshly baked pretzels wafting from the snack food outlet taunted Johnetta's nostrils and stomach. She imagined how the warm brown crust might taste. Salivating, she concentrated on the road ahead of her. She yearned to be so distracted by the early morning traffic that all thoughts of her teeth sinking into the salty pillow of a treat would disappear. One of those large pretzels contained far more dough than she wanted to introduce to the body she'd worked hard to keep reasonably fit. She knew she couldn't give in and buy only half a dozen small pretzel nuggets splashed with salt. Why start a civil war between sodium and the tiny salmon-colored diuretic pill she took daily in her battle against borderline hypertension?

Johnetta drove on and glanced to the left. A huge blue and white sign heralding the new Urgent Care medical office interrupted her pretzel daydream. She was alternately glad for the new center's presence and disdainful of the doc-in-the-box facility that didn't accept her health insurance plan. Word was they turned down most plans and preferred to receive cash at the time of service.

Johnetta turned left at the next traffic light. She slowed her vehicle until it practically crept along the residential street. She perused the scenery, taking in as many details as she could. She spotted a newly installed section of fence in front of one house; a freshly asphalted driveway on the left side of the street; two completely brown arborvitae disrupting a row of healthy plants at the edge of another property; and a child's abandoned tricycle overturned next to a clump of reddish-purple barberry hedges. She made a mental note to repeat this route tomorrow, just so she could look for the little bike.

Some kids have too many toys, she thought, *along with parents who don't teach them how to take care of their things.*

Her phone rang. Johnetta kept her left hand on the steering wheel while she felt her pocket with her right one. She retrieved her cell phone and put its earbud in place.

"Good morning, Harold."

"Mornin', Johnnie. Are you at your desk already?"

"Nope, I'm on the way. What's up?" Johnetta steered her car onto a wide street bordered on one side by a sloping expanse of green open space.

"I'm running late. Car problem." Harold's voice sounded tired and discouraged.

"Did you solve it?" Johnetta asked.

"Did I solve what?"

"Your car problem."

"Oh yeah. It's under control."

Johnetta glanced at the clock on her dashboard.

"I'll be at my desk in five minutes, Harold."

"Okay. Hey Johnnie, did you get the message I left on your office phone last night?"

"You must have left it real late, because the last time I phoned in, there wasn't anything waiting for me." Johnnie looked to her left and right, examining each address as she drove by. She calculated the exact number of houses she would pass before she arrived in front of the one she was most interested in seeing.

"Well I might as well fill you in now." Harold paused. "It's about Reginald Harris. He's not our man for the Shantay Taylor murder."

"What?" Surprised, Johnetta eased her car toward the curb.

"The lab sent the DNA report. There wasn't a match. The sample they found under the victim's fingernails didn't match anyone in the database."

"Oh hell. I thought for sure he was our perp." Johnetta frowned. "Now we're back to square one."

"Yup, and time's working against us." Harold's voice sounded defeated.

"You're right about that."

More than three months had passed, and each day they failed to solve the case, their chance of making an arrest became slimmer.

"At least we have some physical evidence to go on," Harold said.

Johnetta looked at the property beyond the curb. She glimpsed a flash of color and then focused on the evidence Harold mentioned.

"Hey, Harold, did the lab ever identify those fibers found on the girl's underwear?"

"Yeah. They were fibers from inkjet printer paper. And they tested the white particles they scraped off her shoes. Turns out they were specks of old lead-based paint."

"That's right. I remember now." Johnetta chided herself for forgetting those details. Then she reminded herself that this was Harold's case. He was the lead detective and she was perfectly content to follow his directives. Acutely aware of her status as a former retiree, Johnetta no longer sailed with the same gusts of wind that had filled her canvas during her career in Philadelphia. Her competitive urge to lead was still there, but it simmered instead of burned.

"Well, I'm on my way to the station now. Want a donut?" Harold asked.

"In the worst way, but I can't have one. So, no thanks." First a giant pretzel, and now a donut. Johnetta wondered how long she could depend on her self-control to ward off her hankering for something sweet or salty.

"See you soon, Johnnie."

"Right."

Johnetta laid her phone on the passenger seat and looked at the object of her curiosity, a rose-colored brick two-story house sitting about a hundred feet from her car. The lines of the house, softened by age, suggested an English cottage more than the symmetrical Colonial-style structure it was. Although it was autumn and well past the prime mowing season, the lawn had a just-cut shortness. The yews, ilexes, and junipers provided a background for the irregularly curved beds of cool-weather pansies spilling onto the grass. Black metal flower boxes overflowed with densely planted gold and burgundy chrysanthemums and invited Johnetta's eyes up to the second-floor windows.

She admired the property and thought it matched what little she'd observed of its owner the two occasions she'd been in her presence. Everything was well-coordinated and subtly attractive, exactly the impression Johnetta had of the woman who lived there. Johnetta thought this was the kind of property whose exterior beauty promised interior serenity.

As she continued to take in the details of the house, Johnetta visualized its owner. She replayed her memory forged two weeks ago, when she saw Alana Blue stand in front of a file cabinet and extract a client's folder. Johnetta recalled following the line of her profile, starting at her throat and moving to the top of her head. She recollected looking at Alana's lips as they curved upward in a smile. She caught herself imagining how her fingertips would feel if they ever touched the slight indentation in Alana's cheek, and then traced the outline of her precisely cut natural hair as it curled behind the shell of her ear. Johnetta remembered her eyes following the strands of soft hair as they swept toward the back of Alana's head and bloomed into errant waves before descending toward the nape of her neck.

This morning, Johnetta sat in her car and imagined herself stepping on each of the graystone pavers leading to the front door of the house. She inhaled and smelled what little remained of the spent flowers' sweet fragrance. She felt the faint pressure on her forefinger as it pressed the doorbell, and she could hear a woman's voice chirp, "welcome." Johnetta knew her own shy grin would spread completely out of control as she entered the house.

Tapping her steering wheel, Johnetta returned to reality. This morning's surplus of time had dissolved right along with her daydream. She put the car back in drive and pressed the accelerator. By the time she reached the end of the street, Johnetta's mind had arrived at work.

There were two tasks she planned to do as soon as she clocked in. First, she would clear everything from the top of her desk and spread out all the available information about the Taylor case's fiber evidence. Second, she would telephone Alana Blue to tell her Reginald Harris was no longer considered a person of interest. She remembered Alana was on the cusp of leaving the Office of Probation and Parole a couple of weeks ago, so she wondered whether or not she would still be on the job. She wondered also if they would ever run into each other out here in Brighton Township. If ever they did, she planned to tell Alana how much she admired the landscaping and the flower boxes adorning the front of her house.

As Johnetta pulled into her parking stall at Police Headquarters, she wondered about something else. Why was every detail of Alana's profile etched so clearly in her memory?

Chapter Nineteen

"I DIDN'T EXPECT to see you here today." Rafe leaned against the door frame at the entrance of my former office.

"I didn't expect to be here, believe me." I pointed to the computer sleeping on the desk. "I waited 'til the end of the day last Friday, but no one came to check this out and complete my separation paperwork."

Rafe shook her head. "The bureaucracy can drive you nuts, can't it?"

"Yes, it can." I resented driving all the way into the city just to sit on my hands and wait for someone wearing a clipboard and a bored expression to come into the office, power up the computer, sign a paper, and hand me a copy of it.

"And you had to spend your first morning of freedom back here?" Rafe's frown expressed enough disgust for both of us.

"That's right."

"I bet you'll run out of here the minute they check this equipment."

"Well, not exactly. Conrad asked me to meet with Mary Campbell and Stuart Rosensweig. Each one's been given half of my caseload, and one of them will take my probies."

"Am I getting him or her?"

"Neither one. You'll be on your own for the foreseeable future."

Rafe pushed herself away from the door frame and stood perfectly erect.

"What happened to my year of probation?"

"Conrad had a chance to watch you in action. He knows you're more competent than most of the supervising P.O's. And, he's short on supervisors."

"I'm not more competent than you," she said.

"Thanks, but don't sell yourself short."

Rafe walked over to an empty box sitting in the middle of the floor. A used soft drink cup with a trio of dark-brown rivulets congealed on one side shared space atop the box with the office phone. Rafe shook her head.

"I guess it was too much trouble for the cleaning staff to put this back on the desk where it belongs." She leaned down, pushed the phone to one side, and raised her leg high enough to prop one foot on the box.

"Someone probably made a call or two while they sipped their soda. It's still plugged into the outlet," I said.

"Did you have anything to do with Conrad's not reassigning me to a supervisor?"

Her question startled me. Usually candid to a fault, I teetered between not answering and shrouding the facts in doublespeak.

"Everybody's up to here with work." I raised my hand as high above my head as I could. "Having one less probie to supervise is for the good of the unit."

"Right." Rafe rolled her eyes.

"You can take my word for it." I did my best to keep my face expressionless.

"I'd rather take you out for a drink and dinner now that you've left this place."

Rafe's words caught me off guard. She didn't ask if we could see each other. She made a declaration.

"Do you think that's a good idea? My foot's barely out the door."

"And it's a lovely one at that." Rafe looked down at my ankles and then back up to my eyes. "But frankly, Alana, I'm interested in more than your foot."

The phone clanged to life and saved me from having to figure out a response to Rafe's invitation.

"Someone must know you're here," Rafe said. She pointed to the telephone near her foot. "I'd ignore it if I were you."

I let the phone ring twice more before I gave in to my curiosity and picked up the receiver.

"Yes, this is Alana Blue."

"This is Detective Jones…Johnnie."

"Oh, yes. How are you?" I glanced quickly at Rafe and then walked a few feet away from her.

"I didn't know if you'd be there to answer your phone. I thought you might have left your job by now." Johnetta's friendly voice warmed my ear.

"I did. Friday was my last official day, but I had some loose threads to tie up, so here I am back in the office."

Rafe left her perch by the box and strolled to the window.

"Then I'm glad I caught you there." Johnnie paused. "Uh, I phoned to tell you we're no longer looking at your offender, Reginald Harris, for the Taylor murder."

"That's wonderful news, Johnnie." Just that quickly, I forgot I'd severed my connection to Reginald Harris. I wasn't responsible for any part of his life, nor was he obligated to report his comings and goings to me.

"While that's good news for me, I guess it's not a good

development for you, is it?" I asked.

"Nope, it's not."

"I know you and your department will find the monster who murdered that girl. It's just a matter of time, Johnnie."

"I have faith we'll do just that, Alana." Johnetta cleared her throat. "Just as I have faith you and I will get together for coffee or lunch one of these days."

I pressed the phone closer to my ear.

"I'll look forward to it."

"Take care," Johnnie said. "And be in touch. You have my number."

"I will. Thanks for letting me know the good news about my client."

"You mean your former client, right?"

"Right. "

I walked the phone back to its temporary home on the box. Rafe turned her back to the window and watched my movements closely.

"I sure didn't expect to get any phone calls this morning." I felt a need to fill the dead air.

"I didn't think you needed to answer the phone, but obviously you couldn't help yourself."

"You're right. It's hard to stop doing something you've done automatically for so many years."

"Yeah, we all have our hard-to-break habits. Like not wanting to socialize with a co-worker even after you've left the job," Rafe said.

When I didn't confront her challenge, Rafe softened her tone, and gave me a soulful glance.

"So how about having dinner with me some evening soon?"

Maybe it was her determination that appealed to me. Or it could have been the boldness of her invitation coupled with her seductive stare. Perhaps it was the memory of feeling her hand on my shoulder three nights ago at the retirement dinner; or maybe it was the accumulation of all the charged moments we'd spent in each others' presence here on the job. More than likely, it was my sudden loss of routine, along with the smothering loneliness I knew would settle in my being the moment I realized I had unfilled time on my hands.

It may have been all of these things pushing me to accept Rafe's dinner invitation. I don't know for sure. What I do know is all those forces were no match for the inexplicable pull I felt when I'd heard Johnetta Jones' rich, deep voice in my ear.

Chapter Twenty

"SO WHAT ARE you doing on this beautiful autumn day, Mom?"

"I thought I'd gas up and go for a ride, maybe out to that farmers market in Unionville," Johnetta said as she walked to the kitchen window. She examined her favorite blue spruce, and she admired the way its branches cut a pattern against the cloudless sky.

"Sounds like a plan, Mom. Are you going by yourself?"

Johnetta smiled. Although she didn't feel she had to report all of her activities to Tommy, she appreciated the concern wrapped around his question.

"Yes. I'm going by myself."

"I'm not trying to get into your business, Mom," Tommy said. "You know that, right?"

"I know, honey."

"It's just that you're such a good person. I wish you'd meet someone you could spend time with." Tommy paused. "I want you to be happy, Mom."

"Thank you, Tommy. I'm okay, really."

"I don't want you to keep going through life alone."

"And I want you to be less concerned about me. You have your own life to live."

Johnetta stared at the overgrown evergreens in her back yard. For a split second they vanished, only to be replaced by the memory of the neatly trimmed shrubs flanking Alana Blue's front door. She wondered if Alana had installed any fall-blooming plants in her front yard.

"I'm in the middle of a very happy life, Mom. I want you to have one too. And I want you to be safe."

"I'm a cop, remember? I think I can take care of myself."

"Yeah, I know that. Seems like you were retired for only a day before you jumped right back onto the battlefield."

Johnetta hesitated, unsure at first if she should share a job-related incident to him.

"Speaking of the battlefield, a few days ago two of our officers responded to a domestic dispute call."

"You used to say police officers hate that kind of call."

"I still say that."

"What happened?"

"It turned out to be quite a volatile situation. When our guys got there, they heard the husband screaming for help and the wife was yelling all sorts of obscenities, but she wouldn't open the door, so they had to force it open."

"Was anybody hurt?" Tommy asked quickly, his three words sounding as if they were one.

"I'm afraid so. The woman was holding a carving knife. Before anyone knew what was happening, she lunged at the officer closest to her, caught him off guard, and slashed a deep cut in his arm."

"Damn, Mom. That kinda crap happens out in suburbia?"

"You don't know the half of it." Johnetta adjusted her eyeglasses.

"I guess I imagined Brighton Township was a safe haven."

"That's what you're supposed to think. But we have some of the same problems out here as there are in the city. There's just more space between the houses and people tend to keep quiet about their problems." Johnetta paused. "Sometimes I think reporters get paid to keep certain stories out of the newspaper."

Tommy laughed. "I know, right? The last time I looked at your local paper, the only thing I read even remotely related to crime was a list of shoplifting incidents at the mall, and a blurb about somebody's mailbox being smashed. Like that's the only criminal activity going on."

"And do you remember reading where the shoplifters were from?" Johnetta asked.

"Yeah. Philly."

"The crimes committed out here are underreported. I made that discovery after my first week on the force."

Tommy broke into her thoughts. "So did they shoot her or what?"

"Who?"

"The woman who cut your cop."

"No, they didn't have to." Johnetta chuckled softly. "When she stabbed the officer, she shocked the hell out of herself and dropped the knife to the floor. They arrested her, of course."

Tommy was quiet for a few seconds. "So tell me Mom, how is this anecdote connected to my wishing you had a partner?"

"Here's the link." Johnetta left her spot near the kitchen window and meandered into the small dining room. She pulled a chair out from under the oval pine table, and sat down. "The woman wielding the knife reminded me I'd rather be content and by myself than afraid and unhappy with a wacko partner."

Tommy laughed. "Yeah, I hear you. But your relationships were with good people. Only one of your girlfriends was one french fry short of a Happy Meal. And you were a different person back then."

"All right, Mr. Psychologist." Johnetta smiled. "I'll make a deal with you. You find me an unattached, emotionally available gay woman, and I'll date her."

And if she could have Alana Blue's looks and personality, I'd appreciate it. Johnetta thought.

"You're on, Mom."

Johnetta listened to the laughter dancing in her son's voice.

"Hey, it's time for you to start enjoying Sunday with your wife, and for me to hit the road.

"Okay. Talk to you next time. Love you."

"I love you too. Give Sandra a hug from me, please."

Johnetta put the phone down and sighed. Her thoughts lingered on an unpleasant time in her life when her need to have someone by her side outweighed her common sense. Recalling the unwise choices she'd made caused a sudden shiver. Instinctively, she crossed her arms over her chest and rubbed her shoulders.

She pondered Tommy's playful agreement to find her someone to love, and she concluded the likelihood of his introducing her to a woman as interesting and attractive as Alana Blue was nil to none. Johnetta strode purposefully back to the kitchen, hoisted her handbag from the back of a chair, and headed outside to her car.

Although the early afternoon's sunlight heated the vehicle, there was something about the light and the sky that suggested a colder season was on its way. Everywhere Johnetta looked, she saw the muted chrysanthemums still struggling to bloom. Their somber hues radiated a sense of surrender, a willingness to cede to the approaching winds of November and beyond. Even the fullest trees seemed resigned to their maturity as they yielded to shades of gold, red, and orange.

Tranquility seeped into her spirit the way fully developed notes ease out of a saxophone and move through one's soul. She felt all right with the stillness, although somehow incomplete.

A quick glimpse at her gas gauge convinced her to steer her car toward the service station. As she inserted the hose into her gas tank, Johnetta watched another vehicle slowly approach the opposite side of the narrow cement island. She captured a quick glimpse of the familiar profile as the car came to a stop. Alana Blue left the driver's seat and pushed the selection buttons on the gas pump's keyboard.

"Hi, neighbor." Johnetta spoke above the intrusive din coming from a video monitor mounted above the gas island.

Alana turned toward Johnetta. Her face bathed in the sun's spotlight, she squinted before she replied.

"Oh, hi. How are you, Johnnie?"

"I'm just fine, and you?" Johnetta locked the lever on the gas hose, forcing it to keep doing its job automatically. Both hands free, she removed her sunglasses and planted them atop her head.

"I'm well, thanks." Alana beamed at Johnetta. "I didn't recognize you at first."

"That's because I'm not in your office asking about one of your clients."

Alana laughed. "You're right. And the sunglasses were hiding your eyes."

"How's everything going? Are you enjoying your newly found freedom from work?"

Alana nodded vigorously. "I am now that I'm about to begin a part-time gig."

"Already? Whew. You went back to work faster than I did."

"I know. Sad, isn't it?" Pretending to be ashamed, Alana bowed her head.

"Not really. It's proves you're ambitious."

"Or I'm addicted to work." Alana laughed.

"Yeah, that too."

The abrupt click from the end of the nozzle signaled to Johnetta her car was fueled. She glanced at the price and rehung the hose. "Did you say it's a part-time job?"

"Yes."

"That means you're not a full-time work addict, like I am."

"I would think it's difficult to be a part-time detective," Alana said as she watched Johnetta slide her sunglasses back in place.

"That's because there's no such thing as part-time crime."

"Speaking of which, I haven't seen anything in the newspaper recently about the murder investigation."

Johnetta's grin became less apparent than the crease traveling across her forehead."It's taken some unexpected turns, but you can bet we're working on it." She recalled the last chore she'd completed at work a day and a half ago. She could still feel the nagging pain bisecting her shoulder blades as she hunched over the computer screen.

"I have every confidence in your department, Johnnie."

Johnetta stood next to her car and watched Alana finish refilling hers. She waited silently while Alana twisted the gas cover until the locked cap gave up three clicks.

"Do you like taking long walks?" Johnetta asked unexpectedly.

Alana nodded. "In fact, I do."

"Great. Let's plan a walk in the state park. It's not that far from here. We could get coffee afterward." Johnetta made no attempt to conceal the anticipation in her voice.

"That'll be nice." Alana eased herself into her car. "Why don't I give you a call?"

"I'll hold you to that," Johnetta said as she moved toward the driver's side of her vehicle. She opened the door and then waved at the departing Alana.

Seconds later Johnetta drove away from the gas station. She took her time navigating past the strip malls, fast food eateries, and big box home goods stores in the area. Soon she and her car were sharing narrower roads with less traffic. Huge newly constructed houses situated on perfectly landscaped cul-de-sacs fanned out to the left and right of her path. After a few miles, the nouveaux mansions were replaced by old rambling Victorian and Federal-style farmhouses in various stages of disrepair or restoration. Fields began to dominate the vista, vast zones populated by the occasional grouping of rolled hay bales or cows.

Johnetta sought to empty her mind of clutter. Whenever she drove alone through rural areas, she counted on nature to sooth her restlessness. There was something about the earth, the trees, and the sky all coming together in a place like this that never failed to take her away from whatever disrupted her peace. Today was different, however. Brighton Township's unsolved murder case was a metal spike wedged in her consciousness. The obsessive part of her was more than willing to sacrifice her day off and go to her office where she could delve into backgrounds of the newest suspects. But her wiser side remembered all the times when a day away from the precinct in Philly reenergized both her body and brain.

Johnetta's mind flashed to her encounter at the gas station. She didn't understand why she hadn't yet phoned Alana. She felt pleased she could replace the memory of her reticence with today's quasi-invitation issued between the gas pumps.

After driving another five miles, Johnetta saw her destination a few hundred yards ahead. She turned left into the farmers market's gravel parking lot. Driving slowly to avoid kicking up sharp shards of stone, Johnetta found an empty parking space at the end of a long row.

"Shit, I parked crooked." She cursed aloud and backed out of the space, righted her car and then pulled back into the rectangle.

Instead of getting out of the Honda and walking toward the market's entrance, Johnetta remained strapped in the driver's seat. She stared straight ahead and tried to concentrate on her reasons for being there. What was it she wanted to buy? Fresh fruit? Veggies? A bunch of flowers? One of those plump round pumpkins to decorate the front of her house?

Johnetta continued to stare, motionless. She knew she sought something she wouldn't find inside the country market. What was it? Searching for her elusive goal opened a crater of emptiness. Johnetta believed the only way to fill some of that void was to resolve the high school student's murder case. The distractions of work would help her forget there was no one at home to respond to her voice.

As she continued sitting in her car, she mentally shuffled the case's deck of clues and re-examined the hand that had been dealt to the police department. She was pretty sure the perpetrator wasn't anyone they had investigated thus far. Narrowing her recall to the most recent forensic psychologist's report, Johnetta calculated the perp was a newbie, someone whose profile was not yet in any criminal database. The guilty person hadn't planned to murder the girl. It just happened, perhaps as a result of lightning-quick rage or pent up frustration escalating out of control.

Without entering the market, Johnetta turned the key in her car's ignition, backed out of the parking space, and headed toward home. Her trunk was as empty now as it was when she arrived. It contained no bags brimming with fruit and vegetables; no Pennsylvania Dutch shoofly pie tempting her with its thick molasses base; no decorative gourds or dried corn stalks she could tie to the lamp post outside her house. The only things sitting next to her in that Honda were her disappointment about the unsolved murder case and her ever-present yearning for someone who would keep company with her soul, body, and spirit.

Chapter Twenty-one

RUNNING INTO JOHNETTA Jones at the gas station the other day lead me to question why she was single. She was sharp, capable, and mature. Although I didn't believe she was too laid-back to care about the two of us getting together socially, I did appreciate the way she seemed to let time and circumstances determine our meeting. I was thankful for the absence of pressure, and I found that quality in her as attractive as the steadiness of her gaze each time she'd engaged me in conversation.

I had to admit I was curious about Johnnie. I looked forward to seeing her somewhere other than in my office or at the gas station. Maybe I needed to be more aggressive and phone her instead of waiting for her to call me. That only made sense. Try as I might, I didn't always steer myself toward good sense though, even when it was right in front of me.

A perfect example of my tendency to veer away from good sense occurred the day I finally agreed to go out with Rafe. I knew damn well dinner with her was simply a metaphor for something more complicated, something I had no business doing. As interested as I was in getting to know Johnetta, I slid into Rafe's car first. It may as well have had one of those magnetic door signs stuck on the side, saying, "you only live once, why not take a chance?" Fortunately, the day I got into that car, I kept Katey's advice in mind, like a portable GPS mounted to a dashboard.

More than once Katey has opined, "Alana, life happens. But you can stay in control if you navigate with your head, not with your heart."

When I've scoffed at that particular piece of unsolicited advice, Katey has added Jean's shorthand version of wisdom. "Girl, don't make decisions with anything below your waist."

When I left home to spend a few hours with Rafe, Katey's and Jean's words sat right beside me, along with the leftover images from a strange dream I'd had.

My detour toward Rafe began after a late-night mug of coffee accompanied by a seductive phone chat. Thanks to the excess caffeine and Rafe's flirtatious talk, I slept fitfully, if at all. Sometime after midnight vivid images shook me fully awake. In my dream, I heard Johnetta's voice call my name, softly at first, then louder and more persistently. I stumbled toward the sound, but when I got close to it, I saw Rafe, her arms outstretched.

"I'll hold you to that," She kept repeating. "I'll hold you to that."

Rafe's eyes pleaded with me. They bent my will until I melted in her arms. I felt her mouth leave long languorous kisses on my breasts. I reached forward and cradled her hips. My arms and hands moved downward. I grasped the back of one of her thighs and guided her knee to my center. Gasping at the delicious shock of the contact, I cried out and filled the still air in my bedroom with one syllable... Rafe.

Sleep never reclaimed me that night, although I longed to get back to the sweet mirage it offered. Early the next morning, I seemed to move in slow motion. Slightly confused, I heard Johnetta's voice in my ear but I sensed the suggestion of Rafe's mouth covering my body. Fueled by those sensations, I dialed Rafe's phone number and left a one sentence message.

"When would you like to go out for dinner?"

It wasn't like me to pay attention to my physical needs, not to mention cede to them. Somewhere along the path, I completely forgot the voice I'd heard in my dream belonged to Johnetta, not to Rafe Ortiz. I abandoned the road leading to unselfish affection in favor of following the route to indulgence. Or, as Jean later said, I "fast-tracked my way to an unsatisfactory fuck instead of waiting in line for true love-making."

The evening following my dream, I sat across a table from Rafe in a Center City seafood restaurant, sipping Riesling and glancing at her over the rim of my wine glass.

"What made you change your mind about having dinner with me?" Rafe's eyes shone with victory.

"I like rewarding persistence."

"Then I'm glad I kept inviting you." Rafe leaned back. The subdued lighting partially obscured her face and made it difficult for me to tell if her smile was genuine or sarcastic.

"Are you persistent or stubborn?" I asked, already convinced it was the latter.

Rafe's coy smile broadened. "Both. But only about things that matter."

"You're pretty sure of yourself, aren't you?"

"Not really." Rafe wrapped her hand around her glass of tonic. "Although I am sure I want to know you better. I've wanted that for some time."

Her answer sent me directly into the shelter of the large leather-bound menu lying face up on the table.

"Don't you have a smart-ass come back for that, Ms. Blue?"

Feeling trapped and uncomfortable, I changed the subject. "One of my friends told me they make a mean crab cake here."

Rafe smirked. "Yeah, I thought so. You're out of answers."

We spent the next few moments in silence. I was grateful for the silence, and I used it to reclaim control of the situation. I could decide if this date would be a meal and nothing more, just as my dream had been no more than a sensual fantasy.

"Can I assume Conrad's followed through with his plans and not assigned another supervisor for you?"

"He told me he hasn't had time to train anyone new." Rafe turned her glass a full 360 degrees. "

I reached for a roll from the cloth-covered basket the waiter put on the table. I pinched off a piece of the bread, and spoke before putting the morsel into my mouth.

"Has your caseload increased?"

"It's mushroomed. Mine and everyone else's."

"That's not a surprise." I nodded as I watched the waiter put our salads in front of us. "The intention of that last court ruling was to create more space in the overcrowded jails. The decision put more criminals back on the streets."

"That, plus the four of you P.O.'s leaving service," Rafe said, feigning anger.

Her pretense of annoyance amused me.

"Oh, don't be a hater, Rafaela."

"I'm not hating." Rafe aimed her fork at a paper-thin slice of cucumber curled in the middle of her plate. She stabbed it, popped it into her mouth, and then pushed the salad to one side.

"So, what are you doing with all your free time?" she asked.

"Clearly not enough. I've decided to explore a part-time job at a social service agency."

Rafe's expression brightened. "If you're interested in working, why don't you come back to the office? Give us a hand with our bulging client loads."

"No thank you, ma'am. I want to try something new," I said decisively, although I realized this new gig involved working with the same population, a few at a time instead of one hundred plus.

The waiter returned, carrying our entrees. Rafe acknowledged him with a nod.

"All right. Suit yourself." She sighed. "But I certainly miss you....and the others."

"It's nice to be missed." I risked allowing my eyes to linger on Rafe's countenance longer than necessary.

Rafe pointed at my meal. "Looks like those crab cakes are going to live up to their reputation."

Two perfectly broiled lumps of seafood surrounded by a creamy pale yellow sauce stared up at me. A bouquet of bright green broccoli blooming next to grilled fingerling potatoes completed the canvas on the white plate.

I tasted a small bite of crab cake. "Absolutely wonderful."

Rafe looked down at the round dish placed in front of her. Garlicky steam rose from the breadcrumb crust atop her order of shrimp and scallops.

"Your dinner looks tasty also," I said.

I watched her skewer one of the bright pink shrimp. She raised it above the dish, and paused to let drops of butter and olive oil drip from the crustacean. Gazing directly into my eyes, Rafe guided the shrimp-laden utensil toward my mouth.

"Try it, Alana."

Caught with no time to refuse politely, I accepted her offering. I let the shrimp rest on my tongue for a second before I bit into to it.

"This is really delicious, Rafe," I said. "You made a good choice."

"I always make good choices."

Rafe continued staring at me. Her cocky self-confidence was jarring. I thought about the married woman with whom she'd had a career re-routing affair. That episode may not have been such a good choice. Quelling that memory, I offered to share a bite of my dinner.

Rafe reached for my hand, and piloted the forkful of my entrée to her mouth. I watched her close her eyes and envelop the delicately seasoned puff of crabmeat between her lips. She chewed it reverently. Seconds later she half opened her eyes and looked my way.

"Excellent. Just as I thought it would be."

I don't remember swallowing the rest of my meal, nor do I recall much of the remainder of our conversation. More than once I reminded myself to sit back and breathe evenly, despite Rafe's intensity.

Forty minutes after we left the restaurant, we sat in Rafe's car in front of my house. She tapped rhythmically on her steering wheel and matched the beats of the jazz CD spinning in its player.

"Would you like to come in for coffee?" I said.

"No. I'll come in next time."

She seemed sure there would be a next time. I wasn't sure how I felt about her certainty.

"Do you miss the job?"

"Some parts of it." I squinted at the street light's halo above us a hundred feet or so. "I don't miss all the stress and the out-of-control people and situations."

"Yeah. I know what you mean," She said in a subdued, faraway voice.

"Every time I hear about a serious crime that's occurred, I still worry one of my offenders is responsible for it." I frowned as thoughts about the unsolved murder near my neighborhood fluttered through me.

"I bet you miss your co-workers, huh?"

"A few of them. What I really miss is talking with people and exchanging information and a few laughs each day."

"Do you ever find yourself thinking about your probies and wondering what we're up to?" Rafe sounded young and unexpectedly needy.

"Not really." A warning bell went off in my head. I could see Rafe's next question take shape and slip between her lips before I actually heard the syllables.

"Do you ever miss me, Alana?" Her questioning eyes were round wells of expectation.

I turned slightly so I could look directly at her. "Yes. I do miss seeing you."

Rafe placed her hand under my chin. She leaned forward and kissed me.

Her lips engulfed mine with confidence and determination. It was as if my admission of missing her granted her permission to conquer my mouth with hers. Delivered with fury, the demanding kiss was more than I wanted but less than I expected. It lacked an indefinable something I wasn't able to name in that moment.

Rafe's hand moved from my chin to my neck as she pulled me closer to her. All the tension I'd ever felt in her presence merged with the dream I'd had, and despite how I felt after the first one, I gave in to the rest of her kisses without hesitation. Scant moments later, Rafe pulled away.

"Maybe I should forget about waiting 'til the next time, and come inside now."

I hoped my whisper of a smile told her I understood the double entendre lurking inside her suggestion.

"Maybe you should."

Rafe covered my shoulders with her hands. She lifted her left arm and turned it slightly so she could glance at her watch. Bereft of her warmth, my right shoulder cooled instantly.

"It'll have to be the next time, baby. I have to make an early call tomorrow morning."

My mind auditioned a dozen possible responses.

"I have to be somewhere, also. This has been nice."

"Thanks for having dinner with me." Rafe closed the distance between us and once again captured my lips with hers. Again, I surrendered any reluctance I might have had and returned the kiss.

Rafe reached back to her door and pushed a button. The audible click of locks coming undone catapulted me back to the here and now.

"I'll phone you tomorrow," she said.

I walked the stone path to my front door, disabled the alarm system along with a scintilla of my self-esteem, and quickly dismissed the awkwardness I felt when I realized Rafe had abandoned a probable conquest for the sake of an early morning appointment.

She's a professional, I rationalized. *Her job is important to her, and that's a good thing.*

I also dismissed the presence of a wrinkled slip of paper I saw on her car's dashboard seconds before she deftly moved it out of view. I convinced myself the name and phone numbers I saw scribbled on that piece of paper were inconsequential. After all, Selena Garrett was one of Rafe's clients. Why shouldn't she have the ex-offender's contact information jotted down?

Summoned by the answering machine's beep, I walked into the kitchen and found two messages waiting for me.

"Hello, Mother. I'll call back another time. Don't try to call me. I'm busy."

The serrated edge of Nikki's flat voice echoed in my ears. I was glad I missed her call.

The machine automatically segued to the next message.

"Hey, Alana. It's Johnnie. If you're free this Friday, would you like to go for a walk in Fort Lincoln State Park? Give me a call and we'll decide on a time. I hope you're out having fun tonight."

I looked at the calendar hanging above the telephone, and filled Friday's empty block with Johnnie's name and the words "state park." I poured a glass of water and took it with me as I climbed the stairs to the second floor. It wasn't that late, but I was tired. The constant vigilance I'd kept with Rafe tonight had taken its toll. As pleasant as her kisses had been, they felt planned and far from spontaneous; like a necessary step you have to accomplish when following a set of directions.

It wasn't conceit that made me believe Rafe wanted us to see each other again. It was me following Katey's advice to engage my brain and not my heart. Rafe hadn't yet figured me out, and that was an important part of the game she no doubt played with women. Did I wish to see her again? I'd share an evening or two with Rafe. What harm would that do?

Chapter Twenty-two

LORIN WILKES HOPED her boss, Avery Sloan, wouldn't want her to spend the day at the new group home. She preferred being anywhere but there. Located at the northwestern edge of Philadelphia, the Josephine Baker Rainbow Center's facility wasn't far from Lorin's apartment; but it was a distance from her Center City office. The days she had to go to both sites involved a lot of travel time, time she preferred to spend with Kim, if that were possible for both of them.

Lorin rinsed her cereal bowl, put it in the sink, and picked up her cell phone.

"Good morning, Josephine Baker Rainbow Center. Pat Hawthorn speaking," the receptionist sang.

"Good morning, Pat. It's Lorin."

"Hey, darlin', Are we gonna see you today?"

"That's why I'm calling. Avery said something yesterday about my going up to Mount Airy, but she never got back to me."

"Hold on. I'll check with her."

Phone in hand, Lorin walked to the front of her house and opened the door. She bent down to pick up her copy of the morning's Philadelphia Inquirer and scanned the front page while she waited for Pat.

"Lorin?"

"Yes, Pat?"

"Avery says for you to please come into the office this morning. She wants your input about several of the new employers who are willing to hire our clients. She thinks you're familiar with them."

"Great. I'm leaving home in two minutes."

Lorin grinned broadly and pumped her fist in the air. Pleased with her boss' plan, she spoke aloud.

"I can work out of the office in the morning, visit a client before noon, and then meet Kim just as we planned."

After an uneventful commute, Lorin burst through the office door. She beamed at Pat. "Hey, you, have you had your coffee?"

"I sure have, honey." Pat returned Lorin's smile. "And I can tell you've had your dose of caffeine, too."

"Yup. Do you know if Avery wants to see me immediately?"

Pat shook her head. "Probably not."

"Is she in her office? I'll go ask her." Lorin headed toward her boss' office.

"Well, yeah. She's in there. But..." Pat's sentence drowned in Lorin's haste to knock on Avery Sloan's door.

"It's Lorin, Avery."

"Come on in." A warm voice called out.

Lorin marched into the office, expecting to see Avery sitting at her desk. Instead, she saw her sitting in the large wingback chair angled beside the two-seater sofa in front of the window. A sweet fragrance of perfume wafted past Lorin's nostrils. There was a woman seated on the sofa, holding a copy of the Baker Center's Employee Manual and wearing a pleasant smile.

"Oh, I'm sorry," Lorin said. "I didn't know you had someone in here with you, Avery. I can come back later."

"No problem, Lorin. Come in for a minute." Avery smiled warmly at her. "I'd like to introduce you to Ms. Blue."

Lorin stepped into the office.

"Alana Blue, this is Lorin Wilkes, one of our social workers."

Alana began to get up from her seat.

"Please stay seated, Ms. Blue." Lorin stepped closer and extended her hand. "It's a pleasure to meet you."

"Same here, Ms. Wilkes."

"Alana recently ended her career as a parole officer. She has some spare time on her hands, so she's offered to do some part-time work for us."

"That's great. We need all the help we can get." Lorin's clear green eyes shone with enthusiasm. Finished with the formality of the introduction, she searched the woman's face, and zeroed in on her vaguely familiar eyes.

"I thought there might be something I could do here before my skills and contacts get rusty." Alana turned from Lorin to Avery and back.

"Avery will make good use of your skill set. She's a master at matching us with our clients. Right, Avery?"

"If you say so." Avery pursed her lips.

"And I do." Lorin turned toward Alana. "If you were a career P.O., I'm sure you have a lot of experience you can share with us."

"I hope so."

"One of my best friends is a P.O., so I know a little bit about your job." Lorin projected confidence. "I'll look forward to working with you, Ms. Blue."

"That'll be great. But please call me Alana."

"Okay, Alana. Welcome aboard." Lorin turned to leave the two women.

"You're going to be here in the office for a while, right Lorin?" Avery called after her.

"Yes. I'll be working in the back office."

"Good," Avery said. "Alana and I are almost finished here. I'll come back to get you in a few minutes."

Lorin left Avery's office and walked to a large workroom at the end of the hallway. There, she claimed a vacant desk where she began spreading out her paperwork. Her thoughts returned to the woman she'd just met.

Alana Blue...Sounds like a writer's name... or a detective's. She's a good looking woman... Wonder if Rafe knows her? Rafe...Oh my God...Alana Blue is the woman I saw in that deathtrap of an elevator the day I went to Rafe's office. She was Rafe's supervisor... Did Rafe say her supervisor was a lesbian?...After all, we're everywhere. In corporations, non-profits, schools... Schools...Kim. I have to let her know how psyched I am about seeing her today. Jesus, I hope she doesn't have to report home to Lawrence right after work. We haven't had time for as much as a decent phone conversation since our aborted weekend in Rehoboth...

Lorin delayed starting her work long enough to text a short message to her lover. She'd memorized Kim's schedule, so she knew when she would be able to check her cell phone and respond. Lorin typed her message and then put her phone back in her pocket. She was trying to concentrate on the client profiles fanned out on the table in front of her when she heard voices approaching.

"And this is our smaller work space, Alana. Sometimes we meet with clients in here." Avery walked into the room, one stride ahead of Alana.

"Hello again." Lorin chirped as she prayed her phone would remain quiet for as long as her boss was in the room.

"We're just passing through, Lorin. I'm taking Alana on a mini-tour of our quarters."

Lorin nodded at the two women and noted an expression of frank curiosity in Alana Blue's eyes. She wondered if Alana remembered their months-old elevator conversation.

Shortly after Avery and Alana left the room, Lorin's cell phone emitted a series of short beeps. Lorin scanned Kim's response.

"Good. Our plans haven't gone awry. Of course, it's still early in the day." Lorin frowned, afraid to feel too excited about her afternoon assignation.

Chapter Twenty-three

THE FIRST TIME I noticed the hollow in the base of Johnetta's throat was Friday morning. In the midst of taking our walk in the state park, we climbed to the top of an observation platform. Johnetta walked to its eastern ledge. She leaned against the railing and held the binoculars in front of her. I watched her carefully, the way you dare to look at a person when you know she's not aware of your curiosity about her. The deep dimple in Johnnie's soft brown skin revealed itself thanks to her partially unzipped jacket.

"Have you had thyroid surgery?" I asked.

Johnetta continued scanning the horizon. "Parathyroid. Two winters ago."

Seconds later she pivoted and playfully trained the binoculars on my face. "No throat procedures in your recent past. Am I right?"

"Correct." I stared into the lens. "You haven't lost your edge, Detective."

Johnetta lowered the binoculars, letting them rest, suspended by their leather cord, against her chest.

"Oh, I don't plan to ever lose that edge, Ms. Blue."

Something unidentifiable pulsed through me. It forced me to look away from Johnetta and concentrate on the platform's rough-hewn floorboards. When I looked at her anew, I found her offering me the warmest smile I had received in an age.

"I suppose holding on to your edge is a good thing, since you're still in the detective business."

"Yup. It is a good thing."

"Is life on the job going well for you?" I had asked my clients this question hundreds of times, and almost always I'd heard a perfunctory, "Yeah, Ms. Blue, everything's cool."

"Pretty well. In fact, we're getting so close to the perp in the Taylor case, we can smell him."

Johnetta's gentle smile dissolved. She became quiet, and I wondered if she were reminding herself to keep mum about the information she knew.

I wanted to give her a way out of the conversation, so I gestured to the brigade of aged oak and maple trees standing guard at the border of the field spread out in front of us.

"I can see a nest over there, but it's abandoned. I guess the eagles are long gone."

"Maybe they're staying at their vacation home. Everybody

deserves some time off." Johnetta sounded less serious than she had a moment earlier.

"How about you?"

"Oh, I get time off. I'm taking a week in January and another one in February."

"Good for you. Are you going to travel?"

"I'm thinking about it." Johnetta looked at me rather wistfully. "There's this all-woman resort in Florida, real close to a beautiful championship golf course..."

"You should go, Johnnie." I remembered how relieved I used to feel whenever I had the chance to leave work and begin a vacation trip, and I imagined how burdened Johnetta probably felt, having to share the stress of a murder investigation.

"Know anyone who wants to go to the Florida Keys in February?" Johnetta's grin returned.

"I might know one or two people."

We stood there, teetering over the edge of what to say next, until I broke the silence.

"Can I borrow those binoculars?"

"Sure you can." Johnetta hooked her thumb under the field glass's leather strap. She guided the cord over her head and, using both her hands, placed it over mine. I accepted the twin lenses, and in doing so, touched the back of Johnnie's fingers.

"Got 'em?" She asked me softly.

"Yes."

I put the glasses up to my eyes and aimed them at the horizon. With the distant tree limbs sharply defined, I began to scan slowly from left to right.

"See any more nests?"

"No," I said. "I think the information on the interpretive sign is a bunch of lies."

My head and the binoculars moved as one, systematically traveling the entire length of every tree in the distance. "Wait. I see one. It's empty, of course."

"This isn't nesting season. Maybe they'll come back next spring." Johnnie drew close to my ear and whispered. "Where do you see it?"

"Here," I felt for the cord. "Take these back."

"No. Don't lose sight of that nest." Johnetta moved even closer to me. "Keep the cord around your neck, but gradually take the binocs away from your eyes."

I followed her prompt, trying to aim the glasses at the copse of trees where I'd spotted the aerie.

Johnetta took the binoculars from my hands and held them up in front of her eyes. "Okay. Point me in the right direction." Her gentle voice brushed my right ear as she made her request.

I breathed in her fragrance, a mixture of soap and spice, and then turned my head slightly as I guided the field glasses toward the spot where I thought I'd been holding them a moment earlier.

"Do you see the tall sugar maple, the one with a lot of brown leaves still attached to the branches?" It was hard for me to know precisely what Johnetta was looking at. It was harder for me to believe she was using her binoculars while the cord remained hung around my neck.

"Okay. I see it now." Johnetta let a slow whistle pass through her lips. "Damn, it's huge."

I grinned. "Big birds need a big home."

Johnetta eased the field glasses away from her face and handed them back to me. I held them with one hand and slipped the cord over my head with the other one.

I passed them to her. "Thanks for letting me use these."

"You're quite welcome. Do you want to continue our walk?" Johnetta gestured for me to precede her down the platform's stairs.

"Sure. Should we take the paved path or try the grassy one through the woods?"

Johnetta peered at the latter route which lay to our left. After a couple of seconds, she pointed at the macadam walkway and said, "Let's take this one. I know we'd see more of Mother Nature's miracles if we trekked down the unpaved path, but this one looks like it's more populated."

"That sounds like the old safety-in-numbers theory."

"There's something to that old theory, especially in a state park." Johnetta smiled at me.

"Are you always on duty, Detective?"

"To some extent." She sighed, "I guess I've seen too much."

I listened without responding, hoping she'd say more. We walked side by side, matching each other's pace for a good fifty yards before I spoke again.

"So, aside from policing and playing golf, what kinds of things do you enjoy doing?"

"Taking walks, getting to know people, and learning just about anything."

She looked directly at me and smiled shyly.

"A lifelong learner, huh?"

"I suppose so." Johnetta tapped my arm. "What about you? Other than gardening, what activities do you like?"

"How do you know I like to garden?" I didn't remember ever saying anything to her about my love of flowers and landscaping.

"I've driven past your house a few times. Your front yard is beautiful."

I was aware of Johnetta's gaze as she spoke.

"Thanks. I'm proud of all the work I've done in that yard." I beamed. "Although everything's gone to seed by this time of year."

Johnetta nodded knowingly. "I got a quick impression of your place the first day I drove by. It was during the summer. I recall seeing flower beds artfully arranged, shrubs neatly pruned, grass trimmed, color-coordinated window boxes..."

"If that was a quick impression, I wonder how accurately you'd describe my property after a visit." I laughed softly.

"Well, you can invite me sometime soon, and we'll test my observation skills."

Johnetta tilted her head and met my laughter with a chuckle of her own.

I wanted to invite her to my house. I wanted to say the right things to her, but nothing that made me sound like I was too eager for her company.

"I'd love for you to come by. Let me know when you're free."

"Okay."

Then, Johnetta put her palm on the small of my back and eased me toward the right side of the path. A fast moving apparition wearing dark gray athletic gear and a black skullcap streaked past us. The jogger's running shoes barely kissed the ground. His hissed "Thanks" trailed behind him.

"Your hearing is as good as your powers of observation. I never heard him."

She laughed. "My son used to tell me I had teacher's ears."

"I agree with your son."

We stepped back to the center of the path and continued to match each others' stride. We walked so close to each other, our thighs almost touched. I felt the warmth from Johnetta's body radiate through her sweat pants. It warmed the side of me that marched close to her. I felt excitement and also relaxed comfort because of our physical closeness. Most of the time, I was self-sufficient. It dawned upon me that I'd felt protected a moment earlier when Johnetta guided me away from the runner's path.

"I guess I'm so accustomed to being aware of my surroundings, knowing who's in front, in back, or on either side of me is second nature," Johnetta said, not slowing her gait.

"That sounds like a habit I need to acquire." I glanced at her.

You'd think after spending years observing my clients' body and verbal languages I'd be an expert. But the only time I paid attention to the entire environment was in my garden. Like a cinematographer, I knew when each kind of flower was ready to be filmed. I'd memorized the texture, height and width of each plant, and the times of year when beauty filled each area of the yard. No matter what the season was, I could appreciate everything that was there, yet visualize how the entire space would look six months later. As for the rest of the world, I was less observant.

"Are you a nature lover in general, Alana?" Johnetta slowed the pace by half a stride.

"I respect animals. And I absolutely love spending time at the zoo."

"Me, too." She touched my arm. "I swear you can go to the same zoo every week and see something you hadn't noticed the week before."

"Let's go sometime," I said.

"It's a deal."

We sealed the plan by shaking hands.

We walked on and discussed the state of the world, her son, my daughter, and life after leaving a first career. Entire sections of the pine-scented state park floated by without my noticing them.

"That's the parking area over there, isn't it?" Johnetta pointed to the half dozen cars filling the stony lot ahead of us.

"Yes. We've done the circuit."

"Would you like to meet here next week, same day, same time? We could do another health walk," I said.

"Sure. I'd love that." Johnetta gazed at me. "I'm enjoying getting to know you, Alana."

I extended my hand to her. She held on to it firmly and covered it with her other hand. A few steps later found us next to my car. Johnetta waited for me to get in before she turned to walk away. I watched her. Her stride was purposeful, confident. The loose fitting pants she wore failed to conceal the strength of her calves, the power in her thighs, and the taut roundness of her hips. She moved with graceful agility.

Johnetta arrived at her car. She started its engine and then turned her head toward my direction. She smiled broadly and waved. I returned the gesture and backed out of my parking spot.

She followed me for the first few miles. When we stopped at a red light, I looked at her in my rearview mirror. She stared back at me. Her eyes radiated calm and kindness. I wondered what she was thinking, and hoped her thoughts mirrored mine. By the time I reached the intersection where my route parted from hers, I was able to name the feeling that filled me each time Johnnie was close to me today. The feeling was called "safe."

I'd taken care of myself for what seemed like forever, and protected myself for longer than that. To imagine another person could offer me safety after all this time didn't seem possible. To acknowledge that a woman I barely knew could help me feel protected in this world struck me as just short of miraculous.

Chapter Twenty-four

THE SECOND SHE arrived at her car, Nikki saw the piece of paper folded under her windshield wiper.

Who's advertising what now? And what idiot leaves a flier on cars when it's raining?

Although signing out for a half day's absence gave her plenty of time to get to her appointment, Nikki hurried. She snatched the paper from under the windshield blade and tossed it on the passenger seat as she slid behind the steering wheel. She checked her watch's accuracy against the car's clock and hoped the day's wet weather wouldn't slow her drive.

As she glided through the sparse traffic in the neighborhood surrounding her school, Nikki glanced in the visor mirror. Reassured about her makeup and hair, she smiled in anticipation of the afternoon's plans and in appreciation of how clever she'd been to request time off from her job. She'd never done that before and she planned to do it again.

"Oh shit." Nikki cursed the flashing warning signal but she heeded the pulsing yellow light and decreased her speed. As she slowed her car she probed her handbag. Cell phone in hand, she pressed the power button and then immediately heard four tones alerting her she had a text message. She diverted her attention from the traffic long enough to read the words spread across the small screen. It was the second message of the day from the same sender.

Nikki pursed her lips and once again stole a look at the car's digital clock. She tapped out a return message on her phone's keyboard.

On my way.

A few blocks later, Nikki stopped for a red light. Impatient to continue her drive, she thumped her steering wheel and then looked randomly down to her right. The damp piece of paper she'd rescued from her windshield stared back at her. Snagging it just seconds before the light changed to green, Nikki peeled back the two halves of what she thought was an advertisement. She began reading the typed missive.

Her eyes grew large and then narrowed. A sudden heat infused her reddening face as she refolded the paper and set it back on the leather seat next to her. The traffic light gave its permission for her to drive forward, but Nikki's car remained stock still. A horn blared from behind her. Nikki grabbed the edge of the rearview mirror, glared at it icily and yelled,

"Shut the hell up!"

She jammed her foot onto the accelerator and began a profanity laced monologue that continued for ten minutes and stopped only when she parked her car near the corner of a busy intersection. For the next sixty minutes, Nikki remained in her vehicle, alternately seething with rage and then breathing evenly in quiet reflection. Her angry rant resumed when she restarted the car. Nikki cursed every day her husband Owen had been on this earth, and she wished him a most evil end for having betrayed her...with a university student no less.

Chapter Twenty-five

"THANKS, JOHNNIE. YOU don't mind driving into Philly?" Detective Harold Smythe's bushy eyebrows looked like quotation marks surrounding the worry on his forehead.

"No problem. Dr. Mobley is expecting me, right?"

"Yup." Smythe cracked his knuckles. "And she knows you're going to be asking her a few questions about our suspect's comings and goings the day of the murder."

"I'm also going to ask her about his work habits in general." Johnetta reached for her jacket.

"Yeah, like does he get along with his co-workers? Is he a neat-freak or is he sloppy?"

Johnetta nodded. Although she already knew what she wanted to ask, she didn't mind indulging Harold his script writing activity. The interview would be routine, she figured. A forty-minute rain-soaked drive into Philly, an equally long search for a parking space, and a question-and-answer session that might or might not shed light on the suspect's personality and daily modus operandi. She'd ask Dr. Mobley if the suspect had displayed any changes in his demeanor or attitude recently; if he'd done anything uncharacteristic that would multiply their reasons for considering him a person of interest in the Taylor case.

"Okay, Harold. You know where I'll be for the next few hours."

Johnetta plucked a key from the nearby pegboard, signed out one of the department's unmarked cars, and left the building. The roads were covered with thickly matted leaves in various stages of decomposition. A heavy rain shower challenged the car's windshield wipers and reminded Johnetta to monitor her speed. She turned onto a two-lane thoroughfare and immediately headed down a hill. She slowed gradually, well ahead of the stop sign.

Looking to the right, Johnetta realized she was only a few hundred yards from Alana's home. She turned her head, wondering if she'd see Alana's car parked in the driveway.

The last time they saw each other, Alana was in her car, smiling and waving goodbye. Now, as she summoned Alana's image, Johnetta went to that place where she kept all the pretty tender things she'd ever experienced. It seemed that Alana had earned a space there so quickly.

As Johnetta accelerated toward the city, she left the specter of

Alana's beautiful smile at the intersection.

Less than an hour later, Johnetta steered into a parking lot and simultaneously squelched the chatter coming from the car's police-band radio. Tucking her notebook under her arm, she walked across the street to an old brick building where she was to meet with Dr. Caryn Mobley. Intricate carvings adorned the building's massive dark-stained wooden doors. Johnetta grasped one of the door's brass knobs and pulled it toward her. Despite its heft, the door opened without much effort.

Once inside the building, she passed three offices before she arrived at Dr. Mobley's. Two young men in their early twenties, Johnetta estimated, emerged from the office just as she entered. They deferred to her, holding the door open. Johnetta's "Thanks" was overtaken by an authoritative voice aimed her way.

"You must be the detective with whom I have an appointment."

Johnetta nodded at the tall auburn-haired woman. *If you say so,* she wanted to respond.

"Yes, I am," she said instead.

Dr. Mobley ushered Johnnie into her office. "Have a seat, Detective..."

"Jones." Johnetta held her badge at eye level in front of Dr. Mobley.

"I have a full schedule of appointments, Detective Jones, so I'd like to get this interview over and done with."

Johnetta glanced at a small table located on the opposite side of the room. It held a teapot, cups, and a wooden box that no doubt contained tea this woman wasn't about to offer her.

"I have only a few questions, Dr. Mobley. This shouldn't take long at all." Although she wasn't easily intimidated, Johnetta felt pressured to minimize her imposition on this woman.

"I'm going to ask you to remember some details that go back to last summer." Johnetta watched Dr. Mobley look up. She followed her gaze and noticed a strip of paint curling away from the ceiling.

"Lots of luck, Detective. It's getting so I can't remember what I wore yesterday."

Johnetta smiled. "I'm right there with you, Dr. Mobley."

Johnetta dispatched each of her questions about the person of interest. Dr. Mobley couldn't remember anything remarkable having taken place with any staff member on or about the time of Shantay Taylor's murder.

"He's always pretty much the same, pleasant, efficient, adequate but anxious to be better than average."

"Could you describe what you mean when you say he wants to be better than average?".

"Certainly. You see, his colleagues attend most of the staff meetings, and a few of the year's social events. He goes to every single meeting, every colloquium, and every single damn tea, party, and picnic that's held." Dr. Mobley sounded more exasperated than pleased about her employee's conscientious work ethic.

"And you think that means he's eager to be better than average?"

"I've been here for twenty-six years, and I've never known anyone who's attended everything." Dr. Mobley shook her head. "I don't know how that man finds the time to be a husband."

"Have you ever met his wife?" Johnetta asked.

"Of course I have, once or twice." Dr. Mobley rose from her chair and walked to a bookcase near the window. Carefully she moved a trophy out of the way and then picked up a large framed photo from one of the shelves.

"Here's a photo of our staff members with their significant others. It was taken last year." She pointed to the picture's only African-American couple. "There they are."

Johnetta focused on the pair. She knew what the suspect looked like because she had a copy of his file photo inserted under the flap of her notebook. She'd never seen a picture of his wife, though.

"She's very good looking, don't you think?" Dr. Mobley sounded detached as she searched Johnetta's face for some sign of agreement.

"Yes, she is." Johnetta stared at the young woman's features. For a fleeting second, she thought she'd met her. But where?

"So, Dr. Mobley. You've described how faithful he is to his job. Do you have any reason to think his busy schedule here has caused trouble in his marriage?"

"No. No reason at all." Dr. Mobley averted Johnetta's stare. "If you're finished with your questions, Detective Jones … "

Johnetta sensed Dr. Mobley was finished with the interview, whether she had more questions to ask her or not.

"That's it for now." Johnetta extended her hand. She was impressed by the firmness of the other woman's grip. "Thanks for your time, Dr. Mobley."

"I don't want to make your job more difficult, Detective. But if you suspect him of any wrongdoing, I hope you're incorrect. He's very dedicated to his work and he has a solid professional reputation. For what it's worth, I trust him. We meet frequently to discuss all kinds of issues. He's an asset to our department and to our entire organization."

"In that case, I hope my department is barking up the wrong

tree." Johnetta allowed a brief smile. She wanted to have a hand in solving this case, but not if it meant destroying the life of a young black man with a solid future.

Her gut told her she and Detective Smythe were on the right track. She knew they didn't have sufficient reason to pull him in though, or enough evidence to keep him under surveillance. She wanted to do things by the book, not half-assed.

Both the victim and this suspect were African-American. Johnetta was the only black detective on her suburban police force. Those demographics alone compelled her to follow procedures meticulously. She asked herself if her compulsion to do things the right way was similar to the suspect's desire to be better than average. While she felt a special responsibility to protect the murdered girl posthumously by finding her killer, she also sought to avoid arresting the wrong suspect. What would happen to this guy's reputation if he were arrested and proved innocent?

Johnetta breathed deeply as the memory of Khalif Baxter arose like the mirage of water flowing in the middle of a white hot desert. Dismissing her feelings of guilt, Johnetta refocused. *Police work shouldn't be about destroying the lives of black men*, she thought.

As she left Dr. Mobley's office, Johnetta contemplated the woman's description of the suspect. Efficient, pleasant, anxious to be better than the rest. Did he feel constant pressure to perform well? Was he stressed out trying to measure up to his university's expectations? Without intending to, Dr. Mobley may have provided a portrait of the suspect similar to the psychological profile already on the Brighton Police Department's radar screen. The only missing element was the perp's motive.

Feeling cold, damp, and hungry, Johnetta walked a block beyond the lot where she'd parked. The streets were still wet, but the rain was on temporary hiatus. Drawn by the odor of steamed hot dogs, spicy yellow mustard, and sauerkraut, Johnetta stopped at a food truck bivouacked near a busy intersection. She joined the short line of hungry customers. When it was her turn, she decided to skip the chemical-filled-meat in a bun in favor of a large coffee and a cinnamon crumb topped pastry. She knew neither of those items belonged to a food group she needed to consume. But she knew the hot beverage and the flour-sugar-butter concoction would satisfy her hunger, if only temporarily.

Back at the parking lot, she placed the coffee container and the cellophane wrapped bun on the car's roof as she scanned the rows of parked automobiles.

Maybe his car is parked right here. After all, he works in the building I just left, she speculated.

She flipped through her notebook. Rushing past data she

already knew, she found the description of the suspect's car. Then she methodically examined each row of vehicles as she uncapped her drink and blew to cool the dark liquid enough to swallow her first mouthful. Before she could open the pastry wrapper, she heard the guttural chug of a car's engine coming to life. She squinted in the direction of the noise, patiently waiting to see a disruption in the pattern of parked vehicles.

There it was. A late model, light gray VW sporting the suspect's license plate. She watched the car approach the parking lot exit. It stopped and Johnetta could see the driver's window lowering. A vibrant young woman, her hair swirling across the collar of her trench coat, walked rapidly toward the gray car. She began talking to the male driver. She rested her hand on the car's window frame. Seconds later, she bent lower and inclined her head toward him.

Johnetta continued blowing into her coffee cup and taking sips, all the while paying close attention to what looked like a romantic movie scene. She saw the woman's clearly etched profile approach the driver's. A full minute passed before the woman stood upright again. Her hand lingered on the car door. The man's darker hued hand covered the woman's and then quickly brought it to his lips. Following that affectionate gesture, the woman walked in front of the car, opened the passenger side door, and got in. The car's engine continued to idle.

As Johnetta put her coffee cup back on the roof of her car, she recalled the photo she'd examined thirty minutes ago in Dr. Mobley's office.

"Whoa. That woman is not his wife."

The VW moved toward the nearby traffic signal. Just then, the sudden motion of a bright yellow car on the other side of the street grabbed Johnetta's attention. Its female driver jettisoned away from the curb just as the traffic light changed from amber to red. The car's brakes squealed in protest. Its chassis recoiled as it strained to move forward.

Johnetta squinted at the woman whose hands seemed fused to her steering wheel.

"Oh damn, that woman is his wife."

In one motion, Johnetta tossed the uneaten pastry into the back of her car and then threw herself into the driver's seat. She started the engine and backed out of her parking space as quickly as safety would permit, keeping one hand on the steering wheel while she fished in her jacket pocket for the ticket. She approached the automated Pay-To-Park machine, fed it her ticket, and eased a ten dollar bill into the hungry slot. The traffic light switched from red to green the second Johnetta peeled away from the computerized parking attendant without retrieving the money it owed her.

"Keep the change, you little robot. I'm out of here," she mumbled.

For once in her life, Johnetta felt grateful for the horde of cars, buses, bicycles and pedestrians clogging the mid-city traffic artery. Its sluggish pace helped her keep the suspect's and his wife's car in view. She wondered if he knew he was at the front of a three-vehicle parade.

As they got closer to an intersection bordered by a huge medical center, construction trucks caused their procession to move even slower. Johnetta flipped open her cell phone and called her partner.

"Harold? I'm going to be back later than I thought—No, she didn't have any new info for me. But I might be on to something now. It looks to me like our guy just picked up a pretty young thing. What makes it interesting is that his wife witnessed the entire scene, and now she's tailing him in her car. I'm following both of them. Okay, I'll call you back in a few."

The secret parade made its way past the business and commercial area. Turning left onto one of the city's numbered streets, they headed toward the multi-lane flag lined parkway. The three cars drove by the city's storied art museum and then entered a road bordering one side of the Schuylkill River. Rain began falling again; a drenching downpour that soaked the route's sculpture gardens and boathouses named for Philadelphia's moneyed rowing clubs and heavily endowed local universities.

This was a ride Johnetta usually enjoyed, but today she kept her eyes riveted on the gray and yellow vehicles ahead of her. There were three cars separating her from the suspect's wife and at least four playing interference between the wife's car and her husband's. The trio drove in the righthand lane, just under the speed limit. Unlike the path further ahead of them, this part of the road was fairly straight. Johnetta knew if the lead driver were headed home, they'd soon have to maneuver a route with one winding twist after another. In this rainstorm, maintaining visual contact with both cars would challenge her driving skills.

Johnetta slowed her car as she entered a deeply pitched S curve. The lane seemed almost too narrow for the cumbersome vehicle. The curve was so acute, she momentarily lost sight of the wife's yellow car. Just as she steered into the last part of the S, she spotted a flash of yellow about a hundred feet ahead of her. It darted up a steep hill to the right. Johnetta accelerated and made the same turn. She could see the other car's turn signal blinking.

Johnetta knew there was only one place the car could go, into Fairmount Greene, a two-story condominium complex. She slowed and guided her vehicle into the development's entrance. Once she passed the old wooden sign with most of the complex's name faded into oblivion, Johnetta spied her yellow prey gliding into a parking spot at the end of a row of attached houses. She kept her own car moving slowly and stole glances at the other driver as she crept past.

This isn't where they live, Johnetta thought. She drove the perimeter of the development, but she was forced to stop when a school bus, its red beacons flashing, stood stolidly in front of her. Impatiently, she counted the backpack-wearing children who all moved at the same speed: fast, once their feet hit the driveway. Despite their immediate scattering, they didn't disappear quickly enough for Johnetta.

"Dammit!"

The bus finally lumbered on and Johnetta returned to the section where the yellow car was parked. The vehicle was still there, but the driver had disappeared.

"Dammit to hell!" Johnetta gripped the steering wheel. "Which one of these houses did she go to?"

Johnetta set about looking for the gray VW. Failing to see it, she drove to the opposite side of the building complex and then parked her own unmarked vehicle. Once again she examined the information in her notebook. She was correct. The suspect and his wife didn't live here. They had a house eight miles away. For some reason, the suspect's wife had stopped tailing her husband.

Johnetta looked at the crumb-topped pastry in the back seat. Her appetite gone, she opened her notebook and wrote the details of her interview with Dr. Mobley and her chase from one area of Philly to this one. When she restarted the car and began her return trip to the Brighton Police Department, she realized she had far more questions about the suspect than she had answers.

On the drive back, Johnetta thought about the sparse information Dr. Mobley had shared. She regretted the woman's comments failed to shed much light on the perp. When her thoughts turned to Dr. Mobley's photo of the suspect's wife, followed by her actual encounter with the woman, Johnetta figured she hadn't completely wasted her time. There was a story going on, perhaps not one involving murder, but indeed it was one involving drama.

Once she returned to police headquarters, Johnetta parked the borrowed vehicle and signed back in. She had two more hours on the clock before her shift ended. A quick peek inside the office she shared with Detective Smythe told her he wasn't there. No matter. She had a bit of research to do, and she didn't want Harold's acerbic remarks interfering with her work.

She sat at her desk, opened her notebook, and reread every word. Not satisfied, she scoured every police database she imagined could possibly contain information about him. Ninety minutes into her search, she rested her elbows on her desk and closed her eyes. Suddenly, she bolted upright in her seat.

"Oh my God." Johnetta smacked her cheek lightly. "You idiot."

She typed the man's name in the blank Google engine box. Pages of listings appeared. By the time Johnetta skimmed every article on the first five pages she knew more about the study of British literature than she thought should exist. When she perused the first article on the sixth page, she stared in disbelief at the computer screen.

A marriage announcement published by the New York Times related the day, time, and place that Owen P. Reid, Ph.D., joined Nikki Solange Blue in matrimony. The mother of the bride, Alana Blue, gave her daughter away in marriage.

Johnetta read the account twice. Then, with a decisive click, she closed out the website. But she couldn't stop the troubling eddy of questions spinning out of control. How would she tell Alana about her son-in-law's wandering libido? How could she warn her that Owen was a murder suspect, and Nikki could be in danger?And how could she deliver these words to Alana and still expect to be welcomed into this woman's life?

Chapter Twenty-six

RAFE ORTIZ LIFTED her glass and tilted it from side to side, listening as the small chunks of ice collided against each other. She stared at the woman seated across the table. For a brief second she wanted her to be Cynthia, her ex-lover in her former office. Although this woman looked nothing at all like Cynthia, she possessed the same incendiary qualities that once inflamed Rafe's imagination and almost immolated her career.

Rafe stretched her legs under the small pseudo-wood table and examined the other patrons scattered around the room. It was early evening, and the bar wasn't crowded. The acrid smell of singed popcorn mingled with the odor of beer and cologne, splashed haphazardly on the bar's denizens who, an hour before, had been eager to leave their office cubicles and begin the weekend.

Rafe chose to sit at this particular table because she wanted to watch the bar's entrance. You never knew who might wander in.

"You drank that tonic fast. Want somethin' stronger?" The woman leaned closer to Rafe and tried on an enticing smile.

"Nope. I'm fine." Rafe pointed at her empty glass. "I don't do stronger than this."

The woman smiled smugly, as if she had just solved a puzzle. "You in a program?"

"No." Rafe said flatly.

"Then why don't you ever drink anything stronger than tonic or ginger ale? That's no fun."

"I guess that's my business, isn't it?" Rafe relaxed her grip on the empty glass.

She rested her hand beneath the table, spread her fingers and began patting her thigh rhythmically. After playing several five-note scales on her imaginary piano, Rafe once again focused on the unblemished brown face staring back at her. Precisely penciled eyebrows accentuated the woman's small piercing eyes. Rafe thought this woman had the darkest eyes she'd ever seen. They were so dark, Rafe couldn't determine if they were brown or black. Set close together, they gave the woman an almost simian appearance. The woman's broad cheekbones, narrow nose and thin lips gave her a kind of exoticism Rafe couldn't ignore.

"Yeah, baby. It is your business. Frankly, I don't care what's in your glass as long as you're drinkin' it with me." Selena Garrett held Rafe's gaze captive.

Rafe stilled her percussive hand. She stared at Selena and sneered.

"You think we're really dating each other, don't you?"

Selena leaned forward. "Well now, Ms. Ortiz, you come to my job at least once a week, sometimes twice. You phone me every day. You claim you lost the results of my last drug and alcohol test, you haven't made me pee in a cup for a month, and this is the third time we've met for drinks." Selena reached across the table and put her hand on Rafe's. "So, hell yes, baby. Doesn't it look like we're seein' each other?"

"No." Rafe pulled her hand from under Selena's. She looked away from her table mate and stared at the bar's front door.

"Well, you can call it what you want, but I'm pretty sure I'm dating my P.O. And I like it."

Rafe balled her hand into a fist. Whenever she spent time with Selena, she knew she was playing with fire. She felt certain she was holding the matches and she had no intention of risking third degree burns by losing her job.

"I'm not dating you, Selena." She paused. "I'm not dating anyone."

"Sell that story to someone deaf, blind, and stupid, Rafe, but not to me. You probably claim we're not dating because you're talkin' to more than one woman at once." Selena winked. "But right now you're in this bar with me, and the way I see it, we're only one date short of fuckin' each other."

Rafe shook her head and laughed. "Really? Is that how you see it?"

"For real."

"Well, I wouldn't be so sure of all that, Ms. Garrett." Rafe stretched her arms and flexed her fingers.

"Well, I'm as sure about us sexing each other as I'm sure the ice in your glass is goin' to melt." She winked once again and hooked her thumb toward her chest. "If you didn't want this, you should have been more careful, Ms. Ortiz."

Rafe retracted her smile. Maybe Selena had a point. Meeting her in a public venue was a careless move. Had she become so caught up in her fantasies of the two of them seducing each other she was snubbing caution? She wasn't ready to give up her job. She was ready however, for another meaningless sexual diversion. She'd played games like this one before and she was certain Selena had also. They both knew the rules. Move in secrecy, speak half truths, murmur implications of a possible relationship, and then manufacture some reason to rupture the little affair before it went any further. That would work perfectly for Rafe. It always had in the past.

Rafe squinted at her watch, and then said coldly. "You should leave now or you'll be late getting back to the group home. How's that for being careful?"

Selena slid her chair back. "I guess you're not going to give me a lift?"

"No, maybe next time."

"Maybe next time we can meet at your place, Rafe." Selena's lips curved into a salacious grin.

Rafe sat forward and dispatched a matching smile. "Maybe."

"Good. I'll look forward to seeing where you live."

Selena's sentence hung between them, unanswered. Rafe's ringing cell phone hijacked her rejoinder. Glaring at the message on the instrument's screen, Rafe set it face down on the table.

"Don't ignore your call on my account. I was just about to leave, remember?" Selena said.

"No worries. I won't."

Selena laughed softly. "Another one of your women wondering where you are?"

Rafe ignored the question, as well as Selena's tone of voice.

Selena stood and quickly took two steps closer to Rafe. She bent down, and kissed her on the mouth. Startled, Rafe pulled away before Selena could engulf her lips fully.

"See you soon, Ms. Ortiz."

Selena didn't turn around to look back at Rafe. Instead, she simply kept walking. Ghostlike, her form merged with the old battered door separating the bar from the narrow alley-like street outside.

Sensing the suggestion of Selena's lingering presence, Rafe speculated that her daydreams about Selena were probably more satisfying than any reality of their coupling might be. For a moment she considered following the wiser course of action, and enjoying Selena Garrett's naked body only in her imagination, not in her bed. But Rafe thrived on teasing temptation. She'd keep Selena at arm's length until her fantasies weren't enough to gratify her desires.

Rafe knew no one could really love her with the intensity she needed. She'd never met anyone who'd been enough for her, not pretty enough, not independent enough, not clever enough, not affectionate enough. When she compared all of her lovers, their only consistency was their habit of revealing some deficiency the moment they unfolded themselves to her. Every woman she'd ever known had failed to meet her expectations. That included Cynthia. She had been too needy, too demanding of attention. Rafe was on the verge of saying goodbye the day Cynthia's husband arrived at their office and publically threw the shitfit that resulted in her disciplinary transfer.

Rafe picked up her phone and listened to the last message. Her face expressionless, she knew why she no longer entertained daydreams about the caller. She could seduce Alana Blue any time she pleased. A seduction was just about all she wanted from her. Rafe deleted Alana's voice from her phone. She would respond to her message when she was ready, not a moment before.

A whisper of cold air rushed by Rafe as two women entered the bar. She watched them shed their outer garments and claim barstools. The taller of the two summoned the bartender. She extracted a few bills from her wallet and rested them atop the counter.

Rafe's lips played with a smile as she observed her buddy, Lorin, grin unabashedly at the pretty young woman seated next to her.

So that's her main squeeze, Rafe thought. *Not bad.*

Rafe left her table and sauntered toward the bar. Stopping just short of it, she stood directly behind Lorin, placed her hands on her friend's shoulders, and boomed.

"Hey, stranger."

Lorin spun around.

"Rafe." She sprang from the stool and wrapped her arms around her friend. "Oh, man. It's so good to see you."

"Same here."

Lorin's date turned to watch the two women.

"Rafe, meet Kim." Lorin reached out and grabbed Kim's arm. "Kim, this is my buddy, Rafe."

"It's nice to meet you."

"My pleasure, Kim." Rafe enclosed Kim's hand in hers.

"Lorin has mentioned your name to me so many times."

"Always in a positive context, I assume."

"Of course, nothing but positives." Lorin grinned at Rafe. "So how are you, woman? How's the job going?"

"Too many offenders to keep track of, but I'm holding my own."

Lorin turned to Kim. "Rafe's a parole officer. That's how I met her."

Kim's eyes narrowed.

"Don't worry, Kim. Lorin wasn't one of my clients," Rafe said quickly.

"Oh my God, no." Lorin laughed. "My boss at the Baker Center kept assigning me ex-offenders who just happened to be in Rafe's caseload. Every time I turned around I found myself either phoning or meeting with this character." Lorin gestured in Rafe's direction.

"Your girlfriend here is equipped with gaydar." Rafe looked

directly at Kim. "She picked up my vibe and decided we needed to meet for drinks and formally come out to each other."

"That doesn't surprise me." Kim stared at Lorin. "She picked up my vibe also."

"You're good that way, huh?" Rafe teased Lorin.

"Yes she is," Kim said before Lorin could find a response. "She figured me out even before I could put it all together."

Lorin lowered her voice. Her lips barely moved as she continued the narrative. "Kim's not out. She's married. I'm the only one who knows she's a lesbian."

"And that's how I want it, at least for the time being," Kim said. She looked squarely into Rafe's eyes.

Rafe nodded. "No problem. Who you are and what you do is no one's business but yours."

"I told you we could trust Rafe, sweetheart." Lorin regarded Kim lovingly. She caressed her shoulder.

"So how long have you been a parole officer, Rafe?" Kim's voice grew louder.

"Too long," Rafe said with an oft-practiced answer. She perused the seated woman's body. "How long have you known Lorin?"

"For a few months now."

"Oh, newlyweds." Rafe didn't try to prevent a lascivious grin from breaking out on her face. As she watched Kim turn slightly to pick up her glass of wine, Rafe thought she saw a familiar shadow in her profile.

"Which of the city's parole and probation offices are you assigned to, Rafe?" Kim asked.

"Center City."

Rafe saw a flicker of surprise flash from Kim's eyes. Without staring directly at her, Rafe took in the woman's features. "Have we met each other before, Kim?"

"Not that I recall," Kim said quickly and then looked away.

"You're not trying that tired line on my girl, are you?" Lorin chided. She moved closer and put her arm around Kim's shoulders. "That's one of Rafe's most endearing qualities. She thinks she knows every African-American lesbian in Philadelphia."

"Well, she doesn't know this one," Kim said.

"Maybe you have a body double," Rafe said.

Kim inclined her half-empty glass toward her mouth. "Anything's possible."

"Rafe, can I buy you a drink?" Lorin put her hand in her pocket.

"No thanks. I was getting ready to leave when I saw you guys come in." Rafe took a step backwards and began putting her jacket on. "It's been a long-ass week, and I need to go home."

"If I know you, you have a busy weekend planned." Lorin gazed at Kim. "Our Rafaela is dating a mystery woman. The last time I asked about her identity, Rafe wouldn't give it up."

Rafe refused to be baited." She has a name, but just like the two of you, I'm discreet."

"So are you still seeing her?" Lorin persisted.

"Yup."

"Sounds serious."

"Not for a second." The speed of Rafe's response was breathtaking.

Lorin shook her head. "That's Rafe. Love 'em for a moment, but never forever."

"Damn, Lorin. You're giving your girl the wrong impression of me."

"Sorry about that, but it's the reputation you've earned, woman," Lorin said smugly.

"I have to get going." Rafe gave a little wave." Talk to you soon. Good meeting you, Kim."

Kim shrugged away from Lorin's touch. "Nice meeting you as well."

Rafe made her way to the door. Stepping into the evening's chilly wind, she thought about Lorin and Kim.

Better take a page from my book, Lorin, and learn to love for the moment, because your Kim will be gone in a heartbeat. In fact, it wouldn't surprise me to find out she's already left.

Chapter Twenty-seven

JOHNETTA RAISED HER glass and clinked it lightly against mine. "Here's to more movie nights, Alana."

"I second that idea. Especially if we can find films as good as tonight's was." I puckered as I took a sip of the vodka-cranberry-and-limejuice concoction I'd ordered.

Johnetta grinned in amusement. "Is it too tart for you?"

"Let's just say I'm going to let some of the ice melt before I drink any more of it."

"Would you like some of mine?" Johnetta pushed her glass toward me.

"No thanks. I don't want to combine scotch with vodka. You don't want me to be tipsy and sick."

Johnetta sat back in her chair. Her eyelids lowered halfway.

"I think I can handle you tipsy or sober, totally alert or two sheets to the wind."

"You probably can, but only if I want to be handled." If we were going to flirt with each other, I could give as well as get.

"I hear you." Johnetta and I exchanged gazes. After another moment she turned around to see as much of the room as she could.

"This is a cozy little place. I guess it's not gay, is it?"

"Not even a little bit." I looked at the co-ed pairings seated in the booths on the other side of the establishment. "But it's close to the theater and only a couple of blocks from the parking lot."

"And the prices are cheap. My kind of place."

I agreed. I'd been frequenting the movie theater in this small town not far from Brighton Township ever since I read a newspaper article about the building's restoration. Whenever I stepped into the theater's art deco lobby, I was transported back to my childhood, when most Saturdays found my friends and me walking half a mile to see a horror flick or a comedy. The morning Johnnie phoned to ask if I'd like to go to the movies, I suggested we get into "the wayback machine" and drive here, to what I named "the town that time forgot." There was an old-fashioned atmosphere here, along with a spirit of civility I rarely experienced in the city.

Tonight was my third visit to the Tavern on Main. The first time I was here, I'd gone to the movies with Katey and Jean. We ducked into this place in the midst of a storm and had a couple of beers while we waited for the rain to slacken. The second time I slid my feet under a table, I was trying to enjoy an evening with Rafe.

I'd given the tavern's pub menu a glowing recommendation. Five minutes into our visit though, Rafe seemed uncomfortable. The absence of other patrons who looked like us agitated her, and she was convinced the staff conspired to delay waiting on us. We left before we ordered any drinks, but after she complained loudly to the manager. For the rest of that night Rafe fussed with me and questioned my ability to select a good drinking establishment.

Emerging from the memory, I focused on Johnetta.

"Does it seem like the waitress took care of us promptly?"

"Yes. Why do you ask?" Curiosity danced in Johnetta's eyes.

"I was here one evening with a friend and she thought we waited a long time. She thought the waitstaff was ignoring us."

"Maybe that was true then, but not tonight. And besides, you wouldn't put us in a situation like that knowingly."

"You're absolutely right," I said. A flame of self-confidence ignited inside me.

Johnetta nodded toward the bar. "There's another black couple at the far end, and they've been chatting up the bartender ever since we got here."

"Really?" I peered at the row of barstools. When I saw the man and woman Johnetta mentioned, I felt the flame of confidence grow.

"Is it possible you were here with the wrong friend the night she thought the service was slow?" Johnetta winked at me.

"Anything's possible, Detective Jones." I winked right back.

"I like hearing you say that, Ms. Blue, because it gives me hope." Johnetta nodded, then repeated softly. "It gives me hope."

I didn't know exactly what Johnetta was hoping for, nor was I prepared to risk asking. Instead, I shifted our conversation from a personal place to somewhere less threatening.

"What did you like about the film?"

Johnetta looked up at the ceiling for an answer.

"I liked the way the movie had nothing to do with me and at the same time, a lot to do with me."

"What do you mean?"

"A middle-aged woman marries, moves to France, learns French, takes cooking lessons at a famous culinary arts school, and ends up with a successful TV show in America. Another chick works all day in Manhattan, cooks all night every night for a year, writes a blog that get a gazillion hits and becomes famous. Nothing about that story line has a darn thing to do with me." Johnnie looked at me expectantly.

"And?"

"And yet it does have quite a bit to do with me. It's all about the improbable becoming possible. I was a cop in Philly, and I was never hurt or injured. That was improbable. I've retired and begun a second policing career. That's improbable also. Most cops don't retire and then join another police department. Security work? Sure. Another department? Unh, uh. Shall I go on?"

"Sure." I was hooked.

"I've had a couple of bad breakups in which I lost lovers and what I thought were solid relationships, yet I'm more than willing to love again. It's the willingness that's improbable."

She continued. "I believe fervently that anything is possible. In fact, I thrive on possibilities."

I watched Johnetta as she explained her belief in possibility; I saw her sincerity. I didn't respond to what she said because I didn't want to tell her how skeptical I felt regarding possibilities, how I needed to protect myself in case life didn't offer me many more possibilities.

"Do you get what I'm saying?" Johnetta asked.

"Sure. If it's possible for the women in that film to create different lives for themselves, it's possible you can also." I figured my cut-and-dried answer would persuade Johnetta that I wasn't a "possibility" person. And it was too soon for me to want the two of us to be possible.

"That's a start." Johnetta took a deep sip of her scotch. "I don't always say exactly what I want to express."

"A woman of action and few words?" I teased.

"No. I've got plenty of words. Sometimes they act like they don't want to come out."

I smiled as gently as I could.

"I'm patient, Johnnie. Take your time with your words."

"Thanks for your patience." Johnetta looked down at her hands.

"I related to the movie, also," I said. I swirled the little plastic straw in my drink and chanced another gulp of the sour beverage.

"The message I got was, it's okay to acknowledge and indulge your needs. Both of those women loved food. They needed to surround themselves with it. So they dove headfirst into cooking."

"And how does that relate to you? What are some of your needs, Alana?"

"Hmm. I need to feel useful. That's why I'm working part time." I gave Johnetta the most obvious answer I could think of.

She nodded. "Okay, that's one need. What are some others?"

Now it was my turn to look down and stare at my hands.

"I'm sure I have other needs. I just don't think about them much." That was a half-lie. I thought about my needs pretty frequently, but I didn't want to talk about them.

"Maybe you'll share your thoughts with me some other time."

Johnetta nudged her glass forward until it touched the side of mine. Then she added, "I'm patient, also. And I do know how to take my time."

We exchanged shy smiles.

"Do you want another scotch?" I asked.

"No. I'm good with this one." Johnetta lifted her glasses from the bridge of her nose. She seemed to be deep in thought.

"I'm careful with my drinking, Alana. I have to be. For a while, I was enjoying this stuff a little too much. I drank so I could sleep at night, to get through certain anniversaries, to forget crap. It got so the only reason I ever went to parties was to drink other people's liquor."

Johnetta said all of this in a slow, measured pace. The entire time she spoke she looked into my eyes. I believe she was searching for my reaction to her confession.

"We all have our ways of coping with the shittier side of life, Johnnie. You're lucky you recognized the path you were on wasn't a healthy one."

"That's what they told me at Support Services." Johnetta signaled the waitress who arrived, tallying our bill.

"Let me treat you," I said.

"No thanks. So you know, here's the deal. I don't drink off of anyone's dime. That way I can't conveniently drink more than one, two if it's going to be a long evening."

"Is your policy etched in stone?"

We stood up and Johnetta deposited money on the table.

"Nothing is etched in stone. But I'm asking you to cooperate with my rule, at least on our first date. Okay?"

"Okay."

I found myself stealing quick glances at Johnetta as we left the restaurant and walked to the parking lot. I liked the way her slow smile persuaded the cleft in her chin to be more prominent. I enjoyed the feeling I got when I knew her eyes were engaged with mine. By the time we approached my street, my furtive glances changed to a flagrant stare.

Johnetta navigated her car into my driveway. She parked and turned off the ignition.

"I enjoyed myself this evening. Thank you," I said.

"You're welcome, although I believe I enjoyed it even more." Johnetta reached over and ever so lightly touched my arm. Suddenly shy, she withdrew and grasped the steering wheel with both hands.

I was struck by the tenderness I heard in Johnetta's voice and the tentative way she'd just reached out to me. I wanted to feel her skin on mine once again, so I took a turn reaching toward her. I moved my fingertips over the spot where veins gave texture to the back of her hand.

"Alana—"

When I heard Johnetta's voice speak my name, my fingers traveled from atop her hand and migrated to her face. I caressed her left cheekbone and then the soft hollow beneath it leading toward her mouth. Johnetta leaned closer to me. She covered my hand with hers, inviting it to stay exactly where it was. Wordlessly, our lips came together and spoke their own language. We kissed, gently at first. Then, as we realized how much we wanted to enter this new place, we granted our mouths the freedom to kiss more insistently.

"Thank you, Alana."

I smiled. "I think we need to see each other again."

"We will. I promise."

Hours later, in a pleasant pre-sleep haze, I replayed the entire evening from memory.

I hoped replaying our time together wasn't an adolescent thing, that I wasn't wasting my energy when I dwelled on her innuendoes or fixated on recalling her laugh, her fragrance, and the nut-brown color of her skin. I thought about how generously she'd shared anecdotes about her son, and how carefully she'd listened to my anxieties about Nikki. I felt bad for the pain I heard in her voice when she spoke about her deceased partner on the police force.

I resisted sleep for as long as possible so I could keep visualizing Johnnie as she was at the end of our evening together. She'd sat in the driver's seat of her car and looked clear down into my depths. I still felt her hand drawing me close, her mouth meeting mine. Our first kiss began tentatively, as close to being withdrawn as it was to going further. That kiss ebbed, then flowed like a small wave that doesn't know its potential until it grows in spite of itself, surges and finally breaks as it reaches the shoreline.

Johnnie may have anticipated that kiss. I know that I did. Neither of us could have foreseen its power, though. That night, as I landed at sleep's door, I hoped I was one of Johnnie's possibilities. Surely she was one of mine.

Chapter Twenty-eight

OWEN FINISHED TIGHTENING the last of the clips holding the storm door's glass insert in place when he spotted Nikki's car veering into the driveway. He knew she would park in the garage and enter the house through the mudroom, so he gave the insert a tentative push, making sure it was attached securely, and then closed and locked the front door.

He lingered in the foyer, dutifully listening for the sounds of Nikki's arrival. He was eager to go into the den and get settled behind his desk where he would review his lecture notes for the next day's classes. One minute stretched into three as Owen waited to greet Nikki. Impatient, he walked into the kitchen and saw the door leading to the mudroom was still closed. He approached it, calling, "Nikki? Are you—"

The door swung open. Nikki strode into the kitchen. "Am I what?"

"I wondered what was taking you so long." Owen made no attempt to conceal the annoyance in his voice.

"What?" Nikki asked as she slipped her cell phone into her jacket pocket.

"I saw you pull into the driveway, so I decided to wait for you before I went into the den to do some work. It took you forever to come into the house."

"Sorry. I've lost my ability to see through walls. I had no idea you were waiting for me," Nikki said sarcastically as she walked to the kitchen table and deposited her work satchel and handbag.

Owen stepped closer to Nikki and pecked her on the cheek. "So, how was school today?"

"As tiring as usual. This afternoon I had a riot on my hands after I handed out the role assignments for the Thanksgiving play."

"The little movie stars weren't satisfied with their parts?" Owen asked, amused.

"Not one bit. I didn't realize how many prima donnas and dons I was teaching."

"Wait until they realize they have to memorize their lines. I sure hope you have understudies ready to take over when the little Oscar-winning wannabes complain how hard it is to learn their parts."

"That goes without saying."

Owen smiled indulgently at her.

"If you don't need any help with supper, I'm going to start my chores in the den."

"No, I don't need your help." Nikki watched Owen move away from her. "Listen, if you're going to be paying bills, remember to write a check for Dr. Greene. Date it for tomorrow's appointment."

Owen had just reached the kitchen's threshold when Nikki's request stopped him. He turned to face her, his gaze steady, his demeanor serious.

"I've given this a lot of thought, and I've decided I'm not keeping tomorrow's appointment with Dr. Greene."

Nikki frowned. "What are you talking about?"

"I'm not getting anything out of the sessions with her, so I'm discontinuing them."

Nikki was incredulous. "You can't decide to stop going before we've had a chance to talk about it, Owen."

"Yes, I believe I can," Owen said calmly and decisively. "Frankly, I get more from my racquetball games than I get from those forty-five minute bullshit sessions with your therapist."

"But what about us? Don't you think our marriage has improved as a result of seeing her?"

"No. I think our marriage is in the same place it was before we started seeing her."

"Maybe it's Dr. Greene," Nikki said. "Maybe we need to see a different therapist."

"You told me you liked Dr. Greene."

"I do. But maybe she's not as effective with us as she was with me individually."

"Maybe we don't need to see a therapist, Nikki. Maybe all we need is to spend more time together." Owen sounded hopeful.

Nikki didn't answer right away. She held her head high and lowered the timbre of her voice.

"Do we need to spend more time together, Owen? Or do you need to spend less time with that cute little student you've been screwing. The one I saw getting into your car after you kissed her hand. Let's see...I think it was a week or so ago."

The color drained from Owen's face. His silence confirmed Nikki's accusation.

"Is she another one of your legion of adoring fans, Dr. Academic?" Nikki's eyes flashed with anger. "You are such a cliché."

"As are you, my dear Nikki," Owen said, his voice somewhere between smugness and aggression.

"What are you talking about?"

"I'm referring to your sneaking around and taking a female lover while holding on to your grand contempt for your lesbian mother." Owen folded his arms over his chest. Although he and Nikki were the same height, his indignation made him seem taller.

"That's a despicable lie!" Nikki yelled.

"It's not a lie at all," Owen said. "If it were, Lorin Wilkes' phone number wouldn't be listed repeatedly on our phone bill for the past few months."

Nikki remained silent.

"You're romantically involved with her, aren't you?"

Nikki skewered Owen with the razor sharp edge of her furious glare.

"You don't have to admit a thing. I've known about the two of you for a while now." Owen pronounced these words with equanimity.

"And I've suspected your little affair for a while," Nikki spat. "Carelessly, you left all those love poems she wrote to you on your desk. She must be very young, somewhat stupid, and rather inexperienced. Otherwise she wouldn't have written your name in the poetry."

Nikki watched the effect of her last sentence manifest itself in Owen's tightened jaw. Seizing an opportunity to inflict a deeper wound, she went on.

"Obviously, someone else knows all about the two of you. Whoever it is left a note on my car confirming what you're doing."

"Who?"

"I have no idea. It was anonymous. The information turned out to be accurate though, so somebody's out to spoil your game, Professor Reid."

Downshifting quickly from anger to resignation, Owen unfolded his arms. "So what do we do now?"

Nikki's smirk turned to condescension. "It's not all that complicated, Owen. You'll stop seeing your curvy little teeny-bopper, and I'll say good-bye to my distraction."

"Your distraction?" Owen tilted his head slightly. "Doesn't she mean a little more than that to you? As frequently as you phoned and texted each other, aren't you in love with her?"

"In love?" Nikki frowned. "She was more like a crush I needed to explore."

"Oh. Like a phase you needed to go through?" Owen asked sarcastically.

"Exactly. A phase," Nikki said. "And unlike my mother, I'm not stuck in a homosexual mold for the rest of my life. I prefer being married to a man."

Owen frowned. "Let me see if I understand what you're saying. You've been having sex with a female, but you prefer being married to a male. Does that mean you're bisexual?"

"It means I'm not really a damn lesbian, Owen," Nikki yelled.

"And you probably think the two of us can work through this mess."

"We have to. We'll talk about it with Dr. Greene." Nikki sounded dismissive as she looked at the digital clock on the microwave oven. "Why don't you go to the den and get started with your work while I figure out what to make for dinner?"

Owen stared at Nikki in disbelief. After a full minute, he shook his head and left the kitchen. As he walked slowly to the den, he chastised himself for failing to shred the poems and ignore the sexually graphic innuendos he had received from the first-year student. He knew better than to respond to the suggestive remarks and keep that poetry, especially after the girl's tragic death. Bringing the verse home where Nikki might find it and jump to all sorts of conclusions was beyond stupid.

Now, there was an anonymous note to consider. Owen wondered who had written and left it for Nikki. Was the sender one of his university colleagues? Was it another English Department assistant professor eager to make his presence known while besmirching Owen's reputation in advance of next year's grueling competition for tenure?

He yearned to clear his mind of all his marital detritus. He was desperate to have the luxury of concentrating on work. If only he could spend the next few hours planning his lecture, or reading a couple of chapters of his doctoral student's dissertation. He was certain he'd lose himself in its contents, or at least enrobe himself in his fantasies of meeting with her behind the closed doors of his office.

Owen didn't know that Nikki was watching his back as he walked toward his study. He wasn't aware of her standing near the entrance to the kitchen and waiting for him to close the den's door and erase the strip of sunlight that usually streamed out to the hallway this time of day. He didn't see her make her way to the far end of the kitchen, flip open her cell phone, and perform a task she'd been meaning to do for a while now. He didn't hear Nikki tap a sequence of numbers, then hit "send," and bid Lorin Wilkes a terse, final goodbye.

Chapter Twenty-nine

"DON'T GIVE IT all away, Alana. Keep some for yourself."

I stared blankly at Katey as we walked toward a table, balancing our trays laden with bagels and coffee.

"What do you mean?"

"I'm saying you need to take your time with whatever's developing between you and Rafe."

We sat down and Katey handed me a couple of napkins.

"I'm a big girl, Katey. I know what I'm doing."

That statement stretched the truth. I wasn't always sure what I was doing, especially now with Rafe's intermittent appearances and Johnnie's presence in my thoughts.

"I'm willing to bet you haven't seen all there is to Rafe's character. Based on what I've heard..." Katey stopped herself in mid-sentence.

I reached across the table and touched her hand.

"I know you're trying to protect me, and I appreciate that."

"I don't want you to get hurt, Alana." Katey pursed her lips, the way she always did whenever she was trying to decide if she should keep her next words in custody. "And Rafe doesn't have a good track record with women."

My self-defense system wanted to hear more about Rafe's history, but my easily wounded ego longed to be deaf on demand.

"She's not relationship material, Alana. You are."

I glanced out the café's window, and saw people of all sizes, ages, and colors streaming by. I yearned to be one of those pedestrians, scurrying to any destination other than the place where Rafe's elusive truth resided. I inhaled deeply and looked once again at Katey.

"I hear what you're saying."

I wanted to tell her I'd already discovered Rafe's enthusiasm for what she labeled "hooking up," along with her distaste for permanence.

"Katey, do you notice women don't talk face to face with each other these days?"

"What do you mean? We're talking to each other face to face right now."

I leaned forward.

"I mean unattached women seeking relationships. We contact each other by cell phone and email. Sometimes the emails go unanswered for days, and then we don't know how to interpret the damn silence."

Katey listened carefully as I continued my rant.

"Or we send text messages back and forth. Then the texts become briefer and less frequent. Before we realize it, communication has shut down completely."

"It's a new world, huh?" Katey smiled.

"You can say that again. After the texts dwindle in size and number, you figure someone else must be enjoying the long phone calls and all the honey-laced electronic wishes you used to receive, because for sure you're not getting them any longer."

Katey's lips lost their smile. "It sounds to me like you've already seen Rafe's commitment-phobic side."

I nodded. "I know Rafe and I aren't headed toward anything serious."

"At least you realize this now, before you get in any deeper."

"That's true."

I had explored Rafe, and she'd explored me as deeply as either of us cared to. I'd concluded we may have gone to the same parties, but we danced to different tunes. We were not meant to enjoy the same music.

"Jean's known Rafe longer than you have. Want to know what she says about the situation?"

"Okay, let's hear it."

"Jean said, and I quote her, 'Alana has the skills to swim in the deep lane of the pool, so why the hell should she waste her time paddling in the shallow end?' "

I grinned. "That's perfect."

Katey patted my hand.

"We're going to have to find you a swimming partner who's as comfortable in deep water as you are, honey."

"Right."

I imagined Johnetta Jones diving into a pool, but I wasn't ready to speak her name to Katey, because I didn't know yet if Johnnie and I would venture to the deep water or simply float in the safe end.

"I have to run, Katey. I promised a social worker at the Baker Center I'd help her with a difficult interview."

"That's my Alana." Katey's eyes sparkled. "Promise you'll have dinner with Jean and me one night real soon?"

I put my hand over my heart. "You have my word."

Katey and I embraced each other tightly.

I left the cafe and walked at a brisk pace to the Josephine Baker Rainbow Center. A block short of my destination I noticed a female cop standing next to a newspaper kiosk. At ease, with her hands at her sides, she nodded at the passersby. I'd seen Johnetta wear this same relaxed manner, all the while taking note of everything crossing her field of vision.

Johnetta...Johnnie. No doubt she'd been obliged to walk a beat or station herself on a hectic street corner during the early days of her career in the city. She must have been strikingly handsome, her uniform pressed to a fair thee well, and her highly polished shoes reflecting the sunshine. How many women had glanced her way in those days? How many had been bold enough to invite her glances? If I had stood near Johnnie on that busy street corner, would I have nodded at her? Would I have returned the next day, hoping to see her again? Would we have spoken to each other and traded meaningful smiles? I hoped so.

Deep in thought, I arrived at the Baker Center before my daydream about Johnnie ended.

Pat, the receptionist, greeted me warmly. "Well, good morning, Alana. It's good to see you as always."

"Good morning to you too, Pat. Is Lorin here?" I realized the heat in the office felt good after my walk in the cold breeze.

"Not yet." Pat held her pencil above the schedule book. "She has an appointment in a few minutes, so I bet she's on her way. Would you like some coffee or tea while you're waiting for her?"

"No, thanks. I just finished a cup." I shrugged my arms and shoulders out of my jacket. "If it's okay, I'll wait for her in the conference room."

"Sure, dear. Go on back."

I walked through the narrow hallway and noticed the door to the director's office was closed.

When I arrived in the conference room I sat down at its round table. Framed newspaper clippings adorned the wall in front of me. Clearly, in chronicling the Center's struggles and victories, the Philadelphia print media had been kind to this nonprofit agency. The Baker Center played a valuable role by helping ex-offenders get back on their feet.

"Hi, Alana. You're early." Lorin entered the room and placed a mug of tea on the table. "Or I'm late."

"You're right on time." I expected to see the high-energy Lorin. Instead, what I witnessed was her absolute lack of vitality. Lorin's mouth was set in a straight line, not turned up in the smile I'd become used to. Her eyes were downcast and her voice monotone.

"Is anything wrong?"

She sat down and plunked a file envelope on the table next to her tea. Her head sank into her shoulders.

"Everything." Staring into my eyes, Lorin whispered forlornly, "My lover has decided to end our relationship."

"Oh, Lorin, I'm so sorry." I watched tears forge a trail down her cheeks. "How did this happen? When?"

"How? I don't really know. Late yesterday she texted me a Dear John message. I tried calling her, but her phone was turned off. Then, I wrote her a long email, but she never answered it."

Lorin's sadness was palpable. An image of her flashed through my mind. I saw her holding her phone and deciphering the tiny black letters that spelled the end of happiness as she'd known it.

"Were you a couple for a long time?"

"A little more than a year." Lorin wiped away a tear before it began its descent. "I knew it was dicey from the start."

She looked at me, her eyes pleading for understanding or at least for permission to continue explaining.

"She's married."

"That's a tough situation, Lorin." My response held no judgment. Years ago I was married when honesty came knocking at my door and allowed me to admit my truth.

"Tougher than I'd bargained for. I knew being with Kim was wrong, but it seemed so right at the time. I couldn't help myself."

"Did you have any warning...any signs Kim was going to end things?" I wondered if Lorin had seen the opening salvos of the breakup and if she'd ignored the signals just as I'd thought about overlooking the bad-news billboards Rafe posted from day one of our dalliance.

"Many times over. But the difficulties always seemed to disappear whenever we saw each other." Lorin looked off wistfully. "I know I've been foolish. It's just... she's so good looking and intelligent. I couldn't believe she was attracted to me."

"I'm sure she found you attractive and intelligent, also." I wanted so much to console Lorin.

"Can I show you her picture?"

"Sure."

Lorin handed me her cell phone. "I took this one last Saturday. We spent the afternoon at the art museum."

I cradled the phone with the same reverence Lorin showed offering it to me. I peered at the image on the small screen and then brought the phone closer to my eyes. It seemed like entire moments passed before I could find my voice.

"This is Kim? Your girlfriend?"

"My ex-girlfriend now..."

"What do you know about her?" My head snapped up as I questioned Lorin.

"I thought I knew she loved me."

My eyes traveled back to the picture on the phone. "It's possible she doesn't love anyone quite as much as she loves herself."

Lorin looked at me, confused. "Why do you say that?"

"Because Kim is really Nikki, Nikki Reid, my daughter."

Lorin put her hand to her mouth, and I felt she was trying to contain my surprise as well as hers.

"That's why you looked so familiar to me." She shook her head in disbelief. "I thought it was because I spoke to you months ago in that old, broken-down elevator at the Probation and Parole Office."

I strained to remember ever having encountered Lorin anywhere other than here at the Baker Center.

"Now I realize how much you resemble Kim. You have the same forehead and nose, and your laughter is similar to hers."

"That's where the similarities end. Unlike Nikki, I have only one name."

"Is Kim... I mean Nikki married to a man named Lawrence?" Lorin's eyes implored me to tell her more information.

"She is married, but her husband's name is Owen, Owen Reid. He's an assistant professor at—"

"I can't believe this. I absolutely cannot. "

"Excuse me, ladies." Pat knocked on the open door as she entered the room. A compact woman the color of cinnamon preceded her.

"Ms. Wilkes, your client is here for her appointment."

"Come in and sit down, Selena." Abandoning our conversation, Lorin gestured toward a chair. "I'd like you to meet Alana Blue. She used to work for the State Board of Probation and Parole."

I extended my hand. Selena declined to do the same. She nodded in my direction and sat down in a chair other than the one to which Lorin pointed.

"It's good to meet you, Selena." I struggled to push aside the torrent of confusion surrounding Nikki and Lorin, because I suspected the young woman seated across from me had blown into the room on the winds of her own hurricane.

"Same here." Selena measured me with the skill of a monarch's tailor. "I like your haircut, Ms. Blue."

"Thank you." A compliment was the last thing I expected to hear from Selena.

"I think older women should wear their hair cut short, especially if it has some gray in it."

The flip side of Selena's compliment matched my expectations of her. I had forgotten most of the details I'd read a year ago when her case first hit the parole system, but I recalled very well the big picture her reputation painted. Her personality had a straight-edge razor side and she hadn't wasted any time before showing it to us.

"Selena, you know why you're here this morning, right?" Lorin asked.

"Yeah." Selena turned her attention to Lorin. "Your agency is throwing me out of the group home because that bitch who calls herself the house manager can't stand me."

Lorin glanced my way.

"Selena has violated our group home rules one too many times."

"Y'all got too many rules. That's the real problem. We're adults, you know. We don't need all those so-called codes of behavior." Selena nodded decisively.

"You've lived in both of the Baker Center's group homes. You've instigated conflicts with several different roommates, and now you're refusing to obey the curfew rules," Lorin said.

I remained silent, figuring Selena would have plenty to say. I figured correctly.

"I'm a grown-ass woman. I've done my time in jail, I'm holding down a job, I stay drug and alcohol free."

"When was your last D&A test?" I counted on the perennially sluggish pace most drug test results arrived in my former office.

"I don't remember. You'll have to ask my P.O."

"I'll phone her in a few minutes," Lorin said.

"Good. I bet she doesn't know y'all about to put me out on the street."

Agitated, Lorin rose to meet Selena's verbal challenge. "If she doesn't have a clue, I'll be sure to tell her."

I became especially attentive the second Selena referred to her probation officer.

"You do that. But I warn you she won't be happy when she hears I'm homeless." A slow smile began to spread over Selena's mouth. "How I'm doing is real important to her, and she's proud of all the progress I've made."

Something about Selena's smile nudged the needle on my anxiety meter.

"We're all proud of your progress, Selena," Lorin said.

"Not half as proud as Rafaela Constance Ortiz is."

Selena pronounced Rafe's full name with the arrogance of ownership. Then, she favored me with a saccharine sweet smile.

"Since you used to work in the parole office, I'm sure you know her."

I didn't answer.

"She cares so much about me, she's not going to be happy when she hears I've lost my spot at the group home." Selena looked first at Lorin, then at me. "She'll probably let me stay with her for a while until I can find another place to live."

I could no longer remain quiet. "I doubt that. It's against policy."

"Policy? Rafe's not afraid of any damn rules. Screw policy."

"If going against the rules means losing her job, she won't do it." Lorin stood.

"Why don't you sit back down, Ms. Wilkes, and I'll tell you and Ms. Blue about all the ways my P.O. and I have bucked and fucked your policies. We've become very close these last few months."

Selena waited until Lorin took a seat.

"Do you two think my information is valuable enough to keep my bed at your group home and for someone to lock that troll of a house manager in her cave?"

The only thing Lorin and I could do was stare benignly at Selena Garrett.

"Why don't I give you a day or so to reconsider your decision about throwing me out?"

Selena watched us respond with yet more silence.

"I thought so." Selena stood. "Give me a call when you've decided where you'd like me to live...at your group home or with my P.O. lover."

Selena laughed softly. She paused at the door and then turned to face me.

"And don't even think about changing your hairstyle, Ms. Blue. Wearing it short and wavy like that will pull plenty of women...except the one you can't have."

Lorin and I barely breathed until we were convinced Selena had left the building.

"Shit. I don't know what to do, Alana." Lorin covered her face with her hands.

"And I don't know what to suggest."

"First, Kim leaves me. Then I find out her name is really Nikki and she's your daughter. Now it turns out one of my best friends is having sex with the most troublesome client I've had in all the years I've worked here."

"This is a hellish mess, isn't it?" All I could do was confirm what Lorin already stated.

"If I follow my boss's orders, I'll be responsible for my friend's losing her job." Lorin stood and began pacing in the conference room. "I'm fucked six ways out of seven."

"We need time to think about this," I said weakly.

A look of sympathy crossed Lorin's face. "You have some things to deal with also, don't you? You find out your daughter is gay, and one of your former co-workers has crossed a line in the sand with a client..."

"I'm still putting everything together." I had more to contend with than Lorin could possibly know.

I had sensed Rafe's betrayal for a while now, certainly before Selena unmasked it today. I almost took it for granted. I knew there was no way Rafe could avoid answering the challenge named Selena, and I doubted Lorin would be able to convince Rafe to extricate herself from the slick-talking criminal. Moreover, I was convinced Selena would dispose of Rafe the minute their liaison no longer fit her agenda.

Lorin and I exchanged phone numbers and pledged to call each other if and when we figured out a solution to the Selena Garrett debacle. I packed all I'd learned that morning about Nikki and about Rafe and headed home.

Agitation rode the surface of my skin as I turned the key to unlock the front door of my house. After pouring a glass of wine, I offered myself a toast. I remembered the exhilaration I felt a few months ago when I left the title of probation officer in an old dusty office downtown. I realized I had let go of fear, grabbed the balloon of fate, and zealously floated aloft. I vowed to hold on to that feeling. Relinquishing it simply because of Rafe's perfidy or Nikki's self-made disaster was out of the question. I'd taken a fool's chance with Rafe, and spent more than enough years trying to steer Nikki's wagon. I was determined to soar. I'd soar alone if need be.

Draped in my resolution, I finished sipping my glass of wine and then I phoned Johnnie. I convinced myself I was calling her because I wanted to hear any new details she had learned about the Taylor murder case. By the time I placed the phone back on its charger though, I admitted what I'd really wanted was to hear Johnnie's rich contralto wrapped around the words: "Hey, Alana. How are you?"

Having those sounds caress my ears rescued me from today's free-fall into the arms of deceit. Johnnie's increasing presence in my life restored my equilibrium. More and more, I thought about her. Perhaps she was the one who would encourage me to stay aloft, to fly unfettered while she stood close by to catch me if I fell.

Chapter Thirty

IN DEFERENCE TO the inches-thick icy slush covering the road, Johnetta drove to work more slowly than usual. The late November snowstorm had morphed to nothing more than an annoying memory thanks to the rain that now fell. The water drops changed the frosty white coating to a sodden gray mush.

Johnetta glanced at the trees lining her route. Their imposing limbs, still outlined in white, were a photographer's dream come true. She wondered how old the trees were and she speculated which branches might fall victim to their icy weight and come crashing down, dragging electrical wires with them and effectively closing off the road.

Approaching a familiar intersection, Johnetta rested her foot on the brake. The car answered with a series of vibrating thuds. She steadily increased her pressure on the brake until the car came to a standstill. Turning her head to the right, she searched for one house in particular.

Without signaling a turn, Johnetta coaxed the steering wheel to the right. The car's tires blazed a new trail in the softened snow, and Johnetta glanced down at the icy mixture spurting from both sides of the vehicle's undercarriage. She drove slowly past Alana's address, taking in as much as she could see. The driveway's almost pristine surface wore footprints stamped the entire way from the garage to the sidewalk where a small rectangular indentation marred the otherwise perfect area. No doubt the daily newspaper, thrown errantly through the delivery person's car window, had left its imprint on the sidewalk's snowy bed. The path to Alana's burgundy colored front door was unsullied. For the briefest second, Johnetta visualized parking her car and marching triumphantly to that front door. If anyone were to leave footprints on the unmarked path, why couldn't it be she?

What if she did just that? What if she arrived unannounced, rang the doorbell, and asked if she could please come in? What if Alana's eyes lit up at the sight of her rain-dampened gaze traveling from Alana's eyes, to her mouth, her throat, her breasts? What if Alana welcomed her and invited her in to get warm and dry? And what if she told Alana she wanted to do so much more than simply seek shelter?

Johnetta continued driving until she reached the end of Alana's street. She made a wide arc and returned, slowing ever so subtly as she passed in front of Alana's house once again. She imagined the kitchen smelled like coffee and muffins, while the other rooms echoed with Alana's laughter. By the time Johnetta turned back onto the cross street, her daydream began to fade. She felt sure one day soon she would stand in Alana's home and fold Alana in her embrace. If only she didn't have to confront reality and recount to Alana what she knew about her son-in-law, Owen.

Five minutes and four miles later, Johnetta stood at the entrance of the police station. She shook as much rain as possible from her umbrella, scraped her shoes against the huge coir rug spread near the doorway, and clocked in. Separated from her sweet fantasy about Alana, she fell into the rhythm of her daily work routine.

"Good morning, Captain." Johnetta nodded as she crossed paths with her superior.

"It is a good morning, Detective Jones."

The preternaturally taciturn Captain Mulavey offered her a smile instead of the thin straight line his lips usually formed. Johnetta noticed her commanding officer's mouth actually curved upward a bit. His gray eyes, most times set in a steely glare, were on the brink of animation.

"And do you know why it's a good morning, Detective?" he asked her.

"I have to admit I don't know, Captain."

"Because we've received the DNA results for our suspect in the Taylor murder.The FBI lab sent us their preliminary findings. Nothing's final, so we're going to be cautious, but so far, it looks like the suspect you and Detective Smythe have isolated is our perp."

"Good," Johnetta said quietly.

This news divided her spirit. She wanted to resolve the case and bring closure to Shantay Taylor's family, but at the same time, she desperately wanted to spare Alana pain. Johnetta despised the vise-like dilemma holding her hostage. She likened it to maintaining her balance while she danced on the tip of a knife. If she spoke to her superiors about her growing bond with Alana, she'd have to quit the murder investigation. If she spoke honestly to Alana about her involvement with the case, she'd risk Alana's ever trusting her.

"Whenever we go months without new leads, I fear we'll get caught up in new cases, and forget to keep looking for the perps who committed the old ones." Johnetta's eyes narrowed.

"Oh, I never give up, Detective Jones. I don't know what giving up means." Captain Mulavey resumed his customary stern attitude. "By the way, I know I mentioned this to you when you submitted that water bottle for testing, but I'm going to repeat myself. It was real smart asking the suspect's supervisor to hold on to something he'd gripped. Without that bottle, we wouldn't have had any DNA evidence. Good police work, Jones."

"Thanks. No problem."

"I put a copy of the lab paperwork on your desk, and one on Detective Smythe's desk also. The official report should be here in another week or so. We'll wait until then to make the arrest. I've already been in touch with the county D.A.'s office. No one wants any screwups with this case." Captain Mulavey nodded curtly.

"We've waited this long. I guess another week won't hurt us," Johnetta said. *And waiting another seven days will give me more time to figure out what to tell Alana,* she thought.

"One more thing, Detective. We're short-staffed for the next three days because Detective Richard's mother passed away."

Johnetta recalled her young colleague saying his mother was hospitalized and very ill. "I'm sorry. I didn't know."

"Yes. She died last night." The captain cleared his throat. "I need you and Detective Smythe to pull a double shift. You'll do yours tonight, and Smythe will be here tomorrow. Sorry for the short notice."

"That's okay. I had to work a double shift plenty of times in Philly."

"Good. Thanks for your cooperation." Mulavey turned and walked away.

Johnetta quickened her pace. When she reached her desk, the first thing she spotted was the blue folder with "Confidential" stamped on it.

She opened the thin package and began reading. Johnetta shook her head, impatient with all the scientific babble and the tentative tone of the words "preliminary," and "not conclusive" peppered throughout the document. Eager to reach the bottom line, she skimmed entire paragraphs.

At the end of the report's fifth page she found what she was searching for. The DNA material culled from the water bottle was a probable match with DNA material found embedded under three of the victim's fingernails on her right hand. The nearly cold Taylor murder case was suddenly torrid.

"Hey, Johnnie. Morning." Detective Harold Smythe threw his dripping coat onto the molded-plastic chair next to his desk. He held up a familiar white bag with the orange, pink, and brown logo. "Want a donut?"

"I do, but I won't." Johnetta spied the cruller peeping from the top of the bag. She fought hard to convince herself the pastry was slow death disguised as a delicious chocolate-iced treat.

"I admire your self-control, partner." Harold grinned. "I have absolutely none. To me, this is the breakfast of champions."

Johnetta chuckled. "While you're enjoying your breakfast, take a look at that folder on your desk."

"It's not going to give me indigestion is it?"

"Just the opposite."

Harold read for a few minutes and then held the report in the air. "This is great. I wish we could arrest the son of a bitch today."

"I know how you feel, but the captain says we have to make sure every i is dotted and all the t's crossed."

Harold mumbled an unintelligible response.

Johnetta flipped open her cell phone and began tapping out a phone number as she stood and walked out of the office. She leaned against the wall in the hallway.

"Good morning to you as well." Johnetta took a deep breath. She lingered over the sound of Alana's voice and briefly forgot the reason for her phone call.

"Are you at work?" Alana asked.

"Yes, I am." Johnetta paused. "In a way, work is why I've called."

"How so?"

"Well, I have to do a double shift. I know I won't be able to sleep between shifts, so I wondered if you'd like to meet me for dinner and then catch an early evening movie."

"Sure. I guess I could."

Johnetta heard a second's worth of hesitation in Alana's response. "Do you have other plans?"

"Nothing I wouldn't change in a heartbeat."

"You're sure about that?"

"Absolutely sure. One thing I know I'm going to do today is make my famous chili. But that won't prevent me from going to see a movie with you."

"Well, I wouldn't want to get between a woman and her chili," Johnetta said.

"I've got an idea. Instead of going out, why don't you come here after your first shift, have dinner and then relax before you have to return for the second part of your workday?"

Johnetta grinned into her phone. "I accept your kind invitation. What can I bring?"

"Just yourself, Johnnie. What time should I expect you?"

"How about six?" Johnetta hesitated, and then added, "My second shift starts at ten, but you don't have to put up with my company for nearly four hours."

"I can tolerate your company for that long. It seems we always have a lot to talk about."

"That's true. I'll see you later. And thank you."

"I'll look forward to it."

Johnetta slipped her phone back into her pocket. She grappled with the thought of having to arrest Owen Reid sooner rather than later. She feared Alana would believe that gathering information about Owen had been her sole motive for pursuing a connection with her. Johnetta's fear was more chilling than the cold wall tile supporting her back. Its iciness penetrated her jacket and shirt, and traveled clear through her to her backbone. That wall felt like a metaphor of her life: frigid and inanimate before the possibility of Alana Blue began to thaw her frozen hopes.

For more than a year, Johnetta had nurtured the memory of her reaction to Alana. Ever since their contentious first meeting, she'd found herself thinking about the copper-skinned parole officer with the rebellious mixed gray hair and dark, expressive eyes. Although they had been on opposite sides of their debate, Johnetta never forgot the emotions Alana pulled from her that day. She recalled the moment when she stopped caring who was winning their argument. What mattered to Johnetta was the thrill of discovering she wasn't half dead as far as women were concerned. Something, no, everything about Alana suggested Johnetta's numbness was only a perception, not her reality.

Alana represented possibilities. And although Johnetta didn't act on them at that time, she felt less empty simply knowing they existed. The day when she saw Alana's name listed on the first murder suspect's information sheet, Johnetta rejoiced. The morning she walked into Alana's office, Johnetta promised herself she would seize that possibility and run with it. She was drawn to Alana and was no longer willing to deny that fact.

Chapter Thirty-one

OWEN USED HIS knife to scrape a thin ribbon from the top of the butter. He spread it evenly on the slice of whole wheat bread, still warm from the toaster. After cutting the bread into two perfect triangles, he began eating one of them. He angled the newspaper against the basket of fresh fruit standing in the center of the kitchen table and then skimmed the paper's headlines. Owen was convinced of mankind's descent into a quagmire of meanness and immorality. Comforted to find neither a dramatic improvement nor a worsening had occurred while he slept the night before, Owen stacked the newspaper sections, one on top of another. When he was satisfied with the pile's neatness, he extracted the entertainment portion and turned to the next to last page where he found "Today's Look at the Stars."

He zeroed in to read his horoscope, knowing all along he'd forget the augury by the time he'd finished eating his second triangle of toast. Nevertheless, he read the forecast and silently promised himself he would follow the suggestions. Reading, promising, and summarily forgetting were part of Owen's morning rituals, as was inclining his head toward the radio every ten minutes to hear the traffic report.

The latest bulletin was a warning that catapulted Owen from his chair. The ride to the university promised to be a slow one, thanks to the snow-coated roads and the report of an early morning driver who attempted to get through an intersection by shearing off the side of the car in front of him.

"Shit," Owen said aloud. "Kelly Drive is a mess already."

He splashed the remainder of his coffee into the sink and walked briskly to the den where he picked up his briefcase. Stopping at the coat closet long enough to yank a lined raincoat from its hangar, he jammed his arms through its sleeves. Then he headed to the front door. At the last second Owen remembered he'd left his gym bag upstairs.

"Oh, fuck." Owen dropped his briefcase and scaled the steps two at a time. When he reached the master bedroom, he strode to his side of the closet and scooped up the canvas bag he needed for his weekly racquetball date. On his way out, he spotted a slip of paper on the carpet. He was not used to seeing anything out of place in the house he shared with Nikki, so he bent down and retrieved it. Unwilling to retrace his footsteps back to the bedroom where he could throw the paper into a wastebasket, Owen stuffed it into his raincoat's pocket.

He didn't look at the paper again until later that day as he left the gym locker room.

With his hair still wet and his body barely towel dried following his post-racquetball match shower, Owen buttoned his raincoat. He routed through his coat pocket in search of his Irish tweed walking hat. While his fingers groped for the cap, they found the piece of paper.

Owen unfolded the handwritten note. It was addressed to Nikki. In disbelief, he read the message twice. The words assured her that her husband hadn't stopped his philandering ways, not even after one of his playthings had met an untimely and violent death. Now, he was spending time with a doctoral student whom he was "advising." The note included a summons to meet with its author in her office that afternoon. Owen knew where the meeting was to take place, even before he read the address.

"Fuck her! Just fuck her!"

Twin rivulets of water meandered down the side of his face. He swept the moisture away with the back of his hand.

"She needs to keep the fuck out of my personal affairs."

Owen glanced up at the large white clock above the locker room exit. He had barely enough time to get to Nikki's appointment before she would arrive. As he rushed toward his destination, all sorts of questions streamed through his mind.

How did the note writer know his meetings with the grad student involved more than mentoring? After all, he had a legitimate reason for spending time with her. Had the note's author been keeping tabs on his every move? And what did she have to gain by telling Nikki?

By the time Owen flung open the door to the faculty office building, he was out of breath and bereft of answers. He started to go directly to the note writer's office, but he hesitated. He didn't want to act out of control, especially not here, where so many people knew him and where he felt so respected. He needed a moment to think clearly. Otherwise, he'd be no better than some of the students he taught, the immature ones who lacked self-restraint and couldn't harness their passions the way he could, the lovesick females who offered him poetry along with their bodies in exchange for a good grade.

Vowing to be calm, Owen climbed the stairs to the second floor. He took his time and planted his feet on each worn step. He used his slow ascent to plan what he would say once he faced this woman. He wanted to act rationally. The note writer was always quite rational. Despite her reputation for being otherwise, she'd been calm, composed and professional every time Owen talked with her. He had never witnessed the temper tantrums a few of his colleagues described to him during end-of-semester drinks and giddiness.

Dr. Caryn Mobley was always polite to the point of being solicitous with him. She'd bent over backwards to accommodate his course preferences, and she'd provided him with the latest information regarding publication opportunities. Owen couldn't fathom why she'd become involved in what was rightly his business. Why had she contacted Nikki and imposed herself in his personal life?

Halfway to the second floor, Owen had a flashback. He recalled Dr. Mobley squeezing his arm one day as the two of them talked about boundaries between students and professors. She seemed especially bitter when she mentioned female students who believed they could screw their way to a high GPA and ingratiate themselves to male professors eager to add a sexual adventure to their otherwise sterile academic existence.

The afternoon they talked, Owen became so lost in a daydream about one such female student, he missed hearing the fiery edge in her voice as she spat out her words. He let the daydream float away just in time to notice the cold, robotic expression in Dr. Mobley's eyes when she asked if he agreed with her. From that moment, he never doubted Caryn Mobley's resolve to make life an unspeakable hell for any young woman caught having an affair with any of the male instructors in the English Department. Exactly what she might do to the student, Owen hadn't wanted to imagine. Nor had he dared contemplate the punishment she would mete out to any instructor who might commit the deeds he had with several of his students.

Five steps short of the staircase summit, and less than a minute before facing Dr. Mobley, Owen gasped audibly. Dread lodged in his throat and grew tentacles that threatened to wrap themselves around his legs and prevent him from moving. The ancient stair treads under Owen's feet gave up creaking moans, as if they sympathized with him.

Owen stood completely still outside Dr. Mobley's office. He squinted and strained to listen to the voices on the other side of the paneled pine door. He heard nothing. He raised his fist and knocked twice. A female's muffled voice uttered something unintelligible. The voice grew louder.

"Come in."

Owen grasped the tarnished brass knob, turned it, and pushed open the door. Dr. Caryn Mobley sat on the edge of a Queen Anne style chair next to her large desk. She looked up at Owen before she returned her indolent gaze to Nikki, who sat facing her in a matching chair.

"Did he know about our appointment?" She asked Nikki.

Nikki stared at Owen. "Not from me."

"I found a note. You dropped it on the bedroom floor, Nikki," Owen said. "It's time for you to wrap things up here and leave."

"That decision belongs to Nikki and to me, Owen," Dr. Mobley said quietly. "And right now, we're not quite ready to wrap things up."

"What are you telling my wife?"

"Dr. Mobley's been telling me a lot about your little escapades with your students, Owen."

"You and I have already talked about that, Nikki." Owen battled to keep the impatience he felt out of his voice.

"Apparently we haven't talked about all of it."

"Enough of the marital melodrama," Caryn Mobley said. "Owen, I know you have a class to teach, and I have other items on my agenda as well, so let me get to the point."

Nikki squirmed. Owen remained standing, staring at both women.

"Your wife knows about your doctoral student and all the...let's call them "special" dissertation conferences you've been conducting in your office. She didn't know however, about the affair you had with the first-semester freshman. She suspected something was going on when she came across the poetry that lovesick girl wrote to you."

Caryn's gaze took in both Nikki and Owen. "It seems you're both somewhat sloppy when it comes to leaving important pieces of paper scattered around your house."

"Where are you going with this?" Owen asked.

Caryn raised her hands palm up.

"Here's where I'm going, Owen. I told Nikki the freshman's name. She didn't recognize it until I reminded her of Shantay Taylor's unexpected demise."

Owen's eyes darted back and forth from Caryn to Nikki. He felt a searing streak of color suddenly rush to his face, and he began shaking his head.

"Nikki, I didn't have anything to do with that girl's murder."

"That's not what the police think, Owen," Caryn said, speaking softly. "They believe you might have had a hand in it. In fact, one of Brighton Township's finest sat right here in this office and asked me all sorts of questions about your character and work habits."

"What?" Owen felt a wave of nausea rise from his stomach.

"The detective even asked me if I could send her one of your used coffee cups or water bottles so they could get a sample of your DNA."

"I don't believe you." Owen's jaw clenched shut.

Caryn shrugged her shoulders. "Suit yourself."

"Owen, a sexual fling is one thing, but my God, if you killed her..." The tendons along the side of Nikki's neck visibly tightened.

"Nikki, you can't believe I'd be capable of hurting anyone." Desperation pinned Owen's arms to his sides. His eyes pleaded with Nikki.

"Again, enough with the melodrama. Here's our situation." Caryn stood and dominated the small room. The formality in her voice commanded Owen and Nikki's attention the same way it riveted her staff whenever she conducted official faculty meetings.

"The president of the university called to tell me he's been contacted by the Brighton Township Police Department. They inferred an arrest is imminent. I suppose that means their DNA test resulted in a positive match, Owen."

"I didn't kill that girl."

"And I may be the only person who knows you didn't kill her." Caryn pointed to herself. "I may also be the only one who could supply you with an alibi, if I choose to do so."

"What?" Owen was incredulous.

"The girl was killed sometime in the late morning or early afternoon. I'm prepared to tell the police you and I met for hours that day to discuss ideas for new course offerings."

"What about Owen's positive DNA sample? How are the two of you going to explain that?" Nikki asked.

"Oh, the DNA definitely belongs to Owen." Caryn looked directly at Nikki. "Earlier the day she was killed, Owen tried to fondle and kiss her. She scratched the hell out of the right side of his face. That accounts for the police finding traces of his DNA under her fingernails."

Nikki stared at Owen. "I remember that day. You told me your racquetball opponent caused those scratches."

Owen remained silent.

"I'm afraid he lied to you, dear Nikki. Your husband became a bit rough with Shantay, not with a racquetball opponent. She fought back," Caryn said. "Am I right on target, Owen? Didn't you realize you can't manhandle a girl like Shantay, a young woman who grew up in the midst of rough circumstances?"

Owen focused his laser-like stare on Caryn. He ignored her interrogation and began asking questions of his own.

"Why would you want to provide an alibi for me? What's in it for you?"

Caryn smiled beguilingly. She moved closer to Nikki and rested her hand on the younger woman's shoulder. Nikki flinched at her touch.

"Any charges brought against you will be dropped. After a decent amount of time, you'll let Nikki divorce you, freeing her to live her life as she chooses."

Owen shook his head. "This has to be bad dream."

"It'll be a nightmare if you fail to play it the way I've planned it," Caryn said decisively.

"You're out of your mind," Owen said.

"Am I, Dr. Reid? How about if I add a sweetener to the deal? I'll guarantee you earn tenure next year." Caryn's mouth twisted into a cruel half-smile.

Owen's vision clouded over. His mind ached from having to process his likely fate if he didn't accept Caryn Mobley's offer. He hadn't killed that student, but he knew being arrested for the crime would mean he'd never be able to hold on to his teaching position at the university. Even if he were tried and acquitted, he could kiss his academic future goodbye. Earning tenure anywhere would forever elude his grasp.

He looked down at the backs of his hands and fixated on their hue. Usually AWOL from the implications of his racial identity, Owen felt a thunderbolt of reality rip through his consciousness. An electric shock raced from the ends of his neatly trimmed hair, short circuited through his heart, and exited from his argyle and leather covered feet. Here he was, the well-educated Dr. Owen Reid, a black man about to be accused of murdering one of his young black female students, a young woman he had tried forcibly to seduce. He knew his chances of acquittal were nil to none, and he felt closer to Bigger Thomas, a fictional character from a novel he'd never taught, than he'd ever imagined he could.

On the brink of tears, Owen gazed at Nikki. She looked back at him, her stare lifeless, her inanimate mouth resigned to muteness. At that moment, Owen realized sacrificing Nikki and the loveless marriage she shared with him was a small price to pay to avoid going to prison or worse. His eyes shifted to Caryn Mobley and he nodded his consent.

"We're done," he said to Nikki. "We'll work out the details as soon as all the crap with the police is over."

"Owen," Caryn said, "Come back here after your class and you and I will construct the details of our alibi."

Owen turned to leave. The air, which moments before had ceased circulating, began to stir once again. Owen breathed it in deeply and revived his ability to think. As he reached the office threshold, he recalled the summer day when the warm breeze outside this building had calmed the fresh scrapes on his face.

He remembered he hadn't wanted anyone to see the red marks

that ran from north to south over his cheek. He succeeded avoiding curious stares. No one saw him except his doctoral student advisee, and she'd been too polite and needful of his help to risk commenting. Owen's wound went undiscovered until later that day when he was at home. By that time, his blood dotted gym towel had already tumbled through the washing machine's spin cycle. The scratches on his face were reduced to raised lines, instead of the red angry welts that inflated the contour of his cheek. And while Owen peddled his lie about a racquetball mishap, Shantay Taylor lay dead, her limp body dumped in a suburban compost bin.

Owen's mind snapped to attention. He stopped and spun around to face Caryn Mobley.

"No one other than Nikki and one student saw me that day. How did you know I had scratches on my face?"

A smile stretched Caryn's mouth.

"Shantay told me all about it when she got here later that morning. Let's see, if I remember correctly, I asked her how her meeting with you had gone."

"Why did you ask her that?"

"I usually asked her what you'd been up to. Label it curiosity about my competition." Caryn looked down at the floor.

"You were competing with me? For Shantay?" Owen asked.

"Yes, but it wasn't a difficult contest. We used to laugh about your amateur attempts to seduce her."

"Were you trying to seduce her?"

"Of course. She seemed to enjoy all the attention and compliments I gave her." Caryn paused. "That's why I was convinced she was ready for the two of us to go a bit further. Unlike you, Owen, I rarely misjudge the women I pursue."

Caryn looked at Nikki and again, she touched her shoulder. Nikki stared straight ahead, motionless.

"I knew all about Nikki the first time we met at the faculty picnic. Her eyes lingered on mine a few seconds longer than necessary, and she kept showing me that wonderful smile you don't get to see much of."

"But how could you go after a student?" Owen asked.

"You hypocrite." Nikki lashed out at Owen. "That girl's age and status didn't stop you from sniffing around."

Caryn continued. "Shantay was definitely a lesbian, and she never had any objections about getting together with me...until that day. I suppose two of us groping at her the same morning was more than she could tolerate."

"What did you do to her?" Owen pursued the terrible truth that would absolve his guilt, but condemn Caryn Mobley.

"It's more a question of what she attempted to do to me.

Scraping her nails over the side of your face had worked earlier in the day, so she tried to repeat the same tactic with me." Caryn's voice grew faint as she continued.

"It turned out I was the stronger one, despite her youth and stamina. Maybe it was the adrenalin fueling me. I don't know. The second she lunged for my face, I grabbed both her hands and nearly broke her fingers. When she opened her luscious mouth to scream, I wrapped my hands around her throat and squeezed as hard as I could."

"You killed her." A lone tear huddled at the corner of Owen's eye before it spilled over and trailed down his cheek.

Caryn blinked repeatedly. "I guess I did. But you're the person of interest. And I'm your way out."

"What makes you think I won't tell all of this to the police?" Owen said.

"Because when it comes to motive, opportunity, and a positive DNA match, the spotlight is on you, Dr. Reid."

Nikki took advantage of Owen's and Caryn's preoccupation with each other. Very quietly, she got up from her chair.

Caryn wheeled around and addressed her.

"While I'm giving Owen an alibi, I'm also offering you something, Nikki."

"What's that?" Nikki barely whispered her voice devoid of its wrath.

"The chance to escape a stultifying marriage and explore a more exciting and vibrant life, dear one." Caryn tilted her head toward Owen as she spoke condescendingly. "He's intelligent enough, but he simply doesn't have what it takes to stimulate you. All you need to do is play the loyal wife for the duration of whatever transpires with the police. When the dust has settled, you can take off the disguise."

Nikki looked first at Caryn, then at Owen.

"I can do that," she said.

"I'll contact you soon, Nikki," Caryn said. "And I promise I won't write you any more anonymous notes."

Caryn turned to Owen and issued an order. "Be back here in two hours, Owen. We have planning to do."

Owen glared at both of the women. He summoned all his self-control and fought the desire to spit in Caryn Mobley's direction.

Nikki preceded Owen through the doorway. The only sounds they heard as they descended the stairs were the rhythmic clack of her heels and the heavier thud of his soles landing precisely in the middle of each tread. When the couple arrived at the first-floor landing, they looked at each other quickly, and then parted, without uttering as much as a single word.

They found their voices hours later though when, unbeknownst to the other, they each took a turn calling the police.

Chapter Thirty-two

I'D BEEN AWAKE and up for more than an hour when the telephone rang. When I read the name highlighted by the phone's soft backlight, a smile bloomed on my lips.

"Good morning, Johnetta."

"Good morning to you as well." She paused. "Johnetta, huh? You're pretty formal today."

Johnnie's calm warm voice wrapped around me.

Our conversation was brief. Without complaining, Johnnie explained the change in her work schedule. When she wondered aloud if we could spend a few hours together between her two shifts, a quiet joy fluttered through me, a feeling akin to the happiness that accompanies finding the perfect gift for a loved one and then keeping that gift a precious secret until the right moment arrives.

An hour later, as I raided the cupboard shelves and gathered all the ingredients I needed to cook a big pot of chili, I realized how good it would be to see Johnnie. I looked forward to her presence in my kitchen. I was eager to see the table balanced with Johnnie on one side and me on the other. I wanted to hear her laughter reverberate throughout the rooms of my home. I wanted to reach out and touch her arm the way she'd touched mine protectively the first time we walked side by side. I imagined my fingers feeling that which was both new and familiar. They would dance over the sinews of Johnnie's forearm and shyly stop near the crease of her elbow. I wanted, no, I needed to explore Johnnie's mouth once again and taste the fullness of her lips, to smell her subtle fragrance as she stood in my doorway, leaning close enough to me to kiss me goodbye before leaving to begin the second part of her work day.

I began slicing a sweet onion. Soon the odor of sauteed onions and ground beef blended with chili powder and the tomatoes I had chopped. After I transferred the vegetable and meat mixture to the large round crockpot, I added dark red kidney beans and an unmeasured amount of ketchup. Now, while everything simmered, I'd be able to follow through with my plans of paying the bills piled atop my desk.

Even the least complicated plans are frequently disrupted by the unexpected. My phone didn't hesitate to remind me of that.

"Mother?"

"Nikki? Is everything all right? Are you at school?" Nikki

never called me this early in the day.

"I'm sitting at my desk. It's my prep period."

"Is everything all right?"

"I...I just wanted you to know you might hear something on TV or on the radio about Owen."

I heard anxiety in Nikki's voice.

"Something like what?"

I wondered if Owen had discovered Nikki's affair with Lorin Wilkes. Had he assaulted Nikki or done something to Lorin?

"None of it's true. We have to be patient and wait for all the facts to come out."

"Nikki, what are you talking about?"

"Owen may be implicated in a serious crime that occurred months ago."

I felt my heart beating faster, but I didn't say a word. I gave Nikki time to explain.

"Owen's not guilty. Yesterday, I met with the person who committed the crime."

"What?" I couldn't believe what I was hearing.

"I didn't know that fact when I went to meet with her. I learned about it later," Nikki said. "Owen and I know the truth, and that's what counts. I'm telling you about it in case the media gets the story all screwed up."

I felt like I'd suddenly either gone deaf or could no longer process the sounds of English. I tried to understand Nikki's narrative without getting my fear tangled up in her words.

"Are you both safe?" I asked.

"I'm perfectly safe, but Owen will have to save his own ass."

I heard the goodbye in Nikki's voice before she said those two words. I heard her anger and bitterness, also. Balancing my need to offer her support with her need to reject it, I helped her end our conversation.

"Please take care of yourself, Nikki."

I excluded Owen from my request because he always appeared to take care of himself. Hours after I put down the phone, Nikki's words continued to tumble through my mind. Why would Owen be implicated in a crime? How did he know the victim? And why had Nikki met with the person who committed the crime?

A growing uneasiness pulled me to the family room where I turned on the radio, tuning to the all-news station. I listened as the news reader recited the current headlines. Nothing remotely related to Owen, or to his university sailed past my ears. Obviously, the scandal-hungry newshounds hadn't gotten a whiff of Nikki and Owen's situation.

It took me a moment to regroup and remember I'd planned to

grab my checkbook and pay some bills. Before I could walk to my
desk, the phone rang again. In a state of semi-dread, I answered it.

"Alana, how are you? I hate like hell bothering you at home."
Conrad Jackson's powerful voice boomed through the earpiece.

"Hello, Conrad. This is a surprise." I knew I sounded
surprised, and not pleasantly so.

"Are you enjoying your free time?"

"So far. I stay pretty busy."

"Busy is good, Alana."

I looked out the kitchen window and concentrated on the
mound of snow covering the domed top of the bird feeder as I
geared up to hear the real reason for Conrad's phone call. I figured
he was calling about a problem, not simply to trade pleasantries.

"Listen, here's why I've phoned you. I'm sure you remember
your last probie, Rafaela Ortiz."

Was Conrad serious, or was he being sarcastic? Had someone
told him about Rafe and me and our short-lived dance at the edge
of a relationship?

Conrad didn't wait for my answer. "I know you were
burdened with a lot of work when I assigned her to you, but do you
recall why she was transferred to our office?"

"Yes, I remember."

Was he engaging me in some sadistic question-and-answer
game? I'd spent the past few months trying to forget the
circumstances that brought Rafe to my office's threshold. Her affair
with her former co-worker and her hit-and-run episode with me
were like an oil spill, and I'd worked hard to remain untainted by
its viscous residue.

"I can't tell you how I know this information, Alana, but Ms.
Ortiz is intimately involved with one of her clients."

I knew the usually blunt Conrad was describing the situation
as delicately as he could.

"Are you sure about this?"

Conrad's voice grew louder and more agitated. His words lost
their delicate flavor.

"She's screwing the second female client I assigned to her. The
client herself admitted it to a third party. Ortiz' ass is as good as
gone from this office and any other office in the system," Conrad
thundered.

I didn't respond to his anger. Hearing him yell about Rafe's
deeds staved off anything I might have said.

"If you recall, Alana, you were the one who went to bat for
Rafaela. You told me I was wrong for giving her only male
offenders."

Conrad waited for me to defend myself, but there was no way I could offer an argument in favor of Rafe's indefensible behavior.

"Obviously, I used poor judgment, Conrad."

Conrad lowered his voice, perhaps because I was quick to admit my responsibility.

"That's understandable, Alana. You were under a lot of pressure and you thought you were making the right call. We all fumble the ball once in a while."

Conrad didn't know I'd come close to fumbling the ball in the last ten seconds of the fourth quarter, third down, on the one-yard line, and ahead by only one point.

"Is there something you want me to do?"

I couldn't imagine what, other than offer a full confession about my involvement with Rafe, and I wasn't about to do that.

"No. I'm the one on the hot seat." Conrad sounded defeated.

"Her behavior is not your fault, Conrad. Rafe...uh, Rafaela would have engaged in this indiscretion even if she'd had a supervising P.O."

My Rafe-inflicted wounds healed, I was certain I'd spoken the truth. I didn't want Conrad to shoulder the blame for Rafe's habit of collecting people who fit her whims.

Conrad spoke slowly. "I know her screwing around was not my fault, but monitoring her professional behavior was my responsibility. I'll have to pay for this one way or another. I just know it, Alana."

I imagined Conrad with his designer tie unknotted and his mouth turned down.

He continued. "Before you left, you turned in all your notes and records about her, right? There wasn't anything else you may have taken home with you?"

"No. I gave my probies' files to your secretary."

"Yeah, she gave 'em to me. I just wanted to touch base with you to make sure there wasn't more information floating around somewhere else."

"No. I left everything there at the office."

"Okay, thanks. I knew when I called you I was just grabbing at straws, but it was worth it," Conrad said.

"I'm sorry I can't help you."

As far as Rafe was concerned, the best I'd been able to do was help myself.

"It's kind of you to say that." Almost as an afterthought, he added, "We miss you, Alana. You were the best."

"Thanks. I miss you guys also."

"Well, we'll have to get-together over drinks some time. Trade war stories."

"That sounds like a plan, Conrad. Take care."

"You too, Alana."

I hung up the phone and sat down at the kitchen table. While the chili continued to cook, I thought about the boiling vat of soup that threatened to drown Owen and Nikki, and the bubbling cauldron of stew about to engulf Rafe. All I could do was ponder the two situations.

Nikki and her husband were on their own. Rafe had come and gone, leaving less than her shadow as a souvenir. Thanks to her visit, I learned I wanted to love and be loved by someone quite different from her.

I needed a lover whose presence complimented mine, whose gaze enveloped me tenderly, whose full-bodied voice sang caring notes. I was worthy of a lover who would sit across the table from me, spin her dreams as well as her realities, and ask if she could share mine. I required a lover who wouldn't leave the second I trusted it was all right to break down, cry, and say, "I have some needs, and I'm asking you to fill them." I wanted a woman who would show up and stay beside me for more than a butterfly moment. I longed for Johnetta to be that woman.

Chapter Thirty-three

JOHNETTA AND HAROLD trudged away from Captain Mulavey's office. Neither had had time to fully digest all the information their commanding officer shared with them during the past half hour's impromptu meeting.

Although Harold was assigned lead investigator, he learned to follow Johnnie's subtle comments. Seamlessly, he took advantage of her crime-solving instincts and he refused to be intimidated by her age and experience.

He cast a sideways glance at her. "We were on the right track; just a little bit shy of the train station."

Johnetta smiled. "Considering the two of us have never worked a murder together, we've got nothing to be ashamed of."

"We did operate like well-oiled machinery, didn't we? Next time, I'll pay closer attention to your intuition."

"It wasn't my intuition as much as it was my stubbornness." Johnnie paused in front of the restroom. "I didn't want to believe that guy did her. It was too easy, too pat."

"Yeah, but once we got the DNA match, I was sure we had 'em."

"The science is usually reliable, but it's not foolproof." Johnnie winked.

"You met the perp. Are you surprised by the outcome?"

"I'm disappointed I didn't figure it out."

"Give yourself a break, partner." Tiny lines defined the corners of Harold's eyes as he smiled at Johnetta. "You're not perfect. Nobody is."

"I know that. And I know every case is different."

Harold looked at his watch. "It's about that time. You're due back here in a few hours, so why don't you leave now while the leaving's good?"

"I'm out of here right after this pit stop."

Harold held up his hand, as if to stop Johnetta from disappearing into the restroom. "Hey, Johnnie, can I ask you one more question?"

"Sure."

"I remember how pissed off you were when our case against the first suspect didn't work out. Why did you have doubts about the second one?"

Johnetta spoke softly.

"Because he seemed to have potential, Harold. He's the kind of young man who could be my son."

"I understand." Harold nodded and turned to leave. "Good luck tonight."

"Thanks. I'm hoping for a peaceful second shift."

Johnetta entered the bathroom and leaned on the wash basin. While staring at her reflection in the mirror, she reconsidered Harold's last question and spoke a different answer.

"Because the last thing I wanted to do was arrest the son-in-law of the woman I've begun to have feelings for."

Chapter Thirty-four

"REMEMBER EVERYTHING I'VE said to you. It's crucial for Owen and me," Nikki said. She stood up and began walking toward the foyer.

"Everything? You haven't told me very much, Nikki." I watched her walk in front of me and then stop abruptly.

"I've told you all you need to know for right now. In the next few days the media, and maybe even the police might try to contact you. Don't talk to them. Don't give them any information about Owen." The faint lines on Nikki's forehead deepened.

"Whatever's going on must be pretty serious."

I gave Nikki another opportunity to explain why she insisted on my silence about Owen. Instead of grabbing the chance to reveal more, she moved closer to the coat closet.

"Nikki. What has Owen done?"

"He hasn't done anything." She gritted her teeth. "When is your friend going to get here, anyway?"

"Any minute." I turned back toward the living room and glanced at the clock on the fireplace mantel. "In fact, she's running late. Maybe the weather has tied up traffic."

"Well, I really intended to be out of here before your—"

The doorbell's shrill ring truncated Nikki's sentence. As I walked to answer it, it occurred to me this was not only Johnnie's first visit to my home. It was also her first time meeting Nikki.

I opened the door and saw Johnnie standing there, her body turned slightly toward the driveway. She appeared to be staring at Nikki's yellow Mini Cooper.

A sheen of fine mist covered Johnnie's hair, tempting me to touch the softly glistening waves.

"Hello, Johnnie, come in."

"Hi, Alana." Johnnie stepped into the foyer. "Sorry I'm late. I went home after work, showered and changed my clothes. Then I thought I had enough time to make a stop for flowers."

I looked down as Johnnie lifted a bouquet of mixed blooms and offered them to me.

"They're beautiful. You didn't have to do that." I hoped the graciousness in my voice was louder than the frustration I still felt about Nikki's cryptic admonitions.

"I wanted to contribute something to the evening, and I know you like plants and flowers," Johnnie said as she split her attention between me and the third person standing in the foyer. She nodded, acknowledging Nikki's presence.

"Johnnie, I'd like to introduce you to my daughter, Nikki. Nikki, this is Johnetta Jones." I stiffened. I was aware the formality in my voice was more appropriate for a funeral announcement than an introduction.

Johnnie took three steps toward Nikki. I watched her hold Nikki's inanimate hand in her own disarmingly warm one.

"It's a pleasure to meet you, Nikki. Your mother has mentioned you to me more than once." Johnnie's expression was open and relaxed.

Nikki shot me a poisoned look. "Hmm. I can only imagine the things she's said."

I decided not to mumble any platitudes. Johnnie remained quiet also. It was up to Nikki to climb out of the impasse her own remark created.

"So, my mother tells me you're a detective."

"Yes, I work for the local police department." Johnnie stared directly into Nikki's eyes.

Nikki broke the eye to eye contact and swept her gaze over the entirety of Johnnie, starting at her slip-on shoes and ending at the top of her neatly clipped damp hair. I'd seen Nikki do this before with both men and women. And I'd seen how the very boldness of her act could strip away the other person's self-confidence. Because I had witnessed Nikki's expertise in seizing the upper hand in the most casual of circumstances, I believed she was just as proficient at owning the power in more serious relationships. I imagined Lorin Wilkes hadn't stood a chance of holding on to her will once Nikki grabbed control of it.

"You probably have a pretty easy job out here in the 'burbs," Nikki said, almost accusingly.

"Police work is never easy," Johnnie said in a matter-of-fact tone.

Nikki compressed her lips and eked out a patronizing smile. "I suppose it's a good idea to have older officers on the force." Her smile grew more pronounced. "And gay ones also."

I could barely contain my annoyance with her.

"Nikki..."

Johnnie winked at me.

"In some jurisdictions, discriminating against LGBT cops is illegal. More importantly, it's stupid. Hiring older officers is a good policy, Nikki, because we're the ones with all the experience. We've dealt with all kinds of people, from the poorest and neediest to the most affluent and best educated. Some of the things I've seen and heard during my career would curl your hair, my dear."

Nikki ignored Johnnie's response. "I have to be going, Mother. Tomorrow's a workday."

"You're planning to go to work? After what you told me earlier?" If Nikki and Owen were expecting some mysterious uproar involving the police and the press, how could she figure she'd have a routine workday?

"Of course I am. I haven't heard anything that would cause me to stay at home."

Nikki opened the closet door. She tugged her coat from its hangar and hastily put it on while tossing us a perfunctory, "Nice to have met you, Johnetta, talk to you soon, Mother." She unlocked the front door and left the house.

I closed the door behind her and turned around to face Johnnie.

"That's Nikki. Sorry about her older and gay police officer crack."

"She's a grown woman, Alana. You don't need to apologize for her."

I appreciated what Johnnie said as well as her gentle way of saying it.

"Thanks. It sounds like you understand."

Johnnie grinned. "I understand a lady who makes a mean pot of chili lives at this address. And there's a rumor she's offered to share some of it this evening with an over-worked detective."

"I usually advise people to ignore rumors, but in this case, what you've heard is true." I allowed myself a laugh even as I recovered my manners.

"Johnnie, you're still wearing your jacket."

"I was playing it safe, in case you hadn't paid your last heating bill."

"Oh, I paid it all right." I gestured for her to take off her jacket and leave it in the closet.

"I don't need to hang it up."

"Well, do whatever is most comfortable. And I'll put these lovely flowers in a vase."

"Is this okay?" Johnnie pointed at the staircase's newel post.

"Sure."

She pulled her holster from her shoulder and placed it over the wooden post before draping her jacket over the weapon. "Can I leave this here, also?"

"That's fine. I don't have any kids or pets running around the house."

"One of these days, you might have grandkids underfoot," Johnnie said.

My mind flashed to Nikki's photo on Lorin Wilkes' cell phone.

"Not any time soon."

I held onto the bouquet with one hand, and reached for Johnnie's arm with the other one.

"Come on out to the kitchen, and we can talk while I finish making dinner."

"Hold on." Johnnie paused. She entwined her fingers with mine and moved my hand to her lips. She kissed it gently, and then she leaned closer and kissed my mouth.

"I wanted to give you a proper hello, one that would remind you of how we said goodbye the last time we saw each other."

Everything about me softened as I remembered our last kiss. I considered letting go of the flowers and wrapping both my arms around Johnnie's neck. I compromised by kissing her lightly on the tip of her nose.

"Here's a proper welcome to my home," I barely whispered.

"Thank you."

"Come on, Detective Jones. Let's see if you can solve the mystery of what I'm preparing."

Johnnie grinned. "That should be fairly easy since you already clued me in when I phoned this morning."

She let me lead her through the dining room and toward the back of the house. We entered the kitchen, and Johnnie began sniffing the air, redolent of spices, tomatoes, and a surprise baking in the oven.

"Oh, it smells so good in here." Johnnie glanced at the counters.

"Can you figure out what's in the oven?" I asked.

"Let me see." Johnnie closed her eyes and tapped her chin with her fingertips. She opened her eyes suddenly and said, "You're baking cornbread."

"How did you know that?" Slightly disappointed, I'd wanted the game to continue for at least a couple more guesses.

"It's elementary, my dear." Johnnie pointed to an area near the sink. "The empty cornbread mix box is over there on the counter."

I grimaced. "Oh, Lord."

Johnnie bent forward, laughing. I realized this was the first time I'd really heard her react to something funny. Hers was an up-from-the-pit-of-her-stomach kind of laugh. Her happiness climbed a full octave above her regular speaking voice. She sounded young, spontaneous, and free. She ceased being Detective Jones, and instead became joy incarnate.

I caught her fast-moving laugh as if it were a virus, and I giggled right along with her.

"You really do pay attention to all the evidence, don't you?" My question mixed pride along with the pleasure of discovery.

"I do my best." Johnnie's high powered laughter reduced to a simmer. Her eyes shone.

"Have you been working your chili magic all day?"

"I started it this morning. Then I let it rest. That's the secret to good chili. The ingredients need time to blend."

"I can relate. After working all day I need to rest also."

"If you want, you can take a nap after we eat. There's a guest room upstairs."

"I don't want to take a nap, Alana. I want to spend every second here with you."

I felt heat rush to my cheeks.

"I feel the same way, Johnnie. I've wanted you to be here with me for a while now."

Johnnie approached and pulled me close to her. "I'm here, baby."

It felt so good to have her in this familiar space. I wanted to reprise each moment we'd spent together so far this evening. Each moment except the ones that found me stuck on Nikki's verbal barbed wire.

I took the bread from the oven and gave it a few moments to cool before I sliced it. Then, I ladled spoonfuls of chili into two bowls and I put the salad bowl in the middle of the table.

Johnnie stared admiringly at the meal. "Everything looks wonderful."

"Thanks. I hope you're hungry."

"Believe me, I am."

We began eating.

"I haven't had chili this good in an age. Anytime you're preparing it, feel free to invite me for dinner." Johnnie's smile spread from one side of her face to the other.

"I'm glad you're enjoying it."

"I'm enjoying your company as well." The tender expression in Johnnie's melted my heart faster than the piece of warm cornbread liquefied the butter I'd spread on it.

Moments passed without conversation, until my need to share my apprehension about Nikki got the better of me. "Can I talk to you about something?"

"Of course you can." Johnnie held her fork above the plate and waited for me to begin speaking before she continued eating.

"It's Nikki. I think she's in some sort of trouble."

Johnnie put down her fork. Her smile receded.

"Why do you think that?"

"She came here this afternoon to warn me that I might find the police or the news media camped out on my walkway. I asked her why, but she wouldn't explain. She made me promise I wouldn't talk to anyone about her and Owen."

"Alana, Nikki's not in trouble, but I believe her marriage is."

Johnnie cleared her throat and continued. "It's difficult for me to have to tell you this, but for a while, your son-in-law, Owen Reid, was a person of interest in the Shantay Taylor murder case."

My mouth went dry. Long dormant suspicions tumbled out.

"I always knew he was straddling a keg of anger. But I never thought he would..." I couldn't finish my sentence.

Johnnie held up both her hands as if to appease me.

"Don't worry. Although he's not completely off our radar screen, he's no longer a suspect. The Philly police have arrested his department chairperson, a Dr. Caryn Mobley. Allegedly, she confessed to both Nikki and Owen."

A net of confusion covered me. "I don't understand. If she confessed, why is Nikki worried? Why does she think the media is going to show up here at my door?"

I had a feeling there was much more to the story than Johnnie was disclosing. If Nikki and Owen were involved, didn't I have the right to know everything?

"There's still a chance Mobley may try to implicate Owen."

Johnnie's response spurred more questions.

"How can she do that?" I pushed my bowl of chili to one side.

"When we began to suspect Owen might have been involved in the murder, we ran a sample of his DNA. The sample matched another one Forensics removed from under the victim's fingernails."

A lump of half-digested cornbread surged from my belly to the middle of my chest.

"Then Owen is implicated."

"The rest of our evidence was circumstantial. We know something went down between Owen and Shantay. We just don't know exactly what. Owen will have to explain his side of the story to the police."

The dissonance between the soft tones of Johnnie's voice and the ugliness of the situation she described added to my confusion. I looked down at the table and for a moment I thought I saw the salt and pepper shakers doing a little dance. Then I realized why they were moving. My thumb kept hitting the surface of the table. I stilled it and sighed.

"Nikki probably knows what happened between Owen and that girl."

Johnnie nodded. "Probably."

"If Owen's DNA matched the sample from Shantay's nails, doesn't that prove he murdered her?" I struggled to coax my brain back in gear.

"Not necessarily. It means there was some physical contact between the two of them."

"Exactly how was she killed?"

Johnnie lowered her voice to a whisper. "Are you sure you want to hear the details, Alana?"

"I was a P.O. for more than two decades, remember? I've heard my share of details." I counted on that reminder to persuade Johnnie to tell me all she knew. And I counted on it to help me listen to her without feeling any sicker than I did already.

Johnnie's eyes lost their compassionate expression as she began to relate her narrative. She was no longer Johnnie. She became Detective Jones once again.

"Shantay's autopsy revealed she was strangled. The left side of her throat was more traumatized than the right. So, it appears her assailant was right-handed. Owen, as you know, is a leftie. Forensics found bits of old lead-based paint on the soles of Shantay's shoes. The paint couldn't have come from Owen's office. It was repainted last year and the old carpeting was replaced, also. The day I interviewed Caryn Mobley, I saw paint peeling away from the ceiling in her office. A sample of that paint matched what we found on the victim's shoes. When the Philly Police Department's Forensics Division took apart Mobley's office, they found strands of hair that might be Shantay's. They tracked down the rental vehicle they believe was used to transport Shantay's body from the murder site, and they're analyzing hair that was found in its trunk."

Even though I had read worse crime reports during my career, hearing the details of this one left me feeling weak.

"Did she suffer?" I asked.

Johnnie shook her head. "My C.O. thinks it happened fast. Apparently, Mobley got her hands around Shantay's throat before the girl could put up much of a fight."

"But she did struggle?"

"All her life. Her case record with Child Protective Services began when she was three."

"Oh, no." I began shaking my head.

"According to the records, she's been physically, emotionally, and sexually abused since she was a little girl."

"Then, along came Dr. Mobley and Professor Owen Reid," I said unfolding my latent qualms about Owen's tightly buttoned anger.

"Owen was involved with Shantay, but we don't know to what extent." Johnnie examined my face. Her eyes filled with a combination of caution and sympathy.

"I'm sorry you have to be involved with this, Alana, even peripherally."

She reached across the table and touched my hand, but I pulled away from the contact.

"Alana?" Her empathy changed to puzzlement and sudden hurt, the kind of hurt that springs from unexpected rejection.

I ignored her wounded look. "Did you say you interviewed that woman?"

"Yes I did, but Dr. Mobley wasn't a suspect then." Johnnie hung her head for a second before looking up. "I went to the university to ask her questions about Owen."

"How did you get a sample of his DNA?"

"I asked Mobley to hold onto something Owen used, a coffee cup for example," Johnnie said. "She turned in a water bottle."

A kaleidoscope of images spiraled through my mind: Detective Johnetta Jones sitting in my office, questioning me about one of my clients; a conversation with the shy sunglasses-wearing Johnnie, standing on the far side of a gas pump; the state park, and Johnnie's voice close to my ear while her field glasses hung from my neck; her voice calling my name as I drifted through a prophetic dream; finding Rafe instead of Johnnie at the end of that voice; Rafe's perfidious kisses, a prelude to Johnnie's honest affection; my trust riding on the kiss I shared with Johnnie; all the trust I could summon. All the trust I...all the trust...

I glared at Johnnie. "The only reason you've been seeing me was to get information about Owen, right? Our getting together has nothing to do with you and me, does it?"

"That's not true, Alana." Johnnie contorted her features. "That's not true at all."

"The girl's body was found near here. Did you think I was involved in her murder also?" An ache split me in two and yanked me away from all that was logical.

"Of course not," Johnnie said. "I never wanted the perp to be Owen, even before I learned he was your son-in-law. When I researched his background, I could see how gifted he was and what a waste of talent it would be if he was guilty. When I learned you were related to him, I prayed he wasn't the one."

I glared at Johnnie.

"Alana, the last thing in the world I wanted was for you to be touched by all of this shit."

I wanted to believe her, but I wasn't ready. I'd put on my toughest suit of armor and I didn't give a damn if caring and kindness abandoned me forever.

"If Mobley strangled Shantay in her office," I said, "how did the girl's body end up out here?"

"Seven-fifty-four Summit Farm Drive belongs to Caryn Mobley's cousin. Mobley hired two students to rent a car and transport the corpse. The rental records led us to the students. They were both on academic probation, in danger of flunking out of the university, and she had the power to save them. She ordered them to bury Shantay's body at the far end of the back yard where the property abuts a wooded area owned by the Turnpike Commission. But instead of following her instructions, the students took the easy way out and just dumped Shantay in a large compost bin."

As I listened to Johnnie, I concentrated on every centimeter of her face: the eyes I had wanted to become lost in; the broad forehead I'd pictured myself stroking; the strong chin I'd wanted to cradle in my hands; the generous mouth I'd imagined exploring before it travelled over every part of me.

"Alana, please believe me."

Johnnie's entreaty drew me back to the present. Devoid of emotion, I asked her another question.

"When you arrived tonight, did you know the car parked in my driveway was Nikki's?"

"Yes. I recognized it."

"Have the police been following her?"

"No, they haven't had probable cause. But I followed her the day I interviewed Mobley at the university. Nikki was tailing Owen, so the three of us had a little caravan. At some point, I lost Owen. Actually I lost Nikki too, after she parked at a condo development near Lincoln Drive."

"The Fairmount Greene complex?" I asked dispassionately.

"Yes." Johnnie raised one eyebrow.

"Did you know Nikki is a lesbian?" I wondered how much Johnnie knew about my daughter.

"No, I didn't know that." Johnnie leaned forward. "Are you sure?"

"Yeah. I work with her ex-lover at the Baker Center. Lorin is a very nice woman, nicer than Nikki deserves. Lorin lives in Fairmount Greene."

"Has Nikki come out to you?"

"No." I stared at Johnnie, steely-eyed. "I doubt Nikki has come out to herself."

"Alana, the day I followed her, she pulled away from a parking spot like a bat out of hell. She began tailing Owen because she saw him kiss a sweet young thing and then drive off with her in his car. She was the classic jealous wife. That's why I said their marriage was in trouble. It never occurred to me Nikki might be gay."

"Nikki and Owen's marriage has been troubled since their wedding day. But, as you said earlier, Nikki is grown. She's her own person, and I've signed off." I tapped the table with the flat of my hand.

Johnnie leveled her gaze at me. "Please don't sign off on us, Alana. We were just beginning to know each other."

"I can't promise you that, Johnetta. I have a lot to think about."

"You called me Johnetta, not Johnnie. That doesn't sound promising."

I stared at her. Johnetta was a stranger all over again. I wondered when she had planned to tell me she was investigating Owen. Before or after we made love for the first time? I signed off on the two of us as well. How else would I protect my feelings?

"Would you be more comfortable if I left now?" Johnetta asked.

"Yes."

She stood and walked to the foyer. I followed her. Silently, she slipped on her holster and then her jacket.

"I'm so sorry for this." She turned toward the door.

"As am I."

Chapter Thirty-five

I WASN'T TAKEN aback the morning I opened the envelope and read the request that I appear at Rafaela's dismissal hearing. Nor was I astonished when Conrad phoned and told me Rafe intended to challenge her firing. I was angry, but not surprised. Maybe Rafe believed it was okay to be involved with a client, especially if she wrapped her unethical behavior with a blanket of denial.

I didn't mention having to go to the office to Johnetta. Recently there were lots of issues I hadn't mentioned to her. In giving each other space to figure out our feelings, we'd created more opportunities to keep silent about our issues than occasions to share the major and minor events in our lives. The last time we saw each other was the night Johnnie sat in my kitchen and described Owen's connection to Shantay Taylor's murder.

The situation was complicated, and my reaction to Johnetta's dating me while she investigated Owen and Nikki was more convoluted than a labyrinth. I began and ended each day questioning her motives and sincerity. She had arrived in my life, fully compromised by all she knew about me and mine. I neither wanted nor needed all the obstacles she dragged in her wake.

The day of Rafaela's hearing, I decided to drive to the local train station and take the commuter line into the city. I didn't mind hiking the three blocks between the train terminal and my old office building. The mid-December cold felt good to me compared to the train's arid over-heated air.

Puffs of white clouds, thick in their middles and wispy thin at their borders, dotted the deep blue sky as I joined the post-lunch hour pedestrians rushing back to their jobs; eyes focused straight ahead, legs forging on mechanically, minds already engaged in the afternoon's duties. Walking felt far better to me than pondering the questions Rafe or I might be asked if the hearing officers quizzed either of us about our relationship.

On purpose, I opened the door to the building only two minutes before the appointed time. I wasn't here to socialize or track down former colleagues. I was here to participate in an unpleasant bureaucratic ritual. Whether my statements helped or damaged Rafe's defense made little difference to me and probably no difference at all to her.

I avoided the decrepit elevator and climbed the stairs to the third floor's hearing site. With my luck, this would be the day that old lift would hurtle to the basement, taking me and whatever I had to say about Rafe's job performance with it.

The pebbly surface of the glass in the anteroom's door prevented me from seeing who was there. I pulled it open and crossed the room's threshold. There, a few yards away, sat Selena Garrett in all her bold splendor. Her legs crossed provocatively, she rested the current issue of *Journal of Contemporary Criminal Justice* against her thigh.

"Ms. Blue." Selena looked up and fixed her predatory gaze on me. "I knew you'd be here. You used to be Rafe's supervisor, right?"

"For a short while."

"Oh yeah. Now you're workin' for that lame Baker Center, aren't you?" Selena put the magazine on the end table next to her chair.

"Yes."

I was fairly certain my monosyllabic answer wouldn't deter Selena from attempting a long chat with me.

"Yeah, you're workin' with Ms. Wilkes, Lorin." Selena clicked her tongue against her teeth. "She's the one who dropped the dime on me and Rafe."

"If I remember correctly, you're the one who mentioned to us how close you and Ms. Ortiz were."

I knew better than to bait Selena, but I couldn't let her get away with blaming Lorin for Rafe's misdeeds.

In shocked disagreement, Selena pulled back her head so far, her chin disappeared. Narrowing her eyes, she went on the offensive.

"I mentioned all that to you and Ms. Wilkes 'cause I knew for a fact you two were family. I thought you'd have our backs. But Lorin had to run her mouth to her boss who then told Rafe's boss."

I remembered every detail of that afternoon. Lorin was jammed between hell and inferno. Once Selena told us about Rafe's abuse of duty, Lorin had to report it or risk being fired herself. There was no way she could have protected her friend. Adding unemployment on top of Nikki's defection from their relationship would have been disastrous for Lorin.

"Maybe Ms. Wilkes felt she didn't have any choice." I stared directly into Selena's eyes lest she think I was trying to get a glimpse of the two brown orbs spilling over the shirred ruffles of her low-cut blouse.

"She had plenty of choices. She made the wrong one, though." Selena's mouth twisted the way it would have if she'd bitten into a thin-skinned lemon.

One of the two doors leading to the inner office opened. A woman's voice called, "Ms. Garrett, come in please."

"Talk to you later, Ms. Blue." Selena stood up. "I'm sure you'll have good things to say about Rafe when it's your turn to testify."

I looked at Selena, but I didn't respond. She paused directly in front of me.

"Or maybe you won't. We both know Rafe can be a bitch when she wants to." Selena winked. "Then again, so can I."

Hurricane Selena disappeared into the inner office just as the door on the opposite side of the room opened, and yielded Rafe.

Rafe looked down at me and proffered a half nod. "Hey, Alana. Thanks for being here."

"Hello, Rafe. I didn't think I had an option."

"Probably not, if you want to keep receiving your pension checks." Rafe smiled at her own remark. "But I appreciate your showing up, and I'll be grateful for anything good you have to say about me."

"Anything good I have to say about you, or about how you do your job?"

"How I do my job."

I gazed at the doorway through which Selena had vanished.

"Why did you begin an affair with her, especially after what happened in the West Philly office?"

"She was available, and I felt like it." Rafe's quick flat-voiced answer held not an ounce of emotion.

Just as quickly, I asked, "Does that statement apply to us also?"

Rafe rubbed her chin a couple of times.

"Pretty much."

Rafe sat down on a bench directly across from me. For the next five minutes, we sat in silence. Finally the door to the inner office opened, and the voice summoned me. I stood and took one last look at Rafaela. I wanted to say something meaningful to her, some phrase she would think of the next time she found herself on the verge of ejecting a woman from her life. Instead, I settled for the only words I could think of.

"Goodbye, Rafe. And good luck."

Inner peace put its comforting arm around my shoulder and escorted me into the next room.

"Please sit down, Ms. Blue."

A woman sitting at the head of a long table pointed to a chair.

"Alana, it's good to see you." Standing halfway, Conrad put six inches between his rear end and his seat. He stretched across the table and shook my hand. "Sorry it has to be under these circumstances.

"It's good to see you also, Conrad."

My former boss appeared to be as well dressed and adequately fed as he was the last time I saw him.

"I'm Constance Graham, the hearing officer."

The woman's crisp voice interrupted our reunion. She patted a sheaf of papers stacked in front of her on the table.

"Your notes concerning Ms. Ortiz's job history are complete. They're quite detailed."

I nodded. "If that's the case, why am I here?"

Ms. Graham favored me with an insincere smile.

"Because I have one or two questions to ask you."

I searched Conrad's face in an effort to find a clue about Constance Graham's queries. Instead of returning my glance, he busied himself staring down at the table.

"As I said, your notes are quite thorough. They're objective and professional."

"I was always objective and professional."

Ms. Graham leveled her gaze at me.

"Ms. Ortiz has overstepped her boundaries, first with a former co-worker in another office, and now with a client, Selena Garrett. When we first interviewed Selena, she intimated that Ms. Ortiz had been less than professional with you during the period when you were her supervisor. Can you corroborate that information?"

I felt my face flush. "That's not true. Ms. Ortiz never acted less than professionally with me, nor I with her."

Not missing a beat, Ms. Graham asked, "And what about after you left your job?"

I lowered my voice in an attempt to harness my annoyance. "Anything I've done after leaving my job is my business, and no one else's."

Constance Graham smacked the stack of papers in front of her.

"With or without proof that Ms. Ortiz consorted with you, we've reached our decision. And it's a fair one, considering her probationary status."

She turned to the still silent Conrad. "Do you have any questions for Ms. Blue?"

"No, nothing."

"Well, I have one." I spoke up. "Now that you've accepted Selena Garrett's testimony as gospel, what's going to happen to Ms. Ortiz?"

Conrad cleared his throat. "I'm not sure we're at liberty to discuss that, Alana."

Constance Graham sat back in her chair.

"Ms. Ortiz's employment here is terminated. This was her second serious violation, and we see no indication she regrets what she's done."

"Don't worry, Alana," Conrad said. "We know there's nothing you could have done to prevent what happened. You bear no responsibility here."

"But, Conrad, you knew what might happen when you assigned Selena Garrett to her caseload. You set her up to fail. Why?" I protested even though I knew Rafaela was wrong and Constance Graham's decision was right.

Conrad returned his attention to the conference table while Constance Graham sat erect. Her strident tone buried any response Conrad might have struggled to stutter.

"The issue is settled, Ms. Blue. By the way, Selena Garrett was extremely cooperative with us in this matter, so we've assigned her to another parole officer. The new P.O. is going to meet with Selena's attorney who has already agreed to file the necessary paperwork to revisit her case and shorten the term of Selena's parole."

"What a surprise," I said.

Selena had executed a deal. She turned Rafe in to the system in exchange for less time on parole.

It was clear I had nothing more to contribute other than my meticulously written work notes. I excused myself from the sham of a hearing and left Conrad and Constance Graham feeling secure about their decision. When I returned to the waiting room, I thanked God Selena and Rafe were nowhere to be seen. I exited the building the same way I'd entered it, without seeing any of my former co-workers. As I rejoined the throng of people on the city streets, I thought about my brief conversation with Rafe. I realized my final words to her had been far from eloquent. I realized also that I truly didn't care.

I boarded the train for the return trip to Brighton Township. As I let the seat absorb what was left of my anxiety, I watched the cityscape's panorama whiz by the train's clouded windows. Lulled by the vehicle's hypnotic motion, I stared mindlessly at the passing scenes of defunct industry and underfunded attempts at urban renewal. Miles later, when we pulled into the route's first suburban station, I saw a line of black and white police cars on the street below the platform. I found their lack of color stark, perhaps because I'd become used to seeing Brighton Township's navy and yellow squad cars. The Brighton Police Department... Johnetta...Johnnie.

I fished for my cell phone, dialed her number, waited.

"Alana?"

"Hello, Johnetta. I know you're at work, but I thought I'd give you a call. If you're busy ..."

"I'm not too busy to talk to you." Johnetta's words rushed into my ear. After a second, she continued. "I've missed you, Alana."

"I've missed you, too."

I began missing her the moment I watched her walk away from my home. Dejected and unable to mollify my anger and hurt that day, I had exiled her from our possibilities. Now, hearing her say she missed me gave me hope.

"I wondered if you'd like to come over for coffee and dessert sometime."

"I'd love that. When?"

"Tonight?"

"Tell me what I can bring."

"Just yourself." I hoped Johnetta could hear expectation in my voice.

The conductor stood at the far end of the train car and shouted the name of the next station.

"What's that noise?" Johnetta asked.

"That's the conductor. I'm on the train, on my way home from the city."

"What time do you arrive?"

I looked at my watch. "Twenty minutes from now."

"Okay. Travel safely. I'll see you later."

Four stops later the train approached my station. The sun was setting rapidly, and it seemed like the loss of daylight had ushered in a strong wind. This cold was different from the refreshing breeze I'd felt during my walk to the probation office building. This chill wore the undisguised serious side of winter, the side that forced my eyes to look downward toward the path instead of straight ahead toward my destination.

I was a few yards shy of the spot where I'd parked my car when I heard her voice.

"Your train was right on time."

I looked toward the sound.

"Johnnie, you're here."

"Yes, I am."

Unable to tame my smile, I approached her. We stood toe to toe for a second until, oblivious to the other commuters getting into their cars, I leaned in to Johnnie and placed a generous kiss on her mouth.

She grinned. "That was nice."

"It felt good to me, too."

I let my fingertips linger on Johnnie's lips. They were warm, soft. When I took a slow, deep breath, I could smell the body wash and cologne she had no doubt rubbed onto her damp skin early that morning. I wanted to inhale all of her.

I knew I was standing too close to Johnnie to pretend I didn't want to give and receive another kiss. Right then and there, in that public parking lot, I offered her my mouth. The second kiss wasn't the same as the first one. It was more deliberate, hungrier, and vulnerable, filled with the certainty of desire and the promise of fulfillment. We pulled back from each other.

"I didn't expect to see you until later," I said.

"I know. But you forgot to tell me what time you're serving dessert, so I thought I'd come over here and find out." Johnnie's attempt to offer a serious explanation dissolved into a nervous chuckle.

I laughed along with her.

"How about seven o'clock?"

"Okay. Are you sure I can't bring anything?" Johnnie's chuckle became a wide smile.

I looked as deeply into her eyes as I could.

"You can bring four things: your sense of humor, your rakish good looks, your willingness to be patient with me, and your heart."

"That will be so easy." She stroked the side of my face. "And exactly what are you serving for dessert, Alana Blue?"

"All of my trust and all of my possibilities, Johnetta Jones."

I pressed her hand between mine before relinquishing it and stepping back to get into my car. Seven o'clock couldn't get here fast enough.

Other Books by S. Renée Bess

Breaking Jaie

Jaie Baxter, an African-American Ph.D candidate at Philadelphia's Allerton University, is determined to win a prestigious writing grant. In order to win the Adamson Grant, Jaie initially plans to take advantage of one of the competition's judges, Jennifer Renfrew, who is also a University official. Jennifer has spent the past ten years alone following the murder of her lover, Patricia Adamson, in whose honor the grant is named. Jennifer is at first susceptible to Jaie's flirtation, but is later vengeful when she discovers the real reason for Jaie's sudden romantic interest in her. A lunch with an old cop friend reveals that Jaie may very well have ties to Adamson's death.

Jaie is confronted with painful memories as she prepares an autobiographical essay for the grant application. She recalls the emotional trauma of her older brother's death, the murder of a police detective, her dismissal from her "dream" high school, and her victimization at the hands of hateful homophobic students. She remembers her constant struggles with her mother's alcohol-fueled jealousies and physical abuse she had to endure. This wake-up call causes her to look at her life in new ways.

But Jaie is not the only student applying for the grant. Terez Overton, a wealthy Boston woman, is Jaie's chief competitor. Jaie is drawn to the New Englander immediately but is also unnerved by her. She has no clue that Terez is trying to decide whether she wants to accept an opportunity to write an investigative article about an unsolved murder. Writing that article could put her budding relationship with Jaie in jeopardy.

And just when the angst of old memories and the uncertainty of her future with Terez are complicating Jaie's life, her manipulative ex, Seneca Wilson, returns to Philadelphia to reclaim Jaie using emotional blackmail. Senecas actions serve to wound and break Jaie in many ways. Will Seneca drive the final wedge between Jaie and Terez? Who will win the Adamson grant? And what did Jaie have to do with the death of Patricia Adamson?

ISBN: 978-1-932300-84-0

Re: Building Sasha

Sasha Lewis, the uber-competent manager of Whittingham Builders, finds herself drowning in a riptide of distrust as she struggles to maintain her relationship with Lee Simpson. A genius at balancing details, Sasha commits a career-derailing error while being distracted by Lee's threat to burn down their house and its contents.

Lee's flagrant sexual liaisons with a business client, Angela Jackman, and her escalating deeds of emotional cruelty rip apart Sasha. In self-imposed exile from most of her friends, Sasha recalls a brief encounter with Avery Sloan; an encounter destined to become more meaningful when Avery's social service agency hires Whittingham Builders to rehab an old Victorian house.

What hateful acts will Lee perform in an effort to degrade Sasha? How much damage will Sasha endure before she begins to rebuild her spirit? Will Sasha grab Avery's outstretched hand and accept the gentle yet exciting offer of love she sees in this woman?

ISBN: 978-1-935053-07-1

My Life With Stella Kane
by Linda Morganstein

In 1948, Nina Weiss, a snobby college girl from Scarsdale, goes to Hollywood to work at her uncle's movie studio where she's assigned to help publicize a young actress named Stella Kane. Nina is immediately thrown into the maelstrom of the declining studio system and repressive fifties Hollywood. Adding to her difficulties is her growing attraction to Stella. When a gay actor at the studio is threatened by tabloid exposure, Nina invents a romance between Stella and the actor. The trio becomes hopelessly entangled when the invented romance succeeds beyond anyone's dreams. This is the "behind-the scenes" story of the trio's compromises and secrets that still has relevance for today.

ISBN: 978-1-935053-13-4

A Question of Integrity
by Megan Magill

Jess Maddocks is a talented business trouble-shooter who has worked hard to win the respect of her colleagues. When her boss assigns her a special case, Jess relishes the opportunity to prove her worth, unaware that her strict professional boundaries would this time fail her.

Rosalind Brannigan captivates people as easily as others smile. Described as charisma personified, she knows the value of her ability and is ruthless in utilising it to her own advantage. Confident in her mastery of the game, Rosalind assumes the rules will never change.

When Jess's assignment brings these two women together, it sparks an unexpected chain of events that proves life changing to both of them. They are forced to deal with mutual attraction and suspicion whilst an increasingly malignant shadow looms over them. As events unfold they must look to their own integrity as the only guide they have.

This is the first book in the Jess Maddocks series.

ISBN 978-1-935053-02-6

OTHER REGAL CREST TITLES

Be sure to check out our other imprints,
Yellow Rose Books and Quest Books.

VISIT US ONLINE AT
www.regalcrest.biz

At the Regal Crest Website You'll Find

- The latest news about forthcoming titles and new releases

- Our complete backlist of romance, mystery, thriller and adventure titles

- Information about your favorite authors

- Current bestsellers

- Media tearsheets to print and take with you when you shop

Regal Crest titles are available directly from our web store, Allied Crest Editions at www.rcedirect.com, from all progressive booksellers including numerous sources online. Our distributors are Bella Distribution and Ingram.